Tribeca Blues

ALSO BY JIM FUSILLI

A Well-Known Secret
Closing Time

G. P. PUTNAM'S SONS
New York

Tribeca Blues

Tribeca Blues

JIM FUSILLI

G. P. Putnam's Sons
Publishers Since 1838
a member of
Penguin Group (USA) Inc.
375 Hudson Street
New York, NY 10014

Library of Congress Cataloging-in-Publication Data

Fusilli, Jim.
Tribeca blues / Jim Fusilli.
p. cm.
ISBN 0-399-15088-9
1. Private investigators—New York (State)—New York—
Fiction. 2. TriBeCa (New York, N.Y.)—Fiction. I. Title.
PS3606.U85T75   2003   2003046598
813'.6—dc21

Printed in the United States of America
1   3   5   7   9   10   8   6   4   2

This book is printed on acid-free paper. ♾

BOOK DESIGN BY AMANDA DEWEY

To Joe Generelli

First love is first death. There is no other.
There is no death. But all men live forever
And die forever. If this were not true,
We would be more deceived, still more deceived
Than this belief deceives us, whether or not
We think that we believe or we think
Those who believe are deceived. But to believe
That death is the sweet asylum of nothingness:
Is the cruel sick dream of the criminal and the suicide:
Of those who deny reality, of those who steal from
 consciousness,
Of those who are often fugitive, of those who are
 afraid to live,
Of those who are terrified by love, and
 Those who try—before they
 Try to die—to disappear
 And hide.

—DELMORE SCHWARTZ

Tribeca Blues

N.Y. STATE LICENSE: 121383-01   DEA DF 12050612

Elizabeth Williams Harteveld, M.D., Ph.D.
426 East 68th Street
New York, NY 10021
212-555-1990

DICTATED, NOT CORRECTED—24 JUNE

The patient, a 37-year-old male, is a historian by trade who suspended his career following the sudden, violent death of his wife and son some five years ago. He has worked as a private investigator, following at least one year in which he secluded himself from his social sphere, emerging only to provide basic care and companionship for his daughter, now 15.

The patient possesses an intellectual sophistication that at best is manifested in a playful, occasionally charming rhetoric he deploys to resist working through his enduring attitude. At worst, the patient is contentious and aggressive. He demonstrates symptoms of a narcissistic personality disorder encouraged by a repressed, and thus far unknown, conceit which precedes his dominating conscious idea—i.e., my wife and son are dead. Despite his narcissistic tendencies, the patient is now cognizant of his responsibilities to his daughter and his community of friends and associates, and yet he continues to deny that he finds satisfaction in helping these friends and associates, claiming that he becomes involved only because the subsequent investigations help him develop the skills to locate the man who the police suspect is responsible for the death of his wife and son.

In the reverie state, he has on several occasions re-experienced what he believes to be the defining event. However, as his respondent idea—I caused the death of my wife and son by failing to protect them—is fully formed and causative, he refuses to consider any alternatives that might challenge it. Thus, the persistence of his enduring attitude: A man protects his family; having failed to do so, I am not entitled to a man's fundamental rights and pleasures. If he has progressed from his original, intractable positions of self-punishment and self-denial, it is not because his enduring attitude has been worked through, but because the responsibilities of parenthood and the affection bestowed upon him by his daughter and friends have chipped away at its hard shell.

Recently, the patient has tempered his aggression as he has become more fully reintegrated into the larger society. (Is this due to the influence of his new female companion?) It also must be noted that, while he repeatedly states that he rejects psychotherapy as meaningful, he nonetheless returns, if irregularly, for sessions. Curiously, and perhaps promisingly, the patient does not parade his negative emotions toward psychoanalytic psychotherapy in an exhibitionist manner. They surface when he resists alternatives to his respondent idea and cannot work through to a new and plausible enduring attitude, and this suggests that the rejection itself is part of, or a reflection of, his repressed state.

Suggest the patient continue with sessions. EWH to pursue abreaction of emotional responses through further recollection and repetition. Continue to suggest hypnosis as an option (which the patient has soundly rejected). Pursue investigation of familial history and its relationship to the idealization of his spouse. Consider the patient's history prior to the traumatic event. Accept daughter's invitation to dinner at their home?

1

Wallet; money? Eight dollars. ATM card, Amex, MetroCard: in the wallet. Jacket? It's 75 degrees and it's only 8:22.

A little over 90 minutes to get to midtown.

Cab, or the 1 and 9?

Vitamin. Cabinet over the sink.

Bella's manuscript, in the cardboard box; the cardboard box is sealed; the sealed cardboard box is wrapped in brown paper; the wrapped, sealed cardboard box is on the kitchen table wearing a hand-printed label with Bella's careful block letters.

She's asleep upstairs. Last night, on her way to her room, she said what?

"I'm going with Glo-Bug, Daniel and Marcus to the seaport."

"What about dinner?"

"I'll be all right." Bedroom door slams.

A reasonable plan for a Saturday afternoon for a bunch of 15 year olds: skateboarding near Pier 17 off South Street. Shade under the FDR, and the East River, to keep them cool.

Morrie Steiner's address is on the hand-printed label on the brown paper on the cardboard box that holds Bella's manuscript.

As if I'd forget that my agent had his offices in the Brill Building, as if Diddio would let me forget: "Hey, T, the ghost of Phil Spector rattles around up there, man. I mean, it would, if he was, you know, dead. Like Sonny Bono. Or that cheese they say he smoked."

After I drop it off at Morrie's, after I listen to him poke and prod me in an attempt to get me to write again, lunch at . . .

Who responds to poking and prodding?

It's probably time to change the pass code on the locks' keypads. Now it's Davy's birth date, preceded by 44, on the doors front and back.

If someone knows when my son was born and what my number was at St. John's . . .

One more drink of water. Wash the vitamin all the way down.

Take the empty bottle down to the recycling bin. Later.

Need more Badoit. Only one bottle in the back of the refrigerator.

Take the Arts and Leisure section for the ride uptown.

"Dad, if you're going to steal half of my paper . . ."

Forget it. I'll take *Slaughter at Kinmel Hall.* It fits in my back pocket and—

I grabbed the phone on the second ring.

"Terry . . ."

Diddio, and in his voice there was panic, sorrow and fear.

"What, D?"

He couldn't get the words out.

"Just say it, D."

"Leo. Leo's dead, Terry."

Christ. Leo. Oh no.

"Where?"

"At the Tilt. He's— Terry."

"I'll be right there," I told him.

I hung up, grabbed my cell from atop Bella's manuscript and ran out onto Harrison.

He was face-up, empty eyes staring at the musty tin ceiling, his back flat on the grimy linoleum. His arms lay neatly at the sides of his enormous torso, his fingers at his vast thighs.

There was no sign of blood near the body.

"Ah, Leo," I moaned as I stared down at him, thinking about the bad hand he'd drawn, the sad moments he'd spent in painful reflection behind his bar, listening to soaring arias that spoke of loss, abandonment, unfulfilled potential. Leo, who had resigned from this world long before today.

I said, "You moved him?"

Sitting cross-legged on the floor, his heaving back to the pool table, Diddio nodded as he sobbed, and he patted Leo's head, trying to smooth out his oily brown-gray hair. Our long embrace after he unlocked the Tilt's door had done little to assuage his grief.

"Christ. How'd you do that?" Leo Mallard weighed at least 375 pounds.

"He sort of landed on his side, so I, you know, nudged him over," he replied, sniffling, running his thin arm across his nose. "I just . . . I just made him neat."

I came around and was standing now by Leo's wide feet. He wore dark orthopedic shoes. They were scuffed and the bottoms were worn to a sheen.

I caught the scent of stale beer as I studied the room. With the lights on and morning sun slanting through the dust-laden blinds, the Tilt-A-Whirl looked especially shabby, depressing rather than merely off-putting or vaguely threatening.

If someone had killed Leo, he'd left nothing to prove it in the front of the bar.

"Was the door locked when you got here?"

Diddio nodded.

"How'd you get in?"

"I got a key," he said, tears soaking his ashen face.

I reached down, removed the handkerchief from the breast pocket of Leo's old short-sleeved shirt, and handed it to Diddio.

Then I went to the back and looked into the Tilt's lone bathroom. Leo had a crude but oddly effective security system: long nails driven into the window frame, augmented by thin silver tape pressed on the edge of the beveled glass to approximate the kind used in alarm setups.

No one had entered the Tilt through the window. Not this morning.

After a quick peek into Leo's disheveled office, I walked past a moldy tower of long-neck empties in crates, two booths with torn, red plastic seats, and the buck-a-game pool table, and rejoined Diddio.

"Nobody broke in," I said. "Nobody came up on him unless they were here all night." I sat on the floor next to the critic and near our dear, dead friend. "What do you think?"

Diddio shook his head. His unfashionably long Clairol-black hair slapped his drawn, sallow cheeks.

"Heart attack?" A year ago or so, D and I had taken Leo to a cardiologist up on Park, an ace physician I'd read about in *New York* magazine. After the results of all the tests came back, she told us Leo had very high blood pressure, regrettable cholesterol, an enlarged heart and blockages in his legs. Diabetes would soon follow, she said, and then asked if Leo was really only 39 years old.

"Heart attack," Diddio agreed.

"Maybe an aneurysm," I added. "I'm sorry, D."

He sighed. "Leo."

I put my arm across his bony shoulders.

"You were a good friend to him, D."

He nodded as his bottom lip trembled. "We were real friends."

I went to St. John's with Diddio, who signed up to major in rock and pot while tossing in a few journalism courses. College prepared him well for life, at least for his life. He was a successful rock critic, if success is defined as making a living doing what pleases you and still loving the subject of your work. I brought him to Leo's restaurant, Big Chief's, early on. Bella was still a baby, and Marina and I hadn't yet bought the Federal-style house on Greenwich and Harrison, across from Leo's place. They hit it off, but Leo was too busy back then for friendships. Big Chief's, and Loretta, ate up all his time.

"Loretta," I said, breaking the silence.

D pondered. "She's long, long gone," he said finally, summarizing.

I wondered how Loretta would react to Leo's death.

Loretta, who liked to crack the whip. Loretta, who put Leo down in front of the customers. Loretta, who started drinking up what was left of the profits when things started to crumble.

Leo ran the kitchen. Loretta ran the books.

It wasn't the food that killed Big Chief's.

It should've been a good thing for Leo when his wife took off.

But it drove Leo down and down. The city marshal seized the restaurant for back taxes, and Leo didn't resurface in downtown Manhattan until five years later. It was Diddio who stumbled into the Tilt one night on his way to a show at Wetlands. The bar was empty and Leo wanted it that way. When D, hopping from side to side, jiggling, asked him if he could use the restroom, Leo said, "Only if you promise to leave right away."

By then, Marina was represented by Judy Harper, who sold several of her paintings to valued customers who praised Marina's work to their equally well-heeled friends, all of whom appeared to love her affectionate scenes of the Fiorentino ancestral bed in Foggia, Italy. I'd sold my book *Slippery Dick* for a modest advance and, to my infinite amazement, Morrie found a Hollywood production firm, based in Vancouver, to option it.

And so my life, or at least my future, had begun. And it was superb, until five years ago when Raymond Montgomery Weisz took it away.

"Did you call the cops?"

Diddio said no.

"We'd better," I said as I pushed off the floor.

I grabbed my cell, started to punch in the number for the First Precinct, then stopped. I turned to the bar and, pointing, started to speak.

Diddio looked up at me. "Don't worry," he said. "I got it."

"Where did you put it?"

With a snap of the head, Diddio gestured toward the jukebox. "In there."

Leo had kept a .38 tucked behind the bar. He let me use it when I needed to carry.

"It's safe?"

"Terry, man . . ."

"OK." No one knew the Tilt's jukebox as well as Diddio, who changed its menu about seven times a week, pulling compact disks from his warehouse supply the record companies blew him, along with the mixes he and Bella burned. Cases of the CDs were in back and under the bar, where fresh liquor, glassware, paper products and such should've been.

I made the call, pacing toward cobwebs in corners, dead neon signs, and I told the cop at the desk what Diddio had found. He took the address and told me to stay put. Luckily, he didn't ask my name, which is a particularly rancid kind of bile at the First since I helped get Tommy Mango busted down to sergeant.

"They're on their way," I said.

Diddio was behind the bar now, wistfully running a finger along one of Leo's aprons, which the chef, out of habit, had always tucked into his belt, as if he was prepared to return to his old 10-burner gas range and his 80-quart stockpot.

But if Leo enjoyed whipping up a Louisiana dish for friends—a miracle what he could do with the hot plate in his office—he had no intention of running a busy kitchen in a restaurant, whether he owned it or not. He made it clear that Loretta had pounded that ambition out of him, hard and forever.

Christ. Never again the savory scent of green bell peppers, celery and yellow onions, of thyme leaves and cayenne pepper in sweet butter wafting from a well-seasoned frying pan shaken masterfully over an orange coil in back. Nor the fleeting glitter of pride, of satisfaction in Leo's dark eyes when he limped out, hands full of steaming plates.

Never again Leo's salty brand of advice, issued directly, honestly.

No more sentimental Leo.

Or kind Leo, who gave D a second home here at the Tilt, a respite from sweaty rock clubs and his cramped studio on Great Jones.

Fierce Leo, who, fists flying, waded into a gaggle of cops who were squeezing me at my kitchen table moments after I learned Marina and Davy were gone.

"What's going to happen next?" Diddio asked, tears once again gathering in front of his dark eyes.

I came toward him. "I don't get you, D."

"Death is, like, everywhere. All the time." He pointed to the sky beyond the grubby ceiling.

We were standing about nine blocks from where the World Trade Center went down. Throughout TriBeCa, some of the family photos and handmade posters pleading for news of the missing that were put up in the days after the towers' collapse still clung, stubbornly, desperately, to lampposts and phone booths. Faded, ink all but invisible now, snapshots tattered by wind, sun and rain, they were simple testaments to a time set forever for thousands—the moments before their last glimmer of hope surrendered to grief.

"Terry?"

On the subject of death, of dying, I was the wrong guy to ask for insight. I'd spent most of the past five years trying in vain to find solace in an answer, in any answer. Failing that, I tried to ask the right question that might bring a truth to me.

Questions like these: Why did the Madman appear? Why did he kill Marina and Davy?

Why wasn't I with them when he struck?

"D," I said, "people die. That's the deal. And it can happen at any time."

"I know. That's the point," he replied sharply. Shock and sorrow had pushed him to the edge of exasperation and into the lap of sentimentality.

"Yeah, D. That is *the* point."

I turned and looked at him, his vacant expression, his open palms. I was going to tell him that Leo had been engaged in slow suicide: the overindulgence in fatty foods, the lack of exercise—most days he was not so much sedentary as inert—and the weight of the bitterness he carried were evidence of the scheme he'd concocted to wage war on himself. But Diddio wasn't going to buy it. Nor was he going to go for the "he's in a better place now" routine.

"Marina, your son. My Aunt Josey. Everybody we used to see from . . . you know. And now Leo," Diddio counted. He dabbed the handkerchief at his tears.

The wooden stool I'd chosen wobbled until I got myself centered.

We were quiet for a moment, and then Diddio said, "At any time, huh?"

"The whole deal, D. That's why you've got to live while you do." Dr. Harteveld would have been proud of that remark.

"Get it while you can." He mused for a moment, nodding his head, scratching his head, rubbing the rings around his eyes.

I noticed that Leo had begun to go blue at the lips.

Diddio folded the apron and put it on the bar. "I'd better get me some ambition," he muttered.

It wasn't until almost three hours later that we went back to my place. After the coroner's office took the body, we found we hadn't the energy to do anything but stare at the vacant floor where Leo had lain, at his gnarled cane that Diddio had set on his now-empty throne under the TV. We would've cleared out the old cash register, but Leo did that every night before he huffed and scuffled over to his one-bedroom walk-up on Laight Street. Sometimes he had as much as $40 in his pocket.

I went back to Leo's desk and found his old phone book, its brown imitation-leather cracked along the spine. Diddio was waiting for me on steamy Hudson, his key in the lock, his red eyes on the scruffy sidewalk near the door.

"He knew a lot of people," I said as I tapped the book on my thigh.

"Yeah, but he didn't have nobody but us," D replied as we headed south.

We found Bella at the kitchen table, eating graham crackers she'd split in half and carefully stacked. She had the *Times* spread out in front of her; an open page covering her wrapped manuscript. From atop the refrigerator, NPR offered esoteric talk.

Diddio's blues gave it away before I could say anything.

"What happened?" she asked. She wore an oversized Hawaiian shirt, teal except for indolent cockatoos, over red sweat shorts, and when she stood and turned to us, her bare feet squeaked on the floor.

I let the door close behind me. "Bella . . ."

"You're both sad. You, Dennis . . . Something happened. Something happened bad." Then she said, "To Leo?"

"Yeah, Gabby. Leo's . . ."

"Leo's dead. Dad?"

I nodded. "Yes, Bella. That's right."

She stayed still for a few seconds, staring at us, and then she began to tug anxiously at the rainbow of rubber bands around her wrist. And then her eyes began to tear as she tilted her head, as her lip quivered.

"Bella, listen . . ."

As I moved closer to hold her, she dove into Diddio's arms, burying her face against his shoulder.

"I just started liking him," she cried.

"I know, Gabby," D replied, as he stroked her long brown hair. "He was crazy about you. Crazy and proud."

I watched, then I flipped the thin broadsheet page away from the manuscript of the novel we'd worked on, fought over, polished until it sparkled.

"I'm sorry, Dennis," she said as she sniffled. "Real, real sorry."

A moment later, I left the kitchen and went past Marina's paintings to my office in back to call Leo's family down in La Fourche Parish. I decided to start with his sister Ruthie, who sent him via FedEx every edition of the *Times-Picayune.* I could never figure if she thought Leo wanted to know what was happening back in New Orleans or whether she was trying to draw him home.

And while I was on the phone, while I absently played with the computer mouse, I was telling myself my daughter went to Diddio because he needed to be comforted.

2

"This is going to take all day," I said.

Leo's office was too disorganized, too musty and unkempt, to be merely disheveled.

Diddio looked up at me, seemingly cowed by the task ahead.

"We need music," he concluded, as he pushed off the smudged, off-white door frame and went to the jukebox.

I silently bet on music from the '60s. Diddio was nostalgic for an era that preceded him.

In time, quiet chords on an acoustic guitar followed him as he returned. "The Allmans," he said. "'Melissa.' If I'm going to be down, I'll take all the company I can get."

He sat in Leo's chair.

"And sorry I bailed, man. I needed to move around a bit, you know."

"No apology necessary," I told him. Yesterday, after Bella and her friend Daniel Wu had headed off to South Street, skateboards tucked under their arms, D and I shared sesame noodles at Café Franklin and then he disappeared. I spent the evening with Julie and a '97 Bonnie Doon Syrah she brought over. We talked about Leo, then watched Bette Davis in *The Corn Is Green* on Channel 13 before I put her in a cab back to Kips Bay. Diddio covered a Freddie Mercury tribute at the old Felt Forum and crashed. I hadn't realized he had found Leo's body after he pulled an all-nighter on Friday.

Now Julie was at Mass at the Church of Sacred Hearts of Jesus and Mary, and D and I faced a messy mountain of trash and grime, old bills in yellows and pinks, kitchen utensils, empty photo frames and articles torn hastily from nature magazines.

"See anything you want?" I asked.

"The ice pick?" Leo had some of his bills jabbed onto an old-style spindle, the kind OSHA banned in the '70s.

"It's yours." I was going to grab the old frying pan and hang it in my office.

"You know," he said, "Leo did the bills on Sunday."

"He did?" Not all of them, I thought.

"Yep. Fifty-two of them a year."

I tapped my back pocket, where I'd tucked my checkbook. "Bills, then the desk?" I suggested.

"Why not?" Diddio replied. "Who knows what shit we'll find in there?"

We went in, as the gritty singer gave way to a floating, melancholy electric guitar.

All the incidentals, the remnants of an impoverished man's life, were soberly placed in a crate that once held 18 Dixie long necks: dried seasonings, small knives for dicing, his favorite wooden spoon; Colgate tooth powder and a toothbrush, generic brands of over-the-counter cold medicines, a vial of Cipro I got him back in

2001; pencils used until they were nubs, old clotted Bic pens; and an old Motor Bus coffee can that held, I'd bet, more than five thousand pennies. I started another box for things less easily tossed aside: Verdi sung by Vargas, Donizetti by Fleming, Bartoli's Caccini, an assortment of Pavarotti, and familiar Italian operas, jewel boxes and libretti in colorful cases; some New Orleans pop on cassettes nestled in chipped plastic. He had old Christmas cards that he'd tucked back into their envelopes, and birthday cards from Ruthie, and a copy of my *Slippery Dick*. Its limber spine told me he'd read it, and when I looked at it in my hands I saw not the brassy eyes of Connolly's self-satisfied face, but Leo, abandoned and alone, looking for diversion in a book his friend had written.

In the top drawer, which Diddio withdrew and, huffing, lugged out near the jukebox, we discovered Leo's business tools: staples, paper clips, a roll of stamps and a payment book from the IRS. Leo was sending $1,100 a month, more than $13,000 a year, to the government. Juggling his intake somehow, he'd never missed a payment to the Feds.

It was impossible to imagine Leo pulling an extra $1,100 a month out of the Tilt. He used to draw an after-work crowd, young, well-dressed men and women dropping by to hang for a while on their way to the next stop. He greeted them with little enthusiasm, poor service, a very limited selection of cold beverages, and spicy beer nuts. What the Tilt once had going for it was its proximity to the World Trade Center and its brash investment bankers and bond traders who'd use the pool table and listen to Diddio's choices on the jukebox, which had been written up in *New York, Time Out* and, incredibly, a Fodor's guide to TriBeCa. At 8 P.M. or so, they'd clear out to head off to Montrachet, Nobu, Danube, Scalini Fedeli and the other three- and four-star restaurants in the neighborhood.

Since the attacks on the Twin Towers, the Tilt rarely drew more than one or two passersby, a few local old-timers and some devoted travel-guide readers. Habits had changed, vile opportunism had descended, and little guys like Leo were paying.

"Maybe you ought to shut it down, Leo," I said casually, one dour afternoon while the recovery work was still going on down the street with flatbeds and dump trucks rumbling up Hudson, soot and soil kicking into the air with each pothole thud.

"Hey, Terry," Diddio said, jumping down from the pool table, "that's rash, man."

"I ain't closing your clubhouse, D," Leo replied impatiently, without looking up from his newspaper. "Don't you be worrying 'bout that."

"Whew!" Diddio wiped his brow, then he lay back on the table's tatty green felt.

Now, as a folksinger's pretty contralto glided from the jukebox, Diddio jiggled the empty desk drawer back into its slot. We had the office neater and somewhat organized, under water stains on the leaky ceiling, above steel wool crammed into the holes where pipes disappeared into the floor. I'd written nine checks from my account to cover nearly $4,000 in bills, some of which were three months overdue.

Diddio slid the drawer into its slot, then withdrew the last one. From where I stood, I saw a pair of Leo's size 16EEE shoes and an old belt, curled and discarded.

"This belt," Diddio said, as he unfurled it, "could go around me twice."

At least. He had a 28-inch waist, as the leathery patch on the back of his black jeans announced.

He crinkled his nose as he withdrew Leo's black shoes. They were standard-issue rather than the orthopedic brand he'd taken to wearing in the past year or so. At one time, Leo had gotten the things resoled, and then he'd worn down the new bottoms as well.

"Hey."

"Hey what?" I asked.

"There's something in these tugboats."

Gunboats, I thought, but said nothing. Diddio didn't malaprop, even when coming down from an 18-hour buzz.

He dropped the big shoes on Leo's swivel chair. As I inched closer, I saw what he'd seen—a large manila envelope folded into each shoe.

"Look at this," he said, a lilt of wonder in his voice. "One for you, one for me."

I recognized Leo's scrawl on the goodbye envelopes. He'd known he wasn't going to last, and he'd prepared for his exit, writing letters to his friends so he could bid us farewell when he suddenly, though not unexpectedly, finalized his plan.

He looked at me. "Hot shit." Then he said, "What do you think?"

"I think we open them."

"Now?"

"And why not?"

He shrugged, scratched at the top of his head. "Man, I don't know. Like, do we need a ceremony or something? Something?"

I took the envelope addressed to me. "Go change the music," I suggested. "You've probably got something that'd fit."

He ran his fingers along his chin. Then: "Bingo!" And he left the office.

I lifted Leo's shoes from the chair, put them on the floor, and I sat, easing back as I opened the manila envelope he'd addressed to me.

Terry:

You know what this means, bruddy. You know I ain't going to tell you sorry, but I will say I tried not to lie. I didn't have it in me anymore and that says it all, don't it?

I'm not giving anybody any advice, especially you. I never took yours and you never take anybody's, so there's no use. In other words, I'll get right to it.

I want you to keep an extra careful eye on Diddio. He's going to need you now more than he ever did. He's a good kid. Lost like a little ol' raggy dog, of course. But he's got a good heart in him. If he finally finds himself that special girl he's been looking for, you make sure she don't do him like I got done.

Which leads me to my major point—

I want you to go find Loretta Jones.

Bring her to the cops, make her pay for taking my money, my business and whatever all else it was kept me going in this world we're living in. Go with it to wherever it goes. Don't worry about nothing. Keep pushing until it's all like it ought to be.

You find Loretta, Terry Orr, and you make her pay, and you make anybody else pay who's got to.

You've been a good friend, Terry. Do this thing. Set it right.

Leo Mallard

When I finished reading, I folded the handwritten letter and slid it back into the manila envelope. I took a breath and then, as I leaned forward to slip out of the chair, as I prepared to open the other letter-sized envelope, I noticed the silence.

Diddio had cut the music. I tried to remember if I'd even been in the Tilt with him when it was quiet.

Before I could stand to join him by the jukebox, he appeared in the door frame. He seemed stunned and, though not quite frightened, he was less than himself, without his peculiar brand of confidence, his nutty swagger.

"Terry."

"I know," I said. "A voice from beyond. Leo."

What could Leo have written to him? Take care of Terry and Bella. Don't smoke so much pot. Eat right. Exercise. Get some sun. Stop trying to fall in love. Just sidle up to a nice woman and let it flow.

He couldn't have asked him to find Loretta Jones.

"Terry," he swallowed, as he held up the big empty envelope. "He left me— He left me the Tilt."

"Wh— Huh?"

He let himself fall against the frame. "Leo is giving me the Tilt."

"Christ."

"He says free and clear," D said, flapping the envelope, apparently quoting Leo's letter. "Free and . . . I mean, what's that mean?"

I shook my head. "You need a lawyer to tell you." Given Leo's tainted link to the IRS, I couldn't begin to guess what the expression meant to him. "But I didn't see a mortgage book or bills in there, so maybe—"

"A lawyer. Man," he groaned. "Here we go."

I stood, squeezed past him and went toward the long oak bar, the half-empty liquor bottles, the cash register, all of it. Yesterday's FedEx package from Ruthie, blunt with a few editions of the *Times-Picayune*, sat unopened on a stool. The jukebox lid was up, like the wing of a DeLorean.

Diddio followed me.

His letter rested on the pool table.

"Wow," I said. "It's yours. Wow."

I couldn't figure what else I was supposed to say. Did Leo really believe Diddio could run a bar? Diddio, who asks Bella and Daniel to help him with his 1040, who forgets to do his laundry until all his black T-shirts and jeans are too shanked to re-wear? Diddio, who left a rental car outside a Holiday Inn in Cleveland, took a taxi to the airport and didn't remember the white Malibu until he was back in TriBeCa for nearly a week. Who twice had his ATM card seized because he punched in the wrong four-digit code.

I wiped my moist forehead on the short sleeve of my gray T-shirt. It was another unbearably muggy day already, and the overhead fan barely caused a ripple in the thick air.

"He liked you, D," I said finally.

"You think?"

Yes, and he saw in you virgin veins of self-reliance and undiscovered skills in management. I guess.

He followed me. "You got two envelopes?"

I stopped, opened the second, let the contents tumble onto the green felt.

A photo, which landed face-down. A key, and—

"Money," Diddio said, pointing.

—a short stack of bills held together with a rubber band.

"Benjamins." He frowned as he juggled a cube of blue chalk. "I didn't get money."

"You got a bar," I told him. "Don't bitch."

"No, I'm not," he said quickly. "It's just—"

I flipped over the photo.

"Loretta," Diddio said, as the chalk flew out of his hand.

In the glory days of Big Chief's. She was in front of the restaurant, standing on Greenwich. The sun was over the buildings, on its way to the Jersey palisades, and she was in raw light. Her lazy hound dog, a big blond thing, lay at her feet.

"She was pretty good-looking," Diddio observed. "Yeah, I remember now."

I nodded. Loretta had blond hair with a touch of red—in someone of a more genteel disposition, it would be called strawberry blond—pale blue eyes, high cheekbones under a faint complexion, a sprinkling of light freckles, thin lips often drawn tight, even in this photo. When she stood next to Leo, she seemed tiny, but she was about Diddio's height and she was well built, thin in the hips but fulsome on top.

I noticed that the photo had been taken before the hard, weathered look of the persistent drinker had marred her features.

"Never did seem too happy, though," D added. "For a woman who had a dog."

"She was a hard-ass." And a good-looking woman who knew it. "He wants me to find her."

He bent down to pick up the chipped cube. "Why?"

"Bring her to justice, I guess." I shrugged. "Something."

As he stood, I noticed that his face was an odd color, as the blood had rushed to challenge his pallor. "That's what the money's for," he said.

"I guess." I lifted the stack.

"The key. It's for the bar."

"Your bar."

"Holy moley."

"Tell me about it," I agreed.

"Maybe that's why Leo wants you to go get Loretta," he said. "So she don't swoop down and try to take the Tilt from me. You know?"

"Yeah. Maybe." But it was more likely he wanted his revenge dished as cold as could be—from beyond the grave. Not that Loretta would let her guard down, even with Leo gone. D's theory had one thing in its favor: Loretta was a rank opportunist. A nickel never rolled off a table that she didn't grab before it hit the floor.

He looked at me, looked at the money in my hands. The chalk cube once again fell to the grubby linoleum.

"Interesting," I said. "A man owes the IRS, yet he can keep five Gs in his desk for who knows how long."

D started to crawl under the pool table.

"Leave it," I instructed. Waving the money, I added, "I'll buy you a new one."

A muffled "thanks" came up from the tainted linoleum, from beneath hardwood and coarse green felt.

We've changed places: Bella was now back in my office and I was at the kitchen table with her laptop, her Applied Botany text, her marble notebooks, Cedar Pointe pencils and, look at that, an old-fashioned mimeographed sheet of questions, purple ink on white paper. "Explain in detail the primary differences and similarities between angiosperms and gymnosperms."

I wonder if it still has that smell, the chemical—

"We're all set," she announced, returning just as I had lifted the sheet to my nose.

"Good." The central air gave the house a cool, spring-like amiability. Over on West Broadway, grown men in tattered sandals and Yankees T-shirts were jumping under the fire hydrant's arching spray, while on Chambers, window fans were a red-hot commodity, despite the 500 percent markup.

"Tuesday morning, EWR to MSY. Five tickets."

"Five? Who—"

"Dennis. Me, you. Julie. Daniel," she counted, holding up her fingers. "Five."

"Julie?"

"Dad, you bring your girlfriend to a friend's funeral. Obvious."

She nudged me with her hip. She wanted her chair. Bella couldn't do her homework in any other place in the house, nor could she do it without her soft Cedar Pointes. Nor, lately, without removing a yellow rubber band from her wrist and putting it in a perfect circle near the center of the table.

At least she wasn't wearing her fedora.

As I stood, I said, "Bella, let's hold off with the girlfriend stuff."

"Yeah, right," she replied. "You've been seeing her three times a week for over a year, but she's not your girlfriend. *OK.*"

"She's my friend. But that's it."

She reached to boost the sound coming from the little speakers in her laptop. Pulsing dance rhythms made by machines invaded the room.

"And Daniel?" I reached over her shoulder and cut the volume.

With a few flicks of her long fingers, her mother's long fingers, she put the music on pause.

"I need company."

"What about D? And me?"

"You like Daniel."

"Daniel's fine."

Actually, Daniel was much more than fine. He was bright, earnest, witty and thoroughly devoted to my daughter.

"But," I continued, "we're going to a funeral."

"He knows how to behave."

"Bella . . ."

She tapped on the botany textbook. "Dad, I've got to do this and it's not easy."

I assumed she'd chosen the class because her Aunt Rafaela in Foggia ran a florist shop, was a passionate gardener and was Bella's closest blood link to her late mother.

But she picked it, she said, because she thought it wouldn't be easy. Schoolwork wasn't much of a challenge for Bella, even the aggressive curriculum at Walt Whitman. I'd been fighting off suggestions to skip Bella ahead at least a grade since she was five years old.

Marina blamed me for her precociousness.

She said, her Italian accent light, charming, "Who gives a baby a book on Galileo?"

Time-Life had this series . . . "It's got pictures in it," I explained. "Besides, he's Italian, right?"

"She's reading it," Marina replied. Paint had landed on her denim carpenter's jeans, swooshes and dabs of reds, oranges, vibrant greens. "She wants a telescope."

"Oh, Marina, don't exagger—"

"Terry, she is three years old!"

Marina once said that I didn't want a baby, a little daughter. She said I wanted a new friend.

Not true. Not then. Having a baby daughter was great.

So was having a baby son.

"So five to New Orleans?" I asked.

"Dad, please," Bella pleaded without looking up from her text, her scentless mimeograph sheet. "I have to do this, OK?"

She reached out with a finger and let the music play.

3

Newark Airport had improved since my last trip, whenever that was: monorails, which Bella and Diddio found way outrageous and Daniel boarded with a knowing nod, as if he approved; yes, yes, it's fine. As we entered the terminal, we were greeted by forced air, a vague scent of fuel and the kind of mild tension I recalled from the days when I traveled playing b-ball or when Marina went to her openings, with Bella and me tagging along, before Davy was born.

"I got you a *Sporting News* and an *American Legacy*," Julie said as she passed me a yellow plastic sack that wore the vendor's logo.

I juggled my suit bag to the other hand and took the magazines. "What you get? What's—*Mad*?"

She smiled. "That's for Gabriella. Or Dennis." She showed me a copy of *Country Living*.

"Nothing for prosecutors? *Miranda Monthly, Suspended Sentence, Perp Walk Weekly?*"

"Pul-lease. No mention of work, the D.A.'s or Centre Street for the next few days," she said. "I'm paying my respects to your dear friend Leo and his family, and then I'm getting you to show me a good time."

"There's a good time in New Orleans?" I asked.

"So I'm told."

We were greeted at our gate by college-bound students, sleeping on inflated collars, tongues lolling, their legs curled over armrests; and urgent cell-phone shouters in business suits who gestured as if they were conducting the conversation. Discarded pages of *USA Today* cluttered the waiting area, as did carry-ons of all sizes, their handles high, antenna-like. Ignoring instructions, people began inching toward the passageway as soon as the first steward waddled down the ramp, and fit young men who hadn't yet considered having children oozed into the line for the elderly needing assistance and families traveling with small kids.

I was watching Bella distribute the magazines, offering the *Mad* as well as a block of Dentyne to D, who had his Utz baseball cap pulled low to his brow, when I heard my name amid the crackle from overhead speakers.

Bella and Diddio snapped their heads toward me, while Daniel frowned in curiosity.

Who do I know, I thought, who isn't here?

At the check-in counter, a beefy man in white short sleeves handed me a red courtesy phone.

"Hel—"

"Get me my fuckin' money, Terry." A harsh, throaty voice, raspy, shrill.

"Who—"

"It's mine, and you know it's mine."

"Loretta?"

"Everything he had is mine, Terry."

"Loretta, where are you?" My four companions were staring at me, waiting for information. I waved at them, nodding, shrugging to tell them there was nothing to worry about.

"Don't you never mind, and don't change the subject," she barked. "Just get me my money. Don't leave New Or—"

"Loretta, he's got shit," I told her. "And if I find he had a fuckin' dime I wouldn't turn it over to you."

"You think all he had was that piece-of-shit bar? Terry? *Terry?*"

They were boarding our row, and Bella, hand on hip, demanded I catch up.

"Terry!"

"Loretta, go sober up, all right?"

I returned the handset to the thick man behind the counter. Loretta was still spewing when he dropped it back in the cradle.

"First wife?" he asked.

He must've seen me with Julie and the three kids, one of whom was pushing 40.

"Somebody's," I told him. "Not mine."

"Poor soul."

I nodded. "You got that right," I said, as I went to join the jagged line, trying not to think about a gin-soaked woman calling airports at 8:30 in the morning.

I wound up next to pudgy Daniel, halfway toward the back of the narrow jet, but in a deep bulkhead. I could see Diddio four rows up, his head against the drawn plastic window shade, black cap tugged over his eyes. Bella and Julie were across the aisle from the critic, with Bella at the window. As we lifted off, Julie turned, smiled to me. In her pale blue blouse under a blue sweater and charcoal-gray slacks, she looked like an apt businesswoman who the company let bring her child on the trip. I opened *Slaughter at Kinmel Hall* and quickly fell back into the story of duplicity, cowardice and mass murder in North Wales in 1919. It was so damned engaging that I only thought about Marina, Davy and Weisz, the psychotic who killed them, every 20 seconds instead of every 10.

And I was still deep in the book, ignoring the white-noise rush of stale air in the cabin, the dried pancakes, the greasy sausage links, the hapless comedy on the small overhead screen, when I felt a tap on my arm.

"Will you be doing your private investigation work while we're in New Orleans?" Daniel Wu asked.

I turned to him. For the first two hours of the flight, he said nothing, as he contentedly watched streaks of rose-colored clouds, nursed a bottle of water and politely thumbed through the in-flight magazine and *American Legacy*. Daniel was by nature courteous and thoughtful, and behind dark, twinkling eyes nearly hidden by his high, rounded cheeks, seemingly bemused by all he witnessed. Today, under a bulky purple long-sleeved T, he wore big, baggy red shorts and his knees were smooth, with dry wrinkles where his leg bent along the contours of the uncomfortable seat. His black high-topped sneakers, highly stylized with violet plastic squiggles, bold white lines and red Velcro, were placed neatly under the seat in front of him.

"I'm sorry," I said, sliding the ticket stub between the book's pages.

"You'll be working in New Orleans?"

"I suppose you could call it that," I replied.

"After a fashion." He smiled.

"Huh?"

"That's an expression," he told me. "After a fashion."

"You like it?"

He said he did.

"Well, then, I'll be working. After a fashion."

"And what will you be doing, if I may ask?"

Daniel was curious, more so than any of Bella's friends. In him, it was an admirable trait. He seemed to want to understand the world he inhabited, and no fact was too obscure to escape his interest.

"I'll be looking for a woman," I said. "Loretta Jones."

"The one on the phone?"

"As a matter of fact—"

"What did she do?" He shifted his rotund body in his seat so he could face me. I lifted the armrest so he'd be more comfortable.

I figured she'd learned of Leo's death from one of her old boyfriends in the First Precinct, but that wasn't what Daniel wanted to know.

"She embezzled a bunch of money," I told him. "Perpetuated a fraud against the government. Her husband and the government."

"Perpetuated a fraud." He chuckled. "I like that too."

I tried to suppress a smile as I returned to Bodelwyddan.

"Do you have clearance to bring a gun on board?"

This time I put my thumb between the pages. "I'm not carrying," I said.

He frowned. "Is that dangerous?"

I shook my head.

"It could be," he continued. "This woman, we know she is troubled, and now that you are looking for her . . ."

"She's troubled?"

"Stealing is not normal. Lying, not normal. She might even be capable of far worse and, for you, that is a more complicated issue."

"That's it." He had her right, did Daniel Wu.

He said, "Someone who is a thief and a liar has no regard for property or promises. Wouldn't you agree?"

"I'd agree, Daniel."

"What else is there?"

"Well, no one's said she's ever killed anybody," I said, as I stared at the paperback.

"Not such a giant step . . ."

As he paused to consider his own comment, I flipped open—

"And it's a strange city for you."

"Huh?"

He repeated, "It's a strange city for you."

I tried to joke my way out of the conversation. "Well, Daniel, a lot of people say New Orleans is a strange city in itself."

"No, what I mean is, Gabriella says you've never been there."

"That's true."

"Backup."

"Excuse—"

"You'll need backup."

"Not for this I won't, Daniel," I told him, perhaps too curtly.

He paused, frowned. "Am I interrupting?"

I wiggled the book above my lap, my jeans.

"I'm inquisitive," he said with a shrug. "It's me."

"I've noticed."

"Oh."

For all his cheeriness, his innate optimism, Daniel could be sensitive, Bella reported one evening.

"But, it's fine, Daniel. Go on, if you want."

He turned, his shoulders slumping. "I've found it useful to ask," he said softly.

"It's good to ask." I nodded. "But sometimes it's good to observe and see if you can figure it out by yourself."

He paused for a moment, pondering, tossing it around.

"Yes?" I asked.

"Well, I would be inclined to say it's better to ask for help, to cooperate," he replied wistfully. "But I'm going to think about what you said."

He nodded and shifted, and I opened Pomerantz's book. Where was I? Oh yeah, a frigid winter in early 1919 and British troops—

Daniel chuckled. "In itself. A strange city in itself." Then he pushed his small round thumb toward the window, the frail open skies. "I'll watch the clouds."

Before checking in, we paused for a moment to organize in the thin shadows under an ornate verandah, as the Louisiana sun baked the cast-iron railings of a shuttered restaurant on the other side of St. Charles. I ran my finger under the collar of my blue Oxford and rolled my sleeves up an extra notch, as Julie removed her thin sweater and Diddio tugged rapidly at his black T-shirt. Our silent agreement: We'd gotten off the plane and stepped into a *shvitz*. Late summer in Manhattan felt balmy compared to midday off the Warehouse District. One of us was bound to say it, so I went first.

"Big Easy, my ass," I moaned.

"It's just the humidity," Daniel said as he hoisted Bella's backpack onto his shoulder. Behind him, waves of heat rose from the street. "We'll adapt, I'm sure."

Bella smiled with wicked pride, as if to warn me against trying to ruin her good time. I could've sworn she went humph.

Up St. Charles, a big green Cadillac, one Detroit hadn't produced in about 50 years, shone in the sun, its broad, arched hood glowing, its wide grille sparkling like the teeth of a cynical beast.

"Elvis lives," Diddio said, nodding toward the Caddy as it inched forward. He trailed Julie, Daniel and my daughter as they sought the lobby's air-conditioning.

A short, sinewy black man in a black jacket, cream-colored shirt and black bow tie came out of the driver's seat and into the stark sunlight.

"Mr. Terry Orr?" he asked as he made his way around the car.

I nodded.

He had fierce gray eyes, and his skin was drawn tight to his skull. His bony shoulders made it seem as if the hanger was still under his jacket, and his awkward physique made it tough to pin his age. If he'd told me he was 55, I would've believed him. He could've added 15 years to that and I still would've.

He seemed mildly surprised when I stuck out my hand. He shook it, but didn't smile.

"And you are?"

"Willis, sir," he replied. "Miss Mallard would enjoy a word, sir."

He opened the Caddy's back door. Filling the back on the passenger's side was a hefty woman in a fluffy pink chiffon dress and sensible white shoes. The dress's three-quarter sleeves revealed meaty arms that overwhelmed the pearl wristlet meant to accent the white beads on her vast pink bodice. On the seat next to her was a pink hat as wide as a beach umbrella. In New Orleans, pink was the new black, at least for Ruthie Mallard.

Under her flouncy hair, which was as dark as Diddio's dyed mop, she had Leo's face—sad eyes, thin lips, broad nose, an additional chin. But not his pallor: She had bright skin under a dab of makeup, which gave her a somewhat healthy glow.

Yet despite the pink dress, the pleasant smile, her plump body as it nestled in the tufted seat, I could tell there was nothing soft about Ruthie Mallard. I made a silent wager: Within two minutes, this woman is going to tell me what to do.

"Miss Mallard," I said, greeting her.

"Oh no you don't, Terry Orr," she replied in a high, singsong voice. "You and me, we're family, Terry Orr. My baby brother told me all about you and so you know it's so. You just *know* it's so."

Oh boy.

"Now you come on in here. Come on." She shifted her hat to the car's jump seat and tapped the spot next to her. "You and I, we are going to *talk*."

With Willis holding the door, I left the heat, stepped inside and sank into the gray upholstery.

"Some car," I said. After three hours in the sky on a barely padded wooden board, the seat felt like tub butter on my sore ass.

"Terry Orr, this is a 1951 Cadillac Fleetwood Series Sixty Special," she announced. "My mama bought it fresh, and baby Leo and me, we were raised in it."

"Is that right?" I'd been in Yugos with more efficient air conditioners.

"Only eighteen thousand or so of them was built. Did you know that?" she added. "And I'll bet you there ain't but one or two left and none looking like this one here."

I nodded.

"Now, tell me your plans, Terry Orr," she said, as she shifted in the seat.

"I don't get you." When I called to tell her of Leo's death, I mentioned I'd be attending the funeral.

"Now don't you tell me you and your big ol' family came all the way to Louisiana just for my baby Leo."

I said, "As a matter of fact, we did."

"For Leo?" She tilted her head. "Is that a fact?"

"Why else?" I asked with a shrug.

"Ain't that the damnedest thing. Loyalty," she mused. "I can't say I knew my brother inspired it, but you say so, so it must be. Damn."

I didn't respond.

"Well, if you find yourself with time to spare, Terry Orr, I'd say we got everything you want: casino, jazz music, good food and lots of it. You know, character, color. You go see the Garden District and you'll find all sorts of quaint, Terry Orr, you coming from New York, *Three*beca or whatever."

"Maybe we'll take a tour of the bayous," I offered. "I've never seen an alligator."

"See," she said loudly. "*That* is the spirit, right there."

She clapped her hands as if delighted. Willis, who was standing out in the sun with his wrists crossed behind his rump, turned and, with a firm, alert expression, looked in at her. Then he returned to staring down St. Charles.

"Spirit, yes sir," she added.

I smiled, nodded politely. She was playing me and doing a half-assed job of it. The Blanche Dubois–meets–Miss Daisy routine was about as broad as a vaudeville gaffe and no less obvious.

"So, I'd say you and . . . and . . ." She stopped and gave herself a chastening tap on the back of her hand. "I'm sorry, but I do not know the name of your family members, Terry Orr."

"Gabriella is my daughter," I said.

"Gabriella," she said. "Lovely name. Italian?"

She said *Eye*-talian. "Yes."

"And your wife's name?"

"That's not my wife," I said, shaking my head. "Her name is Julie. And then there's Daniel, who's my daughter's friend. And Dennis Diddio."

"Dennis Diddio," she repeated as she put on a wide, knowing smile. "So that is my Leo's great good friend Dennis Diddio. The one with all the . . ."

She wiggled her fingers up and down near her ears, as if a long shock of black hair cascaded along the side of her head too.

"Yes ma'am."

She kept silent for a moment, nodding almost imperceptibly.

"Your time is all planned out then," she said finally.

"More or less. I mean, my daughter has some ideas."

"I must tell you, Terry Orr. I must express my concern."

"About?" I leaned back against the door and its quarter window.

She pointed at me. "I hear say you are some kind of private investigator . . ."

I nodded, shrugged.

"A curious kind?"

"Not really."

"Did you bring with you some form of curiosity that requires satisfaction, Terry Orr?"

She kept saying my name as one, long, vaguely French word.

"I came to say goodbye to Leo," I said flatly.

"And see the alligators."

"There's that, yes."

"Because I had a fear in my mind," she said. "A fear that tells me you might be looking for that cheap harlot who rode him for as long as he had some worth to himself."

Now we were getting to it.

"See, Terry Orr, I knew my baby Leo," she went on. "He wants her back, don't he?"

"I don't get you," I said.

"He wants that Loretta Jones to cry over him. 'Oh my Leo, poor Leo.' Like that."

I shook my head. "Not exactly."

She turned her portly body toward me. "What is it then?"

"He wants her brought to justice," I said.

She hesitated, then smiled. " 'To justice' you say? Well, if that ain't the damnedest thing I ever heard." She tossed her head back and let out a laugh. "Leo. My goodness."

I didn't get her meaning and told her so.

"I had it that he *pined* for her," she replied.

I said no.

"I thought he could maybe want you to find her and drag her to the Halfway Cemetery and have her dive on top of his grave, sobbing and all," she said.

"So she's here? Loretta's in Louisiana?"

"Not that I've been told," she replied. "And believe you me, Terry Orr, I can guarantee I would have been told."

I believed her. She had it out for her sister-in-law. Even the most dubious report of the harlot's return would've gotten her attention.

"No, we're gonna leave Loretta right where she is," Ruthie Mallard said. "Leo don't need her no more."

I didn't reply. That wasn't what Leo wanted, and I'd just told her as much. But I figured all this foolishness was to find out if I'd brought word of Loretta with me, so I went along with it.

"You ought to know, Miss Mallard, that your brother was paying down his debt to the IRS. Any assets Loretta's got may—"

"The IRS. The *IRS*," she bellowed angrily. "Let the IRS, your city marshal, all of them . . . You know what they can do? *They* can follow my baby Leo down the grave and they can go get it from him there."

Again, the chauffeur turned to peer into the Caddy. This time he raised his hands to the car's hot roof. I saw that he wore a shoulder holster stuffed with a snub-nosed .38.

"Oh, I'm telling you, Terry Orr," Ruthie said, "how they hounded that poor boy. Between them and that Loretta . . ." She smiled, reached over and tapped my leg. "If it wasn't for a friend like you, I don't think he would've wanted to live."

I was going to tell her he didn't, but I understood the sentiment and I thanked her.

"And as far as that harlot is concerned, she wanted to go, leave her gone."

She waited a second, turned and rapped the window behind her with a knuckle. Willis opened the front door on his side.

"Yes, ma'am."

"Mr. Orr is going to rejoin his caravan," she said, grinning broadly.

The gun-toting chauffeur peered at me over the front seat, then he turned his gaze to his employer.

"Yes, ma'am."

He came around and opened the door to St. Charles. A blast of thick air greeted me.

I thanked the old man and turned to Ruthie Mallard. "I'm sorry for your loss," I told her.

She lifted her big pink hat and, closing her eyes, calmly said, "Thank you, Terry Orr."

By the time I got up to the room, Daniel had my suit in the closet and my dress shoes on the side of the king-size bed.

"You are scratching your head," he observed.

"Yeah, I guess I am." The room was perfect. He'd even put my copy of *Slaughter at Kinmel Hall* on the nightstand.

"The green Cadillac . . ."

I said, "A quiz, Daniel."

He smiled as he sat on the big bed.

"How would someone who knew me well describe me?" I asked as I ran the cold water at the sink between the rooms of the boxy suite.

"Tall. Fit. Black hair with a little gray. Your eyes are—"

"No, no. I mean—"

"Oh. Your temperament?"

"Well, how about the facts of me?"

Daniel watched as I cupped my hands under the chilly water and splashed my face again and again. The air-conditioning worked fine, but it wasn't enough, at least not yet.

"You are Gabriella's father, and you used to be a writer," he replied when I cut the water, after running my hand along the back of my neck. "Your wife and son were taken from you."

"All of that before the stuff about being a private investigator?"

"Of course." He nodded. "Why?"

I tossed the hand towel into the silver sink.

"Leo's sister knew I was a P.I. but she pretended not to know that Bella's mother was dead."

He thought for a moment. "Yes, she must have been pretending. A friend of yours certainly would've told his sister that fact."

There were two tiny bottles of lukewarm Canada Dry club soda in the mini-bar. I opened one and passed it to Daniel.

"Thank you," he said. He took a long sip.

I said, "The victim's sister doesn't want me to pursue the perpetrator of the fraud."

"If she is more concerned with your position as a private investigator than with your personal tragedy, I would agree." He nodded, as he tried to hold back a curt burp.

I pulled the bottle away from my lips. "She said '*Eye*-talian,' Daniel."

The young man grimaced. "Gabriella told me that as many as forty percent of the people who live in New Orleans are of Italian descent," he replied.

"I believe that's so."

"That was an unnecessary insult, I would say."

"Me too." And condescending.

"What will you do?" He smiled as he stood.

"Well, Daniel, what should I do?" I had my hands on my hips, the bottle engulfed by one of my fists.

"Exactly," he said, beaming.

4

At Big Chief's and, less often, at the Tilt, Leo had spoken of Pib Owen, a chef and restaurateur in the French Quarter who had served as his mentor in the food business. Leo claimed he learned the art of seasoning from his mother, whom he referred to as Big Ruthie, a descriptive name that once brought to mind nothing so much as Leo in drag. Pib, Leo said, taught him how to run a kitchen.

After quick showers, the four of us followed Bella across Poydras to a gumbo place near Jackson Square, then I peeled off to Pib's, calling ahead. I took the long way, leaving the troupe at Dumain, as I set out to kill a few extra minutes so I could catch Owen after his lunchtime crowd thinned. I suppose I could've gone with the others but, having decided to learn as much as I could about Loretta before we went back to ThreeBeCa, I thought a trip to the Voodoo Museum might be distracting. "Come on, Dad. You're going to miss *everything*," said Bella, with the enthusiasm of a happy little girl who just might enjoy her father's company.

Now, I headed west on Dauphine, squeezing through five businessmen who'd wisely left their jackets on door hooks. They were trailed by female colleagues better prepared for the steamy August afternoon: white blouses opened at the collar, short skirts, no pantyhose over tanned legs, sandals. Delivery trucks puttered by, and cabbies at the stand near a chain hotel, dressed down to look extra-local, rested against one long red-and-green Plymouth, settling in for a good conference. One guy removed a fresh toothpick from his shirt pocket, jabbed it into the corner of his mouth, flicked it around with his tongue.

I was thinking Julie and I hadn't exchanged more than a few sentences today when I turned on Toulouse and saw a sign at the corner of the next block. Pib's.

As I drew closer to the storefront, I realized I had no idea if Pib Owen was thin or fat, black or white, tall or short, only a bit older than Leo or a graying knob of an old man.

Turned out he was all of the above—a middleweight with maybe 10 pounds more than he needed on his frame, about 5'9", close-cropped salt-and-pepper hair, and steel-blue eyes and a neat goatee that made him look younger than what I took him to be, which was about 50. Pib Owen was what they used to call in the Deep South a mulatto—half-black, half-white—and his skin was the color of light coffee.

"Goodness," Pib Owen said, as he came out of the kitchen onto Toulouse. "I ain't had nobody look at me like that since I don't know when."

I shook his hand and introduced myself. "Trying to match the man with the image." Sweat was dripping from the back of my hair onto my collar.

"I don't suppose I have an image in New York City, do I?" He smiled as he adjusted his apron. The top of his white cotton uniform bore a laundry mark on the breast.

"If you do, I don't know it."

He nodded, and then, suddenly solemn, he tapped his chest above his heart. "He was a good man."

"You kept in touch with him?" I asked, wondering when Leo might've talked to him about me.

"Not much, no."

Leo had a phone number for Pib Owen in his directory. It looked like it had been written a long time ago.

"Isn't that the way?" I said.

He paused. "I can't say I'm surprised he's gone. But I guess I thought we'd get together someday, talk things over."

"No, he didn't take care of himself," I said, shaking my head. "We tried, but—"

"No, It's not . . . I mean, all the Mallards are big, big folks."

I thought he meant he suspected Leo wouldn't survive his poor health, excessive weight, lazy ways.

"I'm talking about Loretta," he continued. "I knew she'd kill him one way or the other."

Owen reemerged through the screen door, which snapped back with a slap and rattle. He handed me a Dixie and had one for himself.

As he sipped the cold beer, he leaned the sole of one shoe, then his shoulders, against the long brick wall that separated the entrance to his restaurant from the kitchen, escaping the bright rays of the midafternoon sun. From where I stood, I could see through the narrow squares on the screen door into the kitchen where the help continued to clean up from its lunchtime activities while getting ready for the dinner crowd. A young man wearing a black do-rag went at a bunch of bell peppers with a long knife, chopping until he had almost-uniform green pieces on the well-worn cutting board.

"So you're a private eye," Owen mused.

"After a fashion," I replied.

"Ain't never met a private eye."

I lifted the brown longneck. He returned the toast.

"Do I know your work?"

I smiled. "Well, I can't say I busted up a ring of neo-Nazis working out of the Woolworth Building, if that's what you mean."

Nor have I found the Madman who threw my baby son on the subway tracks, who watched as my wife scrambled in vain to save him, who disappeared as the murdering train roared through.

"As long as you ain't a peeper."

"I've never been asked," I told him, "so I never had to say no."

I sipped the cold beer. The faint sound of a saxophone floated from the distance. A familiar New Orleans tune, played with little fire. Apparently, there's no test for skill.

"So, you're looking for Loretta," Owen said. "What makes you think she's here?"

I shrugged. "I'm in town for Leo's funeral. I figured I might ask about her, here and there. Who knows?"

He nodded. Then a thought brought on a thin smile. "I don't suppose Leo got some money for her."

"Might be the other way around." She was already into me for four Gs for the bills he'd missed.

He absently looked at the label on the damp beer bottle, then he shook his head. "That Loretta . . ."

"You know her well?" I asked.

He said no. "Not anymore."

Then he said they first met about 20 years earlier, when the original Pib's was in its second year over on Royal. He needed a part-time bookkeeper: Business was no better or worse than he'd expected, but the financial end was more than he could handle by himself. Before that, he ran the kitchen at a small cash-only place in Lacombe owned by his uncles. Dreaming about having a place of his own in the Vieux Carré didn't include nights in accounting class at the local Voc-Tech.

"Loretta must have been, what, about nineteen, twenty years old back then."

"Maybe a few years older," Owen said. "Not many. She had a year at Dillard, I think it was. Loretta had a few years on Leo. Not that it made a difference. Or maybe it did."

"So Leo was still in high school when you met him?" I asked.

He told me Leo had dropped out. "He wasn't going to go to no culinary institute or nothing, so what did he need school for?" Pib asked rhetorically. "Back in the day, he reminded me of somebody—me."

He came away from the wall and I assumed his spot, grabbing the sliver of shadow. I'd had my eye on the shade for the past five minutes or more. Though I'd stopped dripping, I could feel the effects of the Louisiana sun on the top of my head, my forearms, the backs of my hands.

"All Leo wanted to do was be in the kitchen, working up a little thing here and there," he went on. "You had to like him: a big goofy kid, kind of earnest, as they say. He liked to work, had a nice little flair for it. Big Ruthie used to come by, embarrass him by looking after him. Big Ruthie, she was used to going where she wanted."

I nodded as I imagined Leo as an awkward teen, scuffling to follow his passion. Then I saw him behind the bar at the Tilt, bloated, gray, eyes down-turned, battered by what life had dealt him.

"Loretta saw something in him," I led.

"More like Loretta put something in him," he replied. "I can't say Leo had any kind of big ambitions, you know what I mean? Work the kitchen, make a living for himself, maybe meet a local girl, stay at home in Thibodaux near Big Ruthie and his sister. The easy life. Nice."

But Leo made the move to Manhattan, arriving just before the crest of the Cajun-Creole craze reached New York City. He rode that wave, and Big Chief's became a popular, vaguely esoteric stop. I told Pib the story: As TriBeCa grew, and Wall Street inched north, Big Chief's did a nice lunchtime business. At night, people from all over town, some from Brooklyn and Queens, New Jersey, came to the place they heard about, read about in the *Times,* in Zagat's. Leo served good food in ample quantities, kept the prices reasonable and let good-time music blare. And then there were those beads they gave away, Mardi Gras masks on the wall, green and gold feathers, purple boas, fleur-de-lis flags, $7 Pimm's Cups and Sazeracs, Loretta, a sexy hostess with her dumb old floppy hound dog and all the rest. People loved that stuff. It was as if New York had discovered a lost civilization off the Mississippi. Writers were doing pieces about the culture of New Orleans with the same tone as they used in articles about the jungles of Borneo, about Thira before the volcano. "The roux, that magic concoction, is the guarded secret of the native Cajun chef, a nutty brown underpinning for his creativity, the bedrock of his culinary handiwork. How he whips up this near-mystical potion is as carefully and as ardently shielded as the combination to the family safe." That sort of claptrap. (Leo's carefully, ardently guarded secret: "Don't let it burn.") But he knew how to go with it. "Alchemy," he nodded coyly when asked about his roux by a guy at a table of snickering junior executives from Merrill Lynch. "And, bub, it's easier if you don't be pronouncing the 'x.'"

He was endearing, and he built a loyal customer base.

And for the young couple behind Big Chief's, the success fed a dream that had become a reality greater than the boundaries of the ambition. If my memory was on target, Loretta once talked about franchising, with the goal of making Big Chief's a national brand.

"So, I guess Loretta always had a big vision," I said.

"Oh yeah." Owen nodded. "She wanted something more than what she was going to find here and she set out to get it. Like, I needed her about once a week. But once she hooked up with Leo she was here every day."

"But . . . How do I say this?" I hesitated. "Leo as gravy train? I don't see it."

"I'm saying Leo had talent and she could influence him. You know, he was crazy on her. Big crazy. And that's the only way you're going to get a Mallard to leave Louisiana. Some craziness has got to be involved."

I nodded. Leo was head-over-heels for Loretta when I first met them.

"She was born as cute as a button out there on the bayou," he said, "and she learned how to make it grow, you know what I'm saying? A poor kid, kind of a tomboy, you know, hunting coon and rabbit. But not by the time she got here. Used to be into all kinds of fashion magazines, *Vogue,* whatever. Learning about art and such, *refining* herself, her manners, changing her natural ways. She got herself some kind of sophistication. Cleaning up her French. Putting away her hunting rifle and hounds, her torn T-shirts and tight jeans. New clothes, and a new life, for Loretta Jasmine Jones."

Owen shook his head and smiled. "Remember, I watched that flower blossom."

I couldn't begrudge anyone for trying to change to get ahead. I'd done it myself.

"And in the beginning," he continued, pointing the top of the longneck Dixie at me, "Big Ruthie was with it. Big Ruthie was behind it big."

"What made her change her mind?"

"Big Ruthie?" He chuckled low. "Well, her daughter Ruthie never liked Loretta, true. But it was the bottle that done it for Big Ruthie."

I shook my head in confusion. "Bottle?"

"Loretta put one upside Leo's head," he said. He smacked himself hard on the temple. "Wham!"

I grimaced. "Why?"

"She *overheard,* man," Owen explained. "I think maybe he was telling Big Ruthie he was going north with Loretta. But Leo and his mama was having a big talk."

"And?"

"I saw it. The whole thing." He gestured for me to follow him along Toulouse to the front of the restaurant.

I paused as he pushed open the door, then I went inside. Pib's seated 30 at 12 tables in a square room with a spotless terrazzo floor. Each table wore a napkin dispenser, black ashtray, salt and pepper shakers and a bottle of Tabasco sauce on a white-paper tablecloth, and the kitchen was in full view of the customers who faced it. Above the waitresses' station, the entire menu was painted on chalkboards.

"Big Ruthie and Leo was sitting in the corner there," Owen said, pointing to his left over by the kitchen. "It was about four o'clock. Place was empty."

Now two men working construction sat in the center of the room. Tall iced-tea glasses sat next to their meals, their elbows. The thick man facing me was working on fried oysters.

"I was back in the kitchen," he continued. "What Leo didn't know was Loretta was back there too, working on something or other. She had a little setup, adding machine, papers, her stuff."

Owen moved inside and I followed. A large fan in the corner to my left made the white paper on the tables flutter, but it didn't do much to take away the humidity, the heat.

"Big Ruthie's '51 Caddy Fleetwood was parked out front, ol' Willis leaning on it, bored but with it, if you know what I'm saying."

"Willis."

He said, "Her driver. Neighbor. You know, friend. Big Ruthie wouldn't drive herself." He waved his hand. "That's another story, son."

"Sorry." I smiled.

He nodded. "So there's Leo— I couldn't hear him, but I guess Big Ruthie was asking him, 'Are you sure about this one?' 'Do you know what you're getting yourself into?' That kind of thing. Not that she had something against Loretta, anyway not like Ruthie did. Ruthie thought Loretta was swamp trash making her move. But Mama just don't want her Leo leaving."

"And so Leo didn't show his mother how enthusiastic he was about Loretta's plans?" I asked.

"Her plans and her," Owen replied.

"So Big Ruthie leaves . . ."

"She's not even out the door. Takes a few minutes to drag her big self out to the street, you know."

"And Loretta . . ."

He gestured to a swinging door to his right. "Loretta comes out, crosses the room and, before Leo could get out of the seat, brings the beer bottle down on his head."

"Christ."

"You bet," he said. "Leo went down, blood everywhere, and Loretta's standing over him, screaming, calling him every which name, kicking him while he's on the floor and there he is, bleeding, trying to cover himself up. Big Ruthie came over and she slapped Loretta right in her face. *Boom!*" He pointed to the kitchen. "I saw the whole thing from over there."

He put on a wry smile. "That thing cost Loretta her slice of the Mallards' money."

"The Mallards have money?"

He nodded as he snorted a laugh. "Maybe you ain't heard up there in New York, but there's oil out there in the bayou," he said. "The Mallards used to be richer than shit. They're still doing all right, I guarantee you that. Only there ain't no more 'they.' It's just Ruthie."

Owen reached and pulled out a chair.

"Yeah, Leo gets stitched up and leaves a few days later with Loretta. And that is that."

"When did you see him last?"

"Saw him at Big Ruthie's funeral." He looked at me. "I did like that boy."

"And Loretta?"

"Hell, I ain't never been to New York."

"No, I meant here."

"She ain't coming back," he said, shaking his head knowingly. "Ain't no round-trip ticket in her plans."

A couple of years before, Tommy the Cop told me he'd heard from one of the detectives at the First that Loretta hadn't left Manhattan, that she'd taken her act uptown to find a new stake. Half the stories Mango told were bullshit, but this one sounded like it could be right. Maybe Owen had just confirmed it.

He hesitated, nervously slapping his thumb against the table. "I suppose if you're going to be digging around, talking to folks . . . I might as well tell you. Yeah, I nailed Loretta, sure. She was a pretty young thing and she liked a good time."

I held up my hand. "More than I need to know, friend."

"I mean, she was Leo's girl, but I didn't know he was going to marry her. Not really."

"So she ran around on Leo." I tilted the chair against the wall.

"Son, we were alone in the kitchen, it was a hot night . . ."

"Sounds like love," I said dryly.

He laughed. "You got it. We were real sweethearts."

If two people get together, only they know. And no one is going to find out unless one of them talks. So Owen was certain someone else had learned about that hot night in his kitchen or he wouldn't have mentioned it.

"She told Leo," I said.

"God damn. He tell you?"

You did, I thought. "No."

He scratched the back of his neck. "It works best if he can't trust nobody but her, I guess."

"Sinister."

"Well, I don't know about that," he said. "Something though, huh? Girl had a plan . . ."

He turned to sneak a look at the clock over the waitresses' station.

"I've taken enough of your time," I said as I lifted myself from the chair.

"No, no," he said, waving his hand. "Listen, you had lunch yet?"

I said I did. When I thanked him, I told him I might return, that I was staying in town for a few days after the funeral. What I didn't tell him was how I needed to get back to the hotel to see if I could find a way to get on the Web or go over to the *Times-Picayune* and dig through their morgue.

There was a lot more to the Mallards than Leo had ever told me.

Back on St. Charles, my shirt clinging to my body as if I'd been dunked in the Mississippi, I stopped to look in the windows of Meyer the Hatter, the kind of stylish haberdashery that dotted streets in major American cities until the early '60s. There were about 40 fedoras in the window, all of which were in better shape than the tattered one my daughter cherished. She traded for it a little more than three years ago, giving an old man she met near the Cage on Sixth her favorite beret in exchange. Bella treated it as if it had considerable sentimental value or supernatural powers. I was *not* allowed to put it on my head.

I left the store determined to bring Bella by, to let her see a shop that had been in business since back when her fictional "unassigned detective" Mordecai Foxx skulked around lower Manhattan. As I continued toward the hotel, I let my mind resume its ramble, but it went not to my daughter, her Foxx or a new fedora, or my Marina and our first days in the sunbaked countryside near Foggia, but to Leo picking slivers of brown glass out of his head, and Big Ruthie coming to her boy's rescue. And Loretta's fists and fierce blue eyes, as she stepped back from Big Ruthie's assault, as she calculated her revenge. Was that event the source of Ruthie Jr.'s loathing of Loretta? Could've been. Maybe even should've been.

Cars were backed up on the stretch that led to Route 90 and Route 10, as if rush hour had begun. But a quick peek at my watch told me it was only 3:30. Plenty of time before the real cavalcade began, unless they let people go early here if the humidity exceeds 100 percent.

When I looked up again, I saw, to my surprise, Julie turning the corner in the distance and coming toward me on St. Charles. She hadn't seen me yet, and then she did and she waved, picking up her pace.

I passed the hotel to greet her.

"You escaped?"

She met me with a kiss on the damp cheek. "I think they were glad to see me go."

"No—"

"I'm not offended," she laughed. "I can't keep up with three teenagers."

"How's Diddio doing?"

"He's trying. Your daughter is trying to make sure he's all right," she replied. "But she's got too much energy for me. I surrendered on the way to the Confederate Museum."

Julie had her brown hair tied back, away from her face, but in the heat a few bangs had fallen onto her forehead. As she looked up at me, her cheeks a bit pink from the unexpected exercise, I felt the urge to brush the bangs aside. When I did so, she gave me a bright smile.

Then she hooked her arm in mine. "Tell me what you did."

"Well, it seems Loretta Jones—"

"Not yet," she protested. She pointed to her black flats below her charcoal slacks. "I've got to slip out of these and, Terry, I insist you make me a grown-up drink."

"Fair enough," I said. We headed to the hotel.

She had her bare feet up on the arm of the green sofa, and a vodka-and-tonic in her hand. I'd kicked off my running shoes. The world was on the outside.

Suddenly, it felt right. Though not suddenly: It was always fine. We got along, never bickered. We kept it light. Against all odds, this good woman believed in me.

She rolled the icy glass across her forehead. "Heaven."

Not really. We were in my clean, orderly suite in a serviceable hotel in New Orleans. But I suppose for Julie, after a charmless three-hour flight, a bowl of spicy seafood filé gumbo, a lesson in voodoo rites and a whirlwind stop at the Contemporary Arts Center, lounging on a couch with the AC on high and a cold drink in hand might be close enough to perfection.

I sipped club soda and watched from across the room as she shifted her head on the rigid throw pillows.

"I don't know how you do it," she said, shaking her head.

I sat back. "With Bella? Mostly I'm just sort of along for the ride."

"She's irresistible, Terry."

"Yeah, but I don't think she's obnoxious about it."

"OK. Now, what about me?" Julie joked.

"You're not obnoxious either," I replied.

She tugged at the front of her sleeveless blue blouse, which had dampened in the syrupy air. An ingenuous gesture, unassuming, appealing. "You're such a smoothie."

"Only kidding."

"I suppose it's a compliment," she mused. "Not a very good one, but . . ."

"I wonder if I can do better," I said. "Something there is about you . . . Now, what is it exactly?"

I looked at her. Bella once said that Julie Giada resembled the leisurely courtesan in Manet's *Olympia.* And there were physical similarities: round face, small chin, brown hair, eyes set far apart despite a thin nose. Julie's dark eyes drooped slightly at the outer corners and her skin had an olive tint, courtesy of her Italian grandparents. She was a bit taller than Manet's petite model and had none of her lifeless diffidence.

"What?" she asked.

Lounging on the sofa, thoroughly at ease, she tilted her head and looked at me.

"You ever hear of Victorine Meurend?" I asked her.

She said no.

"She was a model employed by Edouard Manet."

"And?"

"You've seen her," I said. "The painting *Olympia.* She's reclining on a settee, huge soft pillows, a yellow floral throw under her naked body, yellow slippers. She's completely unimpressed, totally blasé, though her maid is bringing her a big bouquet of flowers from an admirer."

"I'm not sure," she admitted. "Is it the way I'm relaxing over here?" She stretched an arm over her head.

"To be honest, you look like her." I made a small circle in front of my face. "The shape, chin, the lips."

"I hope this pleases you."

"You know, one critic said she had a wonderful ugliness."

"Oh—"

"But, Julie, you are beautiful. When you smile, you *beam*."

I heard myself say it, though I had no intention to. I hadn't realized I'd thought it until I said it. Julie could be demure, serious, and she was dedicated to her family, job and church; and patient, particularly with me. And if she was too dutiful, too much the good Italian-American girl raised to stay close to home, to do no wrong and care for others, all I was thinking right now, as she subtly flirted with me, was that she was beautiful, and I was glad I'd told her so.

"Terry . . ." She blushed.

I looked at her. "Yes you are."

"This is so unlike you," she said finally.

"Isn't it." I was with her in this rented suite, but her trust, her generous heart, the glint of sexiness in her eyes, had moved me to another place. I knew I was with her and I was where I wanted to be.

And I was not surprised.

"Let me fix those pillows," I suggested.

She eased her glass onto the coffee table as I pushed out of the chair on the other side of the room.

She lifted her head as I reached for the pillows, and then I kissed her on her lips. She kissed me and I slid my arm under her shoulders, and I felt the warm sweep of her tongue on mine as I lifted her toward me, as I gently went to my knees at her side.

She moaned low as my hand caressed her stomach under her blouse. Pulling back, I saw her face as it glowed with passion, and as I leaned in to kiss her neck, the scent of her moist skin found me, and she moaned my name. I heard her voice, and I kissed her, tasted her, brought her body close to my chest, my heart, and all that I am now, all that I am now, was with her, without hesitation, without judgment, freely, unequivocally.

. . .

She had her head on my chest and I saw the curve of her body as it lay above the sheets, glistening in the wan light that edged through the window shades. I had my hand on her back and she purred softly as she slept, as I stared at the shapes cast by shadows on the bedroom ceiling, at the dark credenza, at my shirt and jeans I'd hurriedly tossed on the chair.

Somewhere in the distance, a drill shattered blacktop as it drove into shale. The hum of the air conditioner, the groan of the mini-bar refrigerator. An empty 50-milliliter bottle of Skyy vodka.

I studied my hand on her back, my veins, small scars, imperfections, and her softness, her skin, her graceful legs.

When it was over, she said my name. And then she opened her eyes, looked down at me and giggled, she shook her head, ran her fingers through her hair.

Instead of easing herself off me, she collapsed on my chest. "Oh my, oh my," she said softly, happily.

I could feel her heart beating. I could taste her on my lips.

"That was . . . Yes," she said. "Mmmm . . ."

I was catching my breath and I put my hands on her head. She leaned back and looked at me.

"You," she said.

Now, after. Memories beckon, but I don't respond.

Am I supposed to feel guilt?

I don't.

Do I?

It has been five years. It had been 1,000 years.

My wife is gone.

What could I have done?

I know what I could've done. Should've done.

I need to be here now. I can't let my mind wander. Think of what is here now.

I brought my hand up along Julie's spine to the back of her neck and drew her tight to my side. She nestled closer, but didn't open her eyes.

Strange room. Generic bedspread, greens and shades of burgundy, tossed on the floor. Bland beige sheets in disarray.

Someone in the room above, people in the room below.

Julie's gold crucifix on the nightstand.

An old sketch in a frame above the small desk. Black lines, gray lines: a statue of Henry Clay in Lafayette Square.

What did D say about Congo Square? Who did he know there?

"Terry," Julie murmured. "Are you all right?"

"Sure," I replied. Why wouldn't I be?

"Tell me we can stay here forever."

"I don't see why not."

She squeezed herself against me. She tugged playfully at the hairs on my chest.

Loretta attacked Leo in front of his mother. Christ.

Leo, once hopeful, happy, success within reach, success in his grasp. Betrayal.

A woman on a trip uptown, infant son in a stroller, heading back home to her husband and daughter. At Lincoln Center, a subway station. People on the platform, waiting. A light in the distance, drawing nearer. The rattle of the train growing louder, soon to be a roar: The Broadway express doesn't stop here. Everyone knows that. It'll fly through, pulling air; it'll speed through. A man, wild red hair, wild eyes, caked in dirt and grime, wearing ragged clothes, leaps from the darkness, from behind broad steel pillars. A woman screams. The baby and his stroller are down in the black water, on the silver tracks. The woman scrambles, tossing herself into the mire to save her baby. The roar, the rushing light—

On the nightstand, the telephone rang.

"Oh, that's not good," Julie said softly.

I blinked my eyes, shook my head. A hotel room in New Orleans. Julie.

Bella, no doubt. Something like, "Dad, meet us at the Napoleon House. Come on. You're missing it."

Or a chauffeur with a gun.

"Yeah, hello," I said, clearing my throat.

"Mr. Orr?" A woman's voice.

"Yes."

"There's a fax for you in the lobby."

I was naked. Julie was naked, and we were comfortably warm in this king-size bed.

"Can you have someone bring it up?"

When she said yes, I added, "Please tell him to slide it under the door."

I heard the bellman and I was thinking, a fax? Who would fax me in New Orleans?

A prank from Bella and Daniel. Together, they made a mischievous pair.

Ruthie Mallard, maybe. Another warning, in case I lost the message in her charade.

I slipped on the shirt I'd been wearing and, in bare feet, went across the prickly carpet to the front door.

"Terry?"

"Just a minute, Jule."

I used my thumb to open the envelope, and I pulled out the waxy page.

My heart stopped and then my blood raced.

"Terry?"

Wrapped in the top sheet, Julie had come up behind me.

I handed her the piece of paper.

As she read it, I said, "I've got to go."

I squeezed past her and I ran toward my clothes. As I dressed, I called and asked the front desk to get a cab ready to take me to the airport. I tried to calculate when the last flight back to Newark, to La Guardia, Kennedy, might be.

I thought of the traffic on 90 as I pulled on my running shoes.

All my other clothes were still in the wardrobe.

"I'll call when I get a flight," I said hurriedly, as I grabbed the bag, packed hurriedly, lifted my return ticket from the desk. "Tell Bella. Tell her to try my cell."

My money was still in my jeans pocket. My wallet, credit cards.

"Terry, wait. Terry," Julie said. She was standing in the living room. "Can I help?"

"No, I don't think so." I had everything.

I threw the bag over my shoulder and I ran out of the bedroom. As I reached Julie, I grabbed the fax, folded it and crammed it in my back pocket.

"Terry, kiss me," she said. Alarmed, she seemed small under the beige sheet.

"OK."

But I didn't. I went by her and let the door slam as I hurried toward the elevator.

5

I knew the facts of her biography as well as my own.

Eleanor Montgomery Weisz was born in 1931 in Berwyn, Illinois, the only daughter of Frank Montgomery, a bartender in nearby Cicero, and Alice Sosnowiec Montgomery, a housewife and part-time piano instructor. A bright girl, Eleanor won a scholarship to Northwestern University, but left in 1949 after her freshman year.

She resurfaced 10 years later in New York City as a secretary in the office of Rudolf Bing, general manager of the Metropolitan Opera. Though on the surface menial, her position with Bing permitted her to meet the stars of the classical-music scene—Mitropoulous, Bernstein, Hurok, Marian Anderson, Maria Callas—as well as members of New York's high society. At 28, she displayed a seemingly natural ease when serving the musicians and their retinues, and since she understood music theory from lessons imposed by her mother, Eleanor was able to distinguish herself from other women in Bing's typing pool.

In hindsight, it's clear she sought a post at the Met in order to infiltrate the New York cultural scene. Articles in music magazines and mainstream media later referred to her unyielding determination in pursuit of a marriage that would bring financial security, status and a life in the arts that far overshadowed what had been achieved by her demanding mother. People who could not be quoted called her arrogant and manipulative. "She simply had too much ambition," said one unnamed associate.

But her scheme wasn't extraordinary, not for an outsider attempting to crack Manhattan's cultural scene, then or now. However, Eleanor chose to launch herself with an extraordinary lie. At some point while working for Bing and the Met, she began to confide to people that she was the great-granddaughter of Aaron Montgomery Ward, founder of the Montgomery Ward retailing empire.

One of the people she told was Harold Arnett Weisz, the enormously successful realtor and philanthropist who was one of the Met's most generous supporters. Mr. Weisz had recently lost his wife of 41 years. Eleanor seized the opportunity presented by his loneliness, his sense of disenfranchisement—it was the first Mrs. Weisz who introduced her reticent husband to the cultural scene—and she subtly affixed herself to the widower, first as a companion, with Bing's blessing, and then as something more. The bookish Mr. Weisz, who began his career in real estate as an accountant, was delighted.

And so, in the spring of 1960, the *New York Times* carried a small tombstone announcing the engagement of Harold Arnett Weisz and Eleanor Montgomery, great-granddaughter of Montgomery and Elizabeth J. Ward.

By that afternoon, Mr. Weisz understood that his fiancée had misled him. Several readers called the *Times* to point out that Montgomery Ward had one child, an adopted daughter Marjorie. In turn, Marjorie Ward Baker had no children.

Eleanor should've known. Montgomery Ward was perhaps the most famous man in Illinois during his lifetime, on the basis not only of the countless stores that bore his name and the Ward Tower in Chicago, but for his public spirit and generosity, attributes he shared with his wife. Mrs. Ward, for example, gave more than $15 million to charities and institutions, one of which was Northwestern, where a 14-story medical center is named in her late husband's honor. A bas-relief of the Wards is in its lobby.

Today, with 24-hour cable news channels and the Web, it's hard to imagine that this scandal passed swiftly from the public eye. The *Times* reporter was blamed for misinterpreting information she'd been given and a correction appeared. In private, Bing was outraged; but when he sought to apologize to his benefactor, he found that the 65-year-old Weisz had forgiven Eleanor and that their marriage plans would proceed. After quietly resigning from her post with the Met, a defiant Eleanor turned up on Mr. Weisz's arm at dinners, socials and concerts, as if nothing untoward had happened. Her brief brush with infamy soon forgotten, she married Mr. Weisz, moved into his grand apartment at 91st and Park, and continued to accompany him to cultural events as warranted.

Eleanor Montgomery Weisz, who wasn't the great-granddaughter of Montgomery Ward (nor 23 years old when married, as she told Bing and her husband), reemerged as a public figure in 1979, when her son Raymond, then 10 years old, performed at a small dinner party at their Park Avenue apartment. As has been roundly reported, he played, flawlessly, Bach's Prelude and Fugue in C Major from *The Well-Tempered Clavier* and Beethoven's Sonata No. 7 in D, Op. 10, No. 3, a performance he dedicated to the memory of his father, who had died four years earlier. The carefully arranged guest list included those in the arts who'd reaped, and might continue to reap, the benefits of Mr. Weisz's estate, which was valued at $480 million.

But Eleanor needn't have been so heavy-handed. Raymond was brilliant, and his talent carried the evening. Within a week, he performed in London for pianist Daniel Barenboim, a former child prodigy whom Eleanor had known through his agent, Sol Hurok, when she was with Bing. Recognizing Raymond's native talent, Barenboim immediately offered to make appropriate introductions.

Young Raymond's career, which brought him such acclaim and such misery, had begun.

"Sir, I need you to stow your tray table and fasten your seat belt."

I looked blankly at the flight attendant as I pushed up the plastic tray, clicked the ends of the seat belt together.

Surrounded by the cabin's darkness, by compliant passengers, she smiled and whispered, "We'll be landing in Newark in about ten minutes."

The overhead light cast a beam onto my lap and onto the back of the fax I'd received. Outside, the starless sky was black, empty.

I flipped over the fax. The clipping had been carefully cut from the *Times* and centered on a white sheet, and photocopied before it was faxed.

The headline above the small box: Eleanor Montgomery Weisz, 72.

The obituary gave the barest details of her life. Hardly a mention of her deceptions, the years of abuse and denial to which she subjected Raymond before he finally snapped. The *Times* said she was born in Berwyn, married very well, endowed museums and orchestras, supported charities, died. She was the first piano teacher of her son Raymond Montgomery Weisz, a prodigy, master of Prokofiev's Eighth Piano Sonata and winner of international competitions. She was bilked out of her fortune by unscrupulous advisors, and had lost license to the buildings her late husband had developed, managed and owned. She saw her Raymond institutionalized for the first time after he was found, hungry and near-naked, living with wolves in the Bronx Zoo, not long after a disastrous Labor Day concert she insisted he perform.

She will be buried tomorrow, following a private service at the Park Avenue Church, at Woodlawn Cemetery in the Bronx.

And, I knew, Raymond Montgomery Weisz, the man who killed my wife and son, would attend.

I had no doubt.

He needs to be certain she's dead.

There is something in my mind that I let simmer but never bring to a full boil because it would require that I find sympathy for the Madman Weisz, that I give him human dimensions, which, despite what Lieutenant Luther Addison says, what Elizabeth Harteveld says, he ceased to have the moment he sprang from the shadows and did what he did.

I have in the pit of my mind an idea that Raymond Montgomery Weisz saw a mother and child on the platform and envisioned himself as the child in the stroller.

He tossed himself onto the tracks in order to kill himself not as he was then, a 29-year-old schizophrenic who'd spent his young life between the concert stage and various psychiatric wards, but a baby not yet corrupted by his mother. And this symbolic suicide had an additional benefit: the gruesome death of the mother.

"Terry, if he did it, we'll make sure he's brought—"

"To justice, Luther? Him in a cell is justice?"

I swear Luther sighed. "Terry—"

"Him under the 2 train is justice. Some kind of justice, anyway."

Or Dr. Harteveld: "Might I suggest that these *extreme* feelings you harbor for this Mr. Weisz—"

"Elizabeth, this man killed my wife and my son," I said. "Do you really believe that what I feel—a desire to beat him bloody to within an inch of his life and then take him by the scruff of the neck and ram him under the next southbound express—is *extreme*? Not me, nope."

Two hours later, I stood in the brick vestibule and, hands on the gold cirmolo frame, stared at Marina's painting, *The Cliffs of Gargano*. But I didn't see the endless blue sky, white water as it lapped the jagged limestone rocks or, in the distance, orange groves where my wife and I had walked, hand in hand, silly in love.

I was searching my mind for Weisz, wondering what he'd do to disguise himself. When he was last seen, scrambling up the steps of the subway station and running frantically on tattered sneakers across the Lincoln Center plaza toward Damrosch Park, his Rasta-style red hair was matted with dirt and his filthy, urine-soaked slacks were held up with twine. The quintessential homeless man, as one of the witnesses called him. A savage, said another.

But how would he appear tomorrow? I knew the red hair was a stone giveaway, so I tried to imagine Weisz with his head shaved, his scalp covered with sores and lesions, but still wallowing in his mad-ness, unable to fully control his rage and unwilling to damper the feral instincts he preferred. I could almost see it: He'd pad east—since he'd spent the night under bushes in Central Park—and he'd enter the gothic church after the service had begun. In his muddled mind, he'd try to draw up whatever dignity he could muster as he moved along the carpeted center aisle. As demons appeared, leaping from stained glass, from behind immovable stone, he'd throw him-self into whatever pew beckoned him, his offensive iodine-and-piss scent, his squalid appearance, shocking everyone who knew him as a well-mannered, meticulously presented child entering from the prompt side of the stage.

I shook my head and looked into the kitchen's darkness, toward the relentless clicking of the stove's clock. Maybe Weisz was receiv-ing treatment somewhere now, living under guard, under an as-sumed name, with endless amenities in a country-club setting, and maybe one of his mother's misguided colleagues would retrieve him for the event. Weisz, in a new suit, buffed shoes, after another night in a warm, clean bed, satisfied by a nourishing breakfast, accompa-nied by the sound of soothing voices, and only a vague memory of the screaming baby in the stroller and the frantic mother who tried to save him. I tried to picture it, and when I couldn't I thought of a photo in my desk of him as a boy, pale with fear in a perfectly tailored tuxedo, moments before his ill-fated concert at Alice Tully Hall. But that was before he was the Madman, the murderer, the monster with the wild yellow eyes, the maniac who emerged from the ether to destroy my life, and Bella's.

. . .

"Hey Dad," she murmured. She'd been asleep.

"How'd it go?"

"Well, we saw a bus named Desire."

Strange to be in the kitchen without the scent of garlic, of broccoli rabe in olive oil, a nice *pollo in tegame al limone* or other dishes made by our housekeeper Mrs. Maoli, who, knowing we'd be in New Orleans, took a brief vacation.

Only Bella's voice kept me from being thoroughly alone with memories and the Madman.

I said, "You didn't call."

"Dad, you left me, remember?"

"Didn't Julie explain?"

I could hear the sound of the shower upstairs and could envision the steam filling the room, wafting around my suit jacket.

"Yes," Bella replied, "But, you know, Leo's funeral is tomorrow—"

"It's a bad coincidence," I said. "There's nothing I—"

"He was your friend, Dad, and mine. And Dennis's."

"I know. I know." I went to the refrigerator for bottled water. White light flooded the room.

"So you aren't only chasing this stupid man but now you have to go his mother's funeral."

The stupid man, the one who changed us forever, is going to be there. It's time, Bella.

"I have to do it," I told her. "I hope you know I wish I could be with you."

"And Dennis, who's miserable without you."

"Bella, I'm really sorry. Please don't make it worse."

She paused. "I don't suppose I have to tell you to be careful."

I could see her toying with her rubber bands, moving them in a pattern only she understood. "It's fine. Really. Don't worry."

I heard her sit up in the bed: the rustle of sheets, a dull thud as she bounced on the mattress. "If he's there, what will you do?"

I said, "I'll call Luther Addison."

"You lie bad, Dad."

"Bella—"

"It's all right. I was thinking, Dad, maybe now this'll be over."

"Could be," I said, trying to add a note she'd find hopeful.

"I think you'd— Wait." She shifted to a softer voice. "Dad, Julie's awake. You want to talk to her? She wanted me to call you before."

I said no. "It's late. Everybody needs some sleep."

"Yes, but she's not asleep—"

"Just tell her I'll talk to her tomorrow, OK? And please give my condolences to Leo's sister."

"Maybe you should give me a good reason to tell Miss Mallard why you're not there."

"You can tell her the truth," I said. I really didn't owe anyone an explanation. Anyone who needed one would never understand. "Keep a tab, Bella, of what we owe Julie or D, OK?"

"The ride to Thibodaux and back is going to cost, like, $300."

"Yeah, like that."

She was silent for a moment. Outside, a car rattled over cobblestones on Greenwich Street.

"It's late, Dad. You'd better say good night."

"Listen, Bella, I . . . I want to—"

"Good night, Dad."

I nodded to the darkness. "Good night, little angel."

I heard her cut the line, 1,300 miles away.

I could've taken the Broadway line to Times Square and shuttled over to Grand Central for the Lex line. But I thought I'd be overwhelmed by morning commuters, rattled in the unfamiliar crush; and I was already agitated, and way too eager for what I knew would happen today. I grabbed a cab on Hudson and told the driver to take Sixth as far north as she could and I kept my hand on the nine-millimeter gun in my navy-blue jacket that lay on the seat next to me as we moved uptown. We did OK until Herald Square, and then it wasn't until we reached Madison in the mid-50s that she could push it over 20 miles per hour again.

I got out at 85th, in front of a Gristedes. As I headed east, I slipped into my suit jacket and, at the corner, eased through a crowd of little kids in camp shirts and shorts on their way west to Central Park. Seeing the counselors corral the eager children, I thought of Bella and her job at the city-run summer camp on Carmine, near her high school, and I realized it was the first time I'd thought of her today.

Moving toward Park Avenue, I walked along the black cast-iron fence of Regis High School, absently running my fingers on the rails. The sun had yet to make its way above the stoic buildings on the east side of the avenue, but it was bright and it was going to be another blistering August day. Above me, the sprawling trees were full, their stout leaves motionless on a windless morning.

On the other side of street, two women in white lab coats on a cigarette break watched as I found the church's side doors shut tight and a gate to a third entrance wearing a thick padlock. I went around and entered the Park Avenue Church by its front doors.

It was 65 minutes before the service was about to begin, and as I passed through the church's dark vestibule, I heard the church's pipe organ. It played somber music—rich minor chords, challenging arpeggio trills in the upper register, vibrating bass notes—and the music filled the vacant church.

The light through the stained-glass windows in the traceries was augmented by simple lamps on thick chains hung from gray stone pillars. A red carpet separated the rows of dark wooden pews. On the altar, candles flickered.

The baroque organ music covered the sound of my footsteps as I went to one side of the back of the church, then the other. To my eyes, the aged church was empty, save for the organist. But I walked to the front and, without hesitation, went behind the formal altar.

No one was there. As I came around, I genuflected, a habit I'd thought had been long ago erased.

The only place I hadn't looked was the sacristy. If Weisz was in there, I'd wait and grab him as soon as he stepped out, in full view of the mourners. I'd drag him into the sun and, since I'd have the nine buried into his temple, no one would intervene.

As I came along the pillars, passing a side chapel under a rainbow of delicate light, I examined each empty pew and listened to the organ. Bach? Toccata and Fugue in D Minor. A guess. Handel? I knew nothing about organ music. I didn't even know if Weisz—

I stopped. Surely, Weisz had at least experimented with organ music, playing a grand pipe organ.

Shifting the gun from my side pocket to my right hand, I went to the vestibule and found the stairs that led to the loft. Amid the brick and stone, the air was cool, motionless, and there was a musty scent. Left hand on the banister, I took the spiral steps confidently—no need for extra precaution while the music played—until I reached the loft door. Partly open, it allowed me to see the spiderweb-like arches in the high ceiling. I could hear fingers tapping on keys while the music seemed farther away; a moment's disorientation. Then I remembered the pipes were high on the stone walls on the outside of the pews.

I came to the narrow landing, put my left hand on the door and shoved it back. It smacked hard on its stop and its glass rattled.

The music halted suddenly. And the woman at the organ—thin, 40ish, round wire-framed glasses—flung her hands in the air and let out an airy shriek.

"They let me," she said, choking on her words. "Practicing. I was just— There's a service."

"Put your hands down," I said. "It's OK."

She wore a light gray runner's jacket, matching pants, sneakers. Her hands still in the air, she nodded nervously, "Gun."

I put the nine-millimeter pistol in my pocket. "Sorry."

She let out a long breath. "You scared the bejesus out of me, Mister," she replied as she sank in relief on the bench.

I smiled politely, self-consciously.

"They ought to lighten up on the security," she said.

"I'll put that in my report," I replied.

By 9:15, I was back on the avenue, stationed on the northeast corner of Park and 85th, in shadows cast by scaffolding. From where I stood, I could spot anyone coming to the church from east or west, north or south. Minus the Hamptonistas on this Wednesday before the Labor Day break, the wide avenue, like the rest of the city, was quiet as it could be and I told myself I'd have few distractions as I watched for one man.

The first few mourners came about 20 minutes later. A group of well-dressed women, all in their late 60s or early 70s, arrived in taxis and greeted each other amicably in front of the church. Minutes later, another cab issued an elderly couple: The hunched man used a cane and leaned heavily on his wife's arm as he negotiated the few slate steps that led to the portal. Two robust middle-aged men in dark suits who were striding amiably past the grass islands in the middle of Park noticed the older couple and scurried to help them.

By 9:55, I'd watched about 40 people make their way into the church. None was the man I wanted, shaven head or wild dreadlocks, ragged clothes or fresh new suit. But two of the people I saw caught my interest and both took me by surprise.

Out of the corner of my eye I spotted one as he walked west on 85th, hands in the pockets of his gray suit, his black flop of hair bouncing with each step. I shifted to gain a better view of him, staying under the scaffolding as he stopped to accommodate a walker with six large dogs on a tangle of leashes. As he reached to pet one skinny long-haired dog, the others leaped toward him and the walker yanked hard on the leashes, scolding the short Frenchman with sharp eyes.

Jean-Pierre Coceau was the only one of the 14 people on the platform who'd witnessed Weisz's murderous act that I hadn't spoken to. A resident of Breil near Nice and the Côte d'Azur who had been on a business trip to Manhattan, Coceau left New York City after speaking to police at the scene and later at the precinct house, where he met then-Sergeant Addison. I learned he was a dealer of original vintage art by illustrators who created those classic French posters as advertisements for Cachou Lajaunie, cigarette papers and the Folies Bergere. I contacted him through the firm he represented, but never received an e-mail in reply. By then I discovered he'd been implicated, and eventually cleared, in some minor embarrassment at the Musée des Beaux-Arts Jules Cheret in Nice, a question regarding the origin of two newly discovered works. But in the end, I decided I didn't really have to speak with him, even after I learned he was running a shop on Columbus Avenue. I had all the information I needed about that horrifying afternoon.

While I was contemplating Coceau's reasons for attending the memorial service for the mother of the man he'd watched kill my wife and son, I saw another familiar man as he left a cab on 85th.

Otto van Kuijk stopped to check the lie of his vest, the crease in his pants, and then he ran his hand over the few gray strands that remained on top of his head. A gold fob crossed the front of his gray suit and he removed the watch at its end. Satisfied that he was on time, he crossed the street and went toward the church.

By then, Coceau had gone inside. Dr. van Kuijk stopped at the edge of the slate steps to let a gray-haired woman who wore a kelly-green raincoat enter before him. He nodded his head graciously, tugged on his jacket, then went up the steps behind her.

A long truck packed with blue bottles of water for the coolers in the doctor's offices and apartment kitchens pulled in front of me on Park. As I edged north to the front of the truck to keep an eye fixed on the church, I asked myself, What is Otto van Kuijk, husband of Dr. Elizabeth Harteveld, doing at the memorial service for Eleanor Montgomery Weisz?

. . .

"I have to see you," I said into my cell phone as I walked away from the church, the last man to leave the service. My head felt as if it could burst.

"I'm afraid that's impossible, Terry," she replied. "I'm actually on vacation. I've only come by my office to—"

"I'll be there in fifteen minutes," I snapped and cut the line.

Elizabeth Harteveld's place was off First, about 25 blocks away.

I pounded on the door until she answered.

She opened it a crack and peered at me through the vertical slit.

"Move back," I spit.

"Terry, this is highly inapprop—"

I shoved the door and went inside.

The waiting room to her basement office was empty. Magazines still in plastic wrapping and shipping envelopes lay in a jumbled pile on the sofa. Like every other shrink in New York City, Harteveld took off for most of August. But she didn't bother to cancel the mail.

"Terry, I cannot see you."

"You're wearing your lab coat," I replied, gesturing toward her. "That means you'll see me."

She hesitated. "Only if it pertains to Gabriella."

"Yeah. It pertains to Gabriella."

I walked past her and went along the white corridor toward her office.

I wasn't going to play her game today. Bella liked the ceremony—easing into the green leather club chair as the doctor went for a moment to retrieve her file from atop her rosewood desk; a few seconds of chit-chat, a maternal yet professional smile; "Shall we begin, Gabriella?" Not me, no. I can see Bella, her hat on her lap, her bowling shoes on Harteveld's Persian rug on the parquet floor. Bella, ready to go. Bella, trusting. She liked Harteveld, who once confessed to me that she had a microphone hidden among the leaves of the green plant on a table next to the club chair.

I sat on the edge of the desk, seething.

Despite the lab coat, Harteveld was out of uniform. Her dark brown hair, which she usually held back in a taut bun, relaxed onto her shoulders, and she wore pressed jeans and a lime T-shirt. The little poms on the back of her white socks stuck out of the rear of her perfect white Keds.

She left her office door open. "Gabriella—"

I cut her off. "Is fine. She's in New Orleans, representing me at a funeral."

"By herself?"

"I don't neglect my daughter," I said, shaking my head. "That's a given now, isn't it?"

She didn't reply and walked toward the chair behind the desk.

"You're not going to want to record this," I said as I turned to watch her.

"You're trying to intimidate me, Terry," she said as she sat. "Is it necessary? We've known each other for quite a while now."

I reached into my jacket pocket and withdrew the pistol. I put it in front of her.

She looked at it. "What am I to do with this?"

"Hold it," I said. "You can't say I'm intimidating you if you've got the gun."

Nodding, she took the nine and slipped it into a side drawer.

"Your face is bright red," she said calmly, "and you're clenching your jaw."

"I'm hot. Physically and metaphorically."

"If you can calm down—"

"Well, I don't think that's going to happen, Elizabeth. I mean, we've known each other for quite a while now. Do I strike you as someone who can just calm down?"

She smiled thinly. She was in her mid-40s, attractive in a proper, judicious sort of way, but today she was trying to look younger. It might work if she smiled more often and less carefully. "Point taken."

I slid out of my suit jacket. Sweat had soaked through my shirt.

She tapped her gold Cross pen on her spotless green blotter. "I don't believe I've seen you in a suit before, Terry."

"What was your husband doing at the service for Eleanor Montgomery Weisz?"

She tilted her head. "I don't understand."

"Your husband, Otto van Kuijk. Eleanor Montgomery Weisz, mother of Raymond Montgomery Weisz. The man who killed my wife and son. Bella's mother and brother."

"Yes, I know who he is," she said as she shifted subtly in the high-back seat. "But my husband . . ." She frowned. "Do you know my husband, Terry?"

I went and sat on the arm of the green leather sofa.

"Otto Andreas van Kuijk III. Born in Dodrecht, Holland; he'll be 65 years old this November. Received his undergraduate degree and did graduate work at the University of Leiden. He came to the U.S. to attend Clark University before moving on to NYU for the combined M.D.-Ph.D. program. As did you, Elizabeth; NYU, I mean. The combined program."

She nodded, her eyes fixed on mine.

"Your husband now is professor of psychiatry at NYU, but he maintains a private practice. His office is at 79th and Park, across from your apartment on Central Park West. He's a fellow of the APA and the American College of Psychiatrists. And he's a member of the Group for the Advancement of Psychiatry, the National Alliance for the Mentally Ill and the National Council on Geriatric Psychiatry. He's not a bad tennis player, though you can easily beat him. His lone vice seems to be his monthly porterhouse at Luger's with his colleagues, given his cholesterol runs a bit high."

"Very impressive," she remarked as she sat back.

"Not really," I replied. "I am a private investigator."

"Are you compelled to have a dossier on everyone you know?"

"Not everyone. Just on the people I ought to."

"I suppose you have one on me," she said.

I didn't reply.

She said, "There is no earthly reason why you need to investigate my husband, Terry."

I stood. "Apparently there is. He knows Raymond Montgomery Weisz."

"I don't see how you can draw that conclusion," she said evenly.

"Sure you do."

She leaned forward and put down her pen. "What I'm suggesting—"

"Elizabeth. I'm not interested in your suggestions today," I said. "I just want to know how you could treat Bella and see me while your husband knew the man who killed the people we love."

She folded her hands on the blotter and kept her customary composure under tight rein. "I have no knowledge that my husband knows Mr. Weisz."

"Elizabeth," I said plainly, "I don't believe you."

"No, Terry, you don't. I've often wondered why."

I'd sat through the service, hanging back in the corner of the second-to-last pew, with my eye on the altar, the attendees, the back door. Under the gray arches, under warm swells of the pipe organ, van Kuijk stayed to himself, sitting next to the gray-haired woman in the green raincoat to fill out a row. When the minister called the service to its end, van Kuijk stood, tamped down his vest, looked at his watch, politely shook the woman's hand and left the church.

"He was there, Elizabeth," I said. "Either you knew or you didn't know. But he was there."

She unfolded her hands and stood, slipping the Cross pen into the breast pocket of her lab coat.

Looking hard at me, she said, "I assure you, Terry, I would not engage in the kind of unethical behavior you're suggesting. I would not betray your confidence. Or Gabriella's."

"Was he treating Weisz?"

She hesitated, then finally said, "I don't know."

"Does that mean he never mentioned him by name?" I asked. "Did he mention a former prodigy, piano whiz, all sorts of awards, a celebrity and now a raging paranoid schizophrenic? How else might he describe him? Animal lover? A misnomer: The man lived in a zoo, for Christ's sake. With the wolves. Wolf Man. Or he lived in the tunnels under the city, a mole rat. Ate out of garbage cans. Skulked around covered in soot, piss, sweat, filth. Hauled in, what, thirty-nine times? Then attacked a woman and her baby. Killed them. Murderer. Sound familiar?"

"Yes, Terry, it sounds terribly familiar," she replied as she came around the desk. "I know it well. From you. While Gabriella has moved beyond—"

"I don't want to say I trusted you, Elizabeth . . . But I expected some level of transparency. The ordinary kind. No special treatment."

She went to the door and dropped her hand on the knob. "My husband never mentioned Weisz. Nor anyone who fits any description you offer. I'm sorry you're upset, but I don't know what I can do."

She was waiting for me to leave. As I lifted my suit jacket, I said, "It's going to be interesting in the van Kuijk household tonight, isn't it?"

"Terry, please."

"What I wouldn't give to be a fly—"

I suddenly realized that Elizabeth Harteveld was upset, though, given her steely exterior, I couldn't tell exactly why. Could've been either of two things: She knew she'd been caught in a duplicitous act, or her husband had concealed information from her that might've affected her treatment of Bella and, by extension, me.

"He knew about us, Elizabeth," I said softly, "your husband. The article in the *Times,* remember?"

About a year ago, a columnist named R. Thomas Coombs profiled me in a *Metro Matters* piece. In the story, Coombs revealed how much Marina's estate was worth, an issue my daughter and I had never discussed. Knowing she'd have access one day to some part of $20 million might affect her, I thought. So I asked Harteveld for advice. She said, "Interesting. My husband asked me the same question. I've never found Gabriella to have any particular awareness of money." I remember this clearly. For one, it's my opinion that Bella is too aware of money. But, more to the point, it was the first time Harteveld gave me a glimpse of her personal life: In my mind's eye, I saw her and van Kuijk at the breakfast table, sharing the *Times* over coffee and toast, discussing what Coombs had written and its ramifications for Bella, who already had too much to consider.

"It mentioned Weisz," I said to Harteveld. "Coombs mentioned him."

The writer had hedged, asserting only that Weisz was "said" to have thrown Davy's stroller onto the tracks. He must've spoken to Addison, champion hedger. Addison, a good man but an all-too-careful cop.

"Your husband knows about Bella and me, Elizabeth."

"Terry, I don't think we should continue this now," she replied.

"What I think—" I stopped myself. Harteveld was stung and she was doing her best to hold it together. There'd be no overt displays of emotions from her. Just an almost imperceptible slump to her shoulders, a subtle lack of focus in her eyes, as she held on to the door, her right hand clasped tightly on its edge, as if she were behind a shield.

"I need my gun," I told her.

I **went west** under the silver lines cast by the Queensboro Bridge, dodging dried pigeon droppings under the squeal and rumble of the Roosevelt Island tram. The sudden darkness gave shade, but no relief from the heat, which rose relentlessly from the mushy black street. Along Second Avenue, babies in strollers went with only diapers and a slathering of sunblock, while their young mothers wore just a bit more: baseball caps, sunglasses, gauzy tops, tailored short-shorts, elegant flip-flops.

I looked at my watch, then dug out my cell phone. I was furious, disappointed, confused, and I needed relief. Tossing my jacket over my left arm, I used my right thumb to punch the 11 numbers, as I kept on toward the N, R or Lex line at 59th.

"Julie Giada."

I said, "Where are you?"

"The Mallard home. Hi."

"How was it?"

"Wait a second," she requested, no doubt to find a bit of privacy. "Well, it was a bit sad, Terry. The four of us. His sister Ruth, a couple of her friends. A few others who seemed like businessmen from around here. That's all, besides an old black man who introduced himself to us as Miss Mallard's chauffeur."

Willis. I wondered if he flashed Julie his .38. But no Loretta. No new awkward scenes with bottles to the head, smacks across the face.

"The priest didn't seem to know your friend, so he talked about his mother and sister."

Poor Leo. Couldn't even have his own funeral.

"Miss Mallard asked Gabriella if she wanted to speak."

"Don't tell me—"

Julie laughed. "She declined, politely. Terry, she was very sweet. How does a fifteen-year-old always know how to say the right thing?"

"She's OK?"

"She's with Daniel, playing with two droopy hounds. Miss Mallard's letting them have the run of the house," Julie said. Whispering, she added, "You didn't tell me your friend's family had money."

"Sorry."

"Well, I don't know if I'd call this place a mansion, but if it's not, it's close enough. White columns, sweeping stairwells, big chandelier."

"Really?"

"I'm out on the lawn now. We're getting white-glove service, Terry. Champagne, hors d'oeuvres. Fresh-cut flowers—azaleas, yellow jasmine, silver bell."

"How's D holding up?"

"He left after the funeral," she told me. "He's upset, of course. But there's something troubling him. I can't put my finger on it."

He owns a bar now, I thought. Diddio needs a plan.

"So where are you?" she asked.

"I'm passing a couple of antique shops on 59th. Doors wide open," I reported. "If you can fit a Louis XVI boudoir under your jacket, you can get away with it. It's hot here. August–in–New York hot."

An overheated bulldog had plopped himself on a worn red carpet that extended from one of the shops. Tongue hanging between the spikes he had for bottom teeth, he looked like he knew he'd been a poor choice for watchdog and didn't care who agreed.

"How was it?" she asked. "The service—"

"He wasn't there," I said abruptly.

"Are you all right?"

"Well, he wasn't there."

Five years now and no resolution. I was ready for him, finally. I was going to take him down. Now I'm back to nowhere, full of anger, uncertainty, frustration, pounding west on 59th, heading nowhere.

She misread my silence. "Terry, do we need to talk?"

I knew what she meant. "Only if you think we do."

"I'd say we've crossed a threshold. We didn't get much time to go over it, but something's different now."

"I had to leave, Jule. No choice," I said. "But you're right. It's different."

"And?"

"And it's good. It's good, Jule."

I'd made it to Third. A lunchtime crowd was funneling its way toward Bloomingdale's. Another crowd was heading to Ranch 1 for chicken and spicy fries.

She hesitated. "What's next?"

"I've got an idea. We'll see." Weisz needs to know she's really gone. I was sure of that.

Through the cell earpiece, I heard a bird's caw, the rustling leaves on a tree, a voice that distracted Julie.

"Say hi to Bella for me," I said.

"Will I talk to you later?"

"Sure," I told her. "Why not?"

I put the phone back in my pocket and kept on toward the subway entrance, no less bitter, no less determined, than I'd been when I left Harteveld's.

7

The white and pink buds of the dogwood trees had long ago baked away in the summer's heat. But even if they had still been on view, feminine and proud on tips of thin branches, I wouldn't be able to see them. At 2:30 in the morning, it was impossibly dark in Woodlawn Cemetery. As it had been at 10:45 P.M., when I scaled the six-foot-high spiked fence on 233rd Street, and 25 minutes later, when I set up my observation post behind the mausoleum of Jacob Doll on the other side of the road, maybe 100 yards from the Weisz tomb.

In one of Bella's old, tattered backpacks, I'd brought along binoculars, a flashlight and four candles in clear glass that I lit and set up on the Weisz mausoleum, a stone structure with a tilted roof, Ionic entablature and columns, thick copper doors and lion's-head-handled base. It wasn't much light, but as the flames wavered they gave me enough to at least see shifting shadows.

When the Madman came, he'd see the candles and, thinking they were part of the burial rite, would press forward.

He had to know that she was finally gone.

She drove him and drove him and hectored him, berated him, battered him, violently transferred all her self-loathing to him, to his fragile psyche, until he snapped.

And then he went far beyond where she pushed him, killing a mother and child.

He wanted to know she would not return. As best he could, he'd focus on that.

He wouldn't know where I was.

Haloperidol, risperidone, olanzapine, sodium valproate, lithium, chlorpromazine, fluphenazine, clonazepam, diazepam, sertraline.

He wouldn't know if that moon up there had wings.

Those squirrels racing through the trees? They talked to Weisz.

I cracked open a bottle of Badoit and took a long drink.

Ten minutes ago, a security van passed by on its rounds, momentarily splintering the silence, its headlights scattering the blackness. Now I could hear the cars on Jerome Avenue and the Bronx River Parkway—not many of them, though. Not at this hour.

When the sound of a car drifted away, in its place was a deep stillness, a seemingly preternatural sense of calm.

I could hear myself breathe. I could barely see my own hands.

To ward off planes, red lights flickered on the roof of the big medical center on the other side of the parkway.

I sat down again, leaning my back against cold stone. A gentle wind tousled the crowded leaves.

I put up my black hood and tucked my hands into my sweatshirt pouch, jostling the nine.

I retied my sneakers.

I was thinking that Weisz could see in the dark. Living in tunnels, at the zoo, foraging for food at night, for clothes, a weapon, he'd developed that skill.

I looked up at the countless stars splashed across the infinite sky. You going to give me enough to get this done?

I heard him before I saw him. Surrounded by such profound silence, even a man who had lived with wolves couldn't approach without making sound.

I stood as soon as I heard the crackle of the branch he'd stepped on. Then I bent down, nestling myself in a crevice at the back of the Doll tomb, bringing my head around to keep an eye on the structure up the road.

There was more rustling in the dark as he came down the slight incline and stepped onto Fern Avenue. He drew closer to his parents' mausoleum, and as he stepped into the dull, quivering light, I saw him.

His features were impossible to detect, but I could see a map of his wild hair, knotty dreadlocks, and the bottom of his pants, caught in the light, were tattered rags.

He was darker than the candle-lit tomb now and I saw the outline of his frame. Weisz had terrible posture. It was part of his legacy, a point all music journalists who covered him referenced. He slouched into himself, hunching over as if trying to collapse his body so he could bring it closer to the keyboard. In some photos, he almost appeared to have a hump on his back.

It was him, the Madman. Raymond Montgomery Weisz. Right there.

The man who killed my wife and son.

I'd have to move closer to get a clean shot at him.

I came off the base of the Doll tomb, stepping gingerly onto the grass.

Weisz didn't turn. He continued to face the mausoleum, where, in daylight, he could see his surname in bronze letters, could see the teeth of the lion that would let him in.

Without moving my feet, I leaned forward against a tree, hands on rough wood, then brought my legs under me.

Weisz slowly crouched down. His feet were flat, knees bent, and he seemed to be sitting on air, his butt inches from the ground.

Then he began to cough—an ugly rattle that didn't immediately stop.

Which gave me a chance to move forward along the tree line and to scuttle around the rotary.

I was exposed; though still in darkness, I was on the road.

But Weisz didn't notice me.

He wiped his right hand on his ragged pants and stayed in his low crouch.

As I inched under branches along the roadside, I saw him tilt his head to look at the flickering candles.

He leaned forward, putting his knuckles on the ground.

And I saw the face of the Madman in the dull, quavering candle-light.

I reached into my pouch and withdrew the revolver.

He was about 150 feet away.

Christ, I was shaking.

I couldn't level the piece.

He was mesmerized by the candles' dancing light. He craned his neck awkwardly.

I needed to move closer.

I shuffled sideways, moving my right foot, then my left, taking long, tight strides.

That Madman, he's the one who threw my baby son's stroller in front of a hurtling express train. He watched as my wife dove onto the soiled tracks to save our boy, watched as the train roared through the station, crushing them, killing them, wrecking my life, changing forever my daughter's world, destroying her innocence, silencing her laughter.

I steadied my right arm by holding it with my left hand at the wrist.

I shuffled toward him, my index finger on the trigger.

And I kicked a tiny pebble.

Suddenly, Weisz turned his gaze toward me.

He looked at me, his head still at an odd angle.

I stood perfectly still and stared down the length of my right arm to the barrel of the nine.

With startling speed, Weisz sprang from his feral position and, at the end of the leap, landed next to the mausoleum, out of my line of fire, out of sight.

I bolted after him, and I skidded as I approached his family's tomb.

Gun high, I turned slowly, cautiously, along the edge of the tomb. But Weisz wasn't there.

He was moving, racing through the woods before us, heading east, away from the moon.

I followed, listening for his footsteps on fallen branches, on stone.

He seemed to know where he was going, even in the blackness.

I had no chance.

But I kept running and listening.

Then I heard the snap of wood in front of me and to my right. It sounded as if Weisz had grabbed onto a low-lying branch and it came off in his hand.

I had to do it now. I squeezed off a shot, sending it toward sound, toward darkness.

I heard a guttural cry, a raw, rumbling groan.

And then, vivid silence.

Until I heard Weisz scampering on a downhill slope.

I kept after him, pushing.

His footsteps slapped the blacktop. He'd left the rugged soil for the pavement.

I'd stand a better chance if we stayed on the road.

If he wanted to leave the cemetery, he was going to have to take the steel fence at the locked gate, and its spikes would ensure that he'd have to slow down as he went over the top.

If I stayed on him, I could grab him at the fence.

If I couldn't get close enough, I'd shoot him again.

I was moving along a level stretch that swung to the south when I heard the sirens.

The patrol car was coming at me from the direction of the front gate. I saw its whirling red-and-white lights in the distance, then its high beams, drawing near. It wasn't coming after Weisz. It was bearing down on me.

I looked to my right. On the other side of a short bridge was Woodlawn Lake.

I scrambled toward the bridge, sliding down parallel to it rather than running over it, as I heard the car continue to approach, its siren growing louder, lights brighter.

I didn't have time to do what I wanted to.

Instead, I pulled myself up along the side of the bridge, reared back and threw the gun toward the lake.

Seconds later, I heard a splash.

I turned, took down my hood, put my hands on top of my head and went up to the foot of the bridge. I arrived as the patrol car thudded to a halt.

I couldn't see beyond the blinding spotlight.

"On your knees!"

I knelt.

A uniformed cop was on me, spinning me around, slapping the cuffs hard on me, as I went face-down onto stone.

"I'm not resisting," I shouted.

I turned my face and saw the other cop's black wing tips. He was wearing his civilian clothes.

He told the cop in blue to get me up.

"Yeah, you're Terry Orr," he said derisively.

He had a thin mustache and kept his dark hair cropped close to his skull.

I made a silent bet with myself that he wasn't thin, but sinewy and muscular under his stylish pale green suit.

"Pat him down."

The uniformed cop, who was at least 10 years older than the black man in pale green, did as he was told. When he came up with my wallet, he tossed it to the guy who was running things.

"I'm going to find a permit for your piece in here?" he asked.

"Piece?" I could see it: concentric circles scattering the stars that reflected on the black water, and the gun sinking swiftly to the bottom of the lake until it landed in the mire, fingerprint oils removed as they mixed with sediment.

The uniformed cop—Sanders, according to his name badge—said, "We heard shots."

Shot, I thought.

"I wasn't hit," I said to Sanders. To the other guy, I added, "I don't carry."

He kept flipping through the wallet.

When he was done, he told Sanders to remove the cuffs.

As I rubbed my wrists, he said, "Was he here?"

I frowned in confusion.

"Weisz," he said. "Was he here?"

I looked at him, nodded.

"Damn," he said to Sanders. "The Old Man was right again."

He turned and went toward the blue-and-white. Sanders gave me a shove, telling me I was getting a ride home.

He told me his name was Renaldo Twist and that he knew Luther Addison and he knew more about me than he cared to. When I asked what he meant, he blew me off, telling me he didn't want to hear what I had to say so I might as well keep my mouth shut. So we went from the Bronx River Parkway to the Harlem River Drive and down to Houston, which ran the width of the island. Varick was as far as Twist and Sanders were going.

As I stepped out, I said "Thanks," grateful not only for the lift but for letting me get Bella's backpack before we left Woodlawn. Twist looked me up and down, his eyes dripping disdain.

"Any fool knows he shouldn't go walking around cemeteries at four-thirty in the morning like some damned zombie," he said. "But no, not you. You just had to be there, didn't you?"

When the blue-and-white took off, I threw the old pack over my shoulder and, as the sun started to send a muted glow over TriBeCa, walked along Varick until Spring, where I picked up Greenwich and went home, passing a bread truck from Arthur Avenue outside the TriBeCa Grill.

As I reached my front door, I understood Twist and Sanders were on their way back to Woodlawn.

But they weren't going to find a gun under the bridge, in the trunk of a tree, in a garbage can. Unless they snorkeled, they weren't going to come across it. If they did snorkel—and Twist looked like the kind of man who'd do what he thought he had to—they wouldn't know whose gun it was, even if they suspected that Weisz couldn't be counted on to know one end of the barrel from the other when all the psychotropic drugs kicked in.

Unless they found his blood on the path.

Unless he collapsed by the gates.

I went up the front steps, punched in the code, entered the empty house.

I wanted to obsess, and I had more than enough rattling around my head to occupy me for weeks. I'd seen Weisz, who is real, who understands, despite his psychosis and the drugs, that he is going to pay for what he'd done. I'd seen van Kuijk, traitorous prick, at Weisz's mother's service, and I'd seen his wife, Elizabeth Harteveld, who may have had to show some fire when she spoke with her husband last night. And I'd seen Coceau, the witness I hadn't talked to, the only one who hadn't told me what he'd seen on the platform under Lincoln Center.

And I hadn't forgotten Loretta, Ruthie's warning or Willis's .38. Or my friend Leo, who wanted justice, even from the grave.

But it was Weisz who once again came through the door with me, followed me into my home.

All that I had spent much, most, of the last five years thinking about until my brain ached as much as my soul did had finally come together. I knew this now: Weisz lives, and someone had protected him. Maybe several people had. Whether they took him into their homes or merely kept silent, they aided him, kept him away from me.

Addison had a man at Woodlawn. He knew Weisz would show.

Did he have someone at the service at the Park Avenue Church?

And why was Twist looking out for Weisz? Because his lieutenant told him he was a murderer? Or because Addison merely wanted to talk to him?

I was still dressed in a black hooded sweatshirt, and my sneakers squeaked on the hardwood floor and on the kitchen linoleum tiles as I paced to the living room and back.

Bella's threadbare pack was on the table, next to her Mordecai Foxx manuscript.

Bella.

Bella, you would've seen that I was right. It's right to take a bad man down. The little things, maybe you can let them slide. But when it's important, you've got to get it done.

You've got no choice.

8

I couldn't say I hadn't intended to nap, since I woke up under the covers. But I didn't want to sleep until 2:30 in the afternoon. By the time I dragged myself, and my stiff right knee, out of bed, and shaved and showered, it was just after 3 P.M.

I knew Weisz would be harder to find now. Not harder than during much of the past five years—at least now I knew he existed. But harder than it would've been if I hadn't faced him down outside the tomb, harder than it would've been if I hadn't heard of Renaldo Twist, who claimed he knew more about me than he cared to.

I also knew it wasn't going to be as I had fantasized—I'd be jogging across town one morning, bounding on concrete as I left the Seaport headed toward Delancey, and I'd see Weisz as he threatened a group of old Italian women clutching their shopping carts as he waved a box-cutter at eye level. Or Bella and I would be leaving the

Cherry Lane Theater and there'd be Weisz, panhandling on Commerce. (In that one, I chase him into Washington Square Park, tackling him at the foot of Turini's statue of Garibaldi.) Or Diddio and I would be leaving Gigino's, the taste of Tuscany still on our lips, and I'd see Weisz on Greenwich, moving toward my home on Harrison, determined to push the issue.

Christ, I was hungry.

I zipped up my jeans, slid into sneakers and went downstairs.

The mail lay scattered on the kitchen floor near the front door. I couldn't think of anything we expected that needed immediate attention, so I went right to the refrigerator. Mrs. Maoli hated that I cut myself slivers of the pricy Parmigiano-Reggiano she bought us at Murray's, instead of reserving it for her special dishes, but I couldn't help it. It was the world's best cheese even when I wasn't famished.

I took the cheese, a Granny Smith apple, a plastic container of green Ascolane olives and a bottle of Badoit to the table, letting the refrigerator close on its own.

By the time I'd finished, I was no closer to an idea of how to find Weisz than I was before I sat down. The obvious one— check in with Addison—was easily swept aside.

As I put the dishes in the sink and reached for one of Bella's vitamins, I realized I had time to go back to the task Leo handed me. For some reason, on this clear, sun-drenched midafternoon, Ruthie's warning gave me a lift. I was in a mood for defiance.

The restaurant was less than half the size of Leo's old place. Someone sliced the space, renting the back part to a three-person architectural firm that put up dry wall, a complex HVAC system and a great old Georgian door on Harrison. The front part was now home to The Red Curry, which wasn't Vong nor even the Thai House Cafe, but it did enough business to stay open for nearly five years.

"Somebody told me your friend used to own this place," said Mary Boettcher, who, with her husband Kitti, ran the restaurant.

We were seated at a table where the big bar once stood at Big Chief's. I expected the scent of chili pepper, cardamom, basil, but no. Just clean air, well cooled. That HVAC system really worked.

"Leo Mallard." I nodded.

She smiled. "I used to wonder if you were mad at us."

"Me?"

"I'd see you and your daughter." She pointed to Greenwich. "But you never came in."

I wasn't socializing when The Red Curry opened. "I was here last year." With Bella, Daniel and their friend Glo-Bug. I'd forgotten I was supposed to pick up stuff for homemade Mexican.

"Let's hope you're not a stranger," Mary Boettcher said.

She looked tired; her hands were red and rough, her auburn hair lifeless. I'd bet she put in 18 hours a day at the 20-seat restaurant. Like everybody else down here whose business survived September 11, she and her husband were trying to build back up to where they'd once been. It was hard, hard work.

"I appreciate you taking time for me," I told her.

"We have to help each other, right?"

I nodded. "I'm trying to understand what caused Leo to lose this place, and what happened after that."

Leo's side of the story—Loretta stole, Loretta embezzled, Loretta ran off; the government invaded—might sound all right to a friend. But there was more to it than that. Ruthie trying to steer me away told me so.

If I was going to track down Loretta, I'd better know the back story.

"I don't know much about it," she said with a gentle shrug. "Gossip."

"Such as?"

"His wife." She shook her head disapprovingly.

I asked her if she'd ever met Loretta.

"Neither her nor him," she replied. "Is he doing all right?"

I told her.

She quickly blessed herself. "I'm sorry to hear that."

"Thanks."

She leaned forward. "Can I ask you a question? Did your friend own this space?"

"No." I stopped. "At least I don't think he did."

"I heard he owned the Tilt-A-Whirl."

"I think that's right."

"Free and clear?"

I smiled. "So I'm told."

"That's a major investment."

I paused. The Tilt itself was probably worth about $12. But the land it sat on was prime real estate in downtown Manhattan. "You're right."

"How could he do that after what happened here?" she asked.

"You mean after the city shut him down?"

She nodded.

"That's what I need to know, I guess," I said.

"You should talk to Patti Pondfield at Fleece Realty," she suggested. "She brokered the deal for us to rent this place."

"Fleece Realty?"

"They're not so bad." As she stood, Mary Boettcher added, "I'll get you her number."

I thanked Boettcher, then walked over to Fleece's office on West Broadway to see Patricia Pondfield. When I entered the storefront, one of her colleagues intercepted me and told me she was out. The woman, who was about five feet in heels and as round as a melon, stood about an inch from me as she spoke, even as I backed away, asking for information on the site of The Red Curry. As she detached herself from me to use her computer, I saw that Pondfield had been named a member of the Platinum Club in each of the past four years. The little blond dynamo had a bumper sticker on her monitor: DIVORCED AND LOVIN' IT!

When she returned, she gave me the name of the site's landlord— Interstate Properties Limited. But the address of its local agent wasn't too promising: Two World Trade Center.

I told the blonde I'd find where they'd moved to, and I left.

Halted for now in the Loretta chase, I paused on the corner of West Broadway, looked at my watch, then up at the gorgeous high sky to make a silent apology to Leo. If he was watching, he already knew he was going to have to wait.

I thought about taking the 1-9 uptown, but I decided I might want to use my cell on the way to the Upper West Side. Bella might call, or Julie. Or Addison.

I went out onto the soft street, and a cab, a gleaming yellow mini-van, arrived seconds later. It had an ample flow of air-conditioning and *All Things Considered* on the radio.

Yeah, it was going my way now.

It wasn't until we reached Gansevoort Street that I remembered why I felt so energetic, so upbeat. I'd ventilated the murderous motherfucker. I'd made him bleed.

Coceau's shop was three blocks north of La Belle Époque, the better known of the vintage French poster shops on Columbus. Coceau's purported specialty was rare antiques advertising posters, originals only. Thanks to his affiliation with antiques dealers in Paris and Nice, his shop had access to extremely rare works by Jules Cheret, the father of the poster as art. Coceau's website claimed his New York shop had the largest selection of rare Cherets in the U.S.

As I understood it, in the late 1840s in Paris, Cheret marshaled his talents to create the first color poster promoting a commercial enterprise, serving as artist and printer. In the years that followed, he was capable of producing on his press thousands of copies an hour of each of his exquisite works. But because they were so widely available, people in Paris at the end of the nineteenth century didn't consider them collectible art, despite vibrant color and imagery, the quality of craftsmanship. Magnificent posters by Toulouse-Lautrec, Bonnard, Cappiello and Grün followed, further legitimizing the medium. But as had Cheret's, most of their posters went up on walls with glue slapped on with horsehair brushes and, shortly thereafter, were tossed into the trash. Only a few of their works, if that many, survived. Hence, the tight market, the high prices, the collectors' fervor.

As I stood in the bright sun on Columbus, sliding bills back into my pocket, I saw that in Coceau's window today was a framed photograph of Jules-Alexandre Grün's *Je Sais Tout,* in which a thinking man with the planet Earth for a head wore a white bow tie and black long coat to promote a group of periodicals. A hand-penned sign taped to the frame announced WE HAVE THE ONLY ORIGINAL IN THE STATES! The poster looked remarkably new.

Coceau did a good job with his front windows. Plenty of eye appeal, real traffic stoppers. To match this work, the easel stood on orange satin and the walls were painted a pale green. It looked great. I wanted the Grün. Anyone would. Anyone who would pay a sizable sum for a poster of a frowning man with globe for a head.

I entered the shop. Behind an ornate oak desk, surrounded by framed and matted posters of ships and exotic seaports, women in pearls and lavish gowns, gleeful dancers with their legs stretching ever higher, bare-breasted coquettes awaiting the return of the slick in a top hat and tails, a young man was thumbing through a thick book of similar works. He didn't look up when I entered or when I stood between the director's chairs that faced him.

"He in?" I asked.

He ignored me as he continued to gloss over posters in the book and toy with the desk set's gold-plated letter opener.

He was a red-haired, ruddy-faced kid who couldn't have been more than 25 years old. Coceau had gotten him a nice gray suit, white shirt and yellow-and-gray patterned tie for his lean body and taught him enough to hold the fort until he returned. But he hadn't taught him how to size up a customer. His insolence wasn't going to work on a man who wanted to talk to his boss. Nor on the next man who came into the shop, who may have enough in his pocket to buy an original Cheret.

I reached over and shut the book with a dull thud. Lettering on its yellow cover screamed at me: POSTERS OF THE BELLE ÉPOQUE. The kid was still learning.

"Yes?" he asked with a flutter of his eyelashes and a thin smile.

I laughed.

He frowned. "What?"

"You got moves, but you don't know how to use them," I said. "And I'm not sure you've got the looks for that last one." I flashed my fingers in front of my face. "You know, the thing with the eyes."

"I do all right," he said sharply.

"Yeah, but who wants to settle for all right?"

He sat back and crossed his leg. "What is it you want?"

"Your boss. Coceau."

"He's not here."

"When's he coming—"

The kid looked past me to the glass door. I turned.

There was Jean-Pierre Coceau, a brown leather briefcase in tow. And I knew instantly that he didn't recognize me.

Thinking I was a customer, Coceau greeted me with a bright look of anticipation.

"I'm sorry to keep you waiting," he said as we shook hands. His French accent was pronounced, though he seemed comfortable speaking English, as he gave what must've been his standard, customer-softening greeting.

"It's OK."

Beads of sweat dotted his forehead under the black curls that lay against his skin. As I looked down at him, I noticed that his blue eyes were complemented by the cobalt shirt he wore open at the collar over a blue-checkered blazer and yellow slacks.

"I have been running to many—"

"I'm Terry Orr," I said. And though I saw he immediately recognized my name, I added, "You saw my wife and son die."

He stopped.

"You went to the memorial service yesterday," I continued. "Is there a reason you did that?"

"Yes," he replied without hesitation. "Your obsession."

He told me to follow him into his office.

He took a one-liter bottle of Volvic out of a small refrigerator he had in the corner and placed it between two glasses on a silver tray on his desktop. I watched as he removed his blazer, slipped it on a hanger and returned the hanger to the coat tree.

The office walls were painted a dark blue, and they matched the curtain that separated Coceau's space from the rest of the shop. He had only one poster in his office, a festive scene by Jules Cheret of a lute player and a dancer, men on horseback, in bright yellows, deep browns and rich, subtle blues.

"I had hoped to avoid you, Mr. Orr," he said as he sat behind the desk, which was thick frosted glass on two simple steel pedestals. His mail was in a yellow folder on his blotter and a letter opener was on the folder. Otherwise, the desktop was empty.

"I know," I replied, "but you were at the church yesterday."

"And you were also?"

I nodded.

"You were disappointed," he said.

"Yes, I was. Were you?"

He shrugged and made a small puffing sound with his lips. "Maybe I am not so sure why I was there, really. I thought you might come. There could be trouble."

Coceau was a small man, slightly built. It was unlikely he could've prevented what I had in mind and I told him so.

"As I say, I don't really have something firm in my mind," he said. "Maybe I could protect him. It's crazy . . ."

"You want to protect Weisz? Why?"

"Your obsession," he repeated. "It is totally unjust. I'm sorry to tell you that."

He leaned forward and took the cold bottle of mineral water.

"I don't understand," I said. "What could be unjust about a man wanting to capture the lunatic who killed his wife and son?"

As he cracked the plastic seal on the bottle, he said, "A lunatic he could be, as you say. But by now I am sure you know Mr. Weisz did not kill your family, Mr. Orr."

He turned over both narrow glasses and began to fill one.

"I don't know that," I said. "I don't know anything like that."

He nudged a glass of water toward me.

"I do. I know Mr. Weisz did not kill your family."

As he filled the second glass and returned the plastic bottle to the tray, I asked, "Really? If he didn't, who did?"

He sipped the cold water. "No one killed your wife and son, Mr. Orr."

"Listen to me, Coceau," I said sharply. "They're dead. I'm sure of that."

"Yes, but it was an accident," he said again. "I'm sorry, but you know . . ." He shrugged.

I came out of the chair. "I spoke to everyone who saw what Weisz did. Everyone who was there, except you. And no one has ever said it was an accident." I shook my head. "An accident? No."

"Mr. Orr, please. You are angry. I understand."

"Angry? No, I'm . . . incredulous. After five years—"

He waved his hand as he placed his glass on the tray. "Please, I don't want to make more bad memories for you."

I gripped the knobs of the back of the director's chair I'd been sitting in. "My obsession, my memories."

"Yes, my dear boy, I have tried to imagine what could be your pain," he said. "But it cannot justify what you have intended to do. But it was an accident, yes. Terrible, terrible."

"The stroller went onto the tracks. How? By itself?"

"Yes, in fact," he replied as he folded his hands together. "It rolled. It fell."

"No," I snapped. "People saw Weisz push it."

"Weisz tried to grab it. I saw it. I saw him."

I stepped away from the chair.

Coceau said, "I was on the northbound platform. The only one. I just missed my train. The police have told you this."

I was staring at him. My heart was racing and my breath was shallow and suddenly labored.

"When the man screamed, the man with the cane, everyone turned. They saw him, his arms reaching."

"No, they saw him shove it," I said. "Throw it."

He shook his head. "They did not."

"They said he threw it onto the tracks. All of them."

"They were reading their newspapers, magazines," Coceau said calmly, "or looking for the train. Listening to music with their earphones."

"But then he— Then he ran."

"Of course he did. He is a crazy man. He is not stupid."

I shoved my hands into my jeans pockets. "Marina reacted. She was— She dove down there fast. Immediately. To save him."

He nodded. "She was very brave, but not fast enough. The train was coming and—"

"Hold it," I said. "'Not fast enough.' What do you mean?"

"She had to come around the pillar. She couldn't move until she heard the scream, of course, because she did not see."

"What do you mean, she didn't see? She was right there. Of course she saw."

"I'm sorry, but she was not."

"No? Well, where the fuck was she?"

"Ah, Mr. Orr, this is the problem. This is why I did not wish to speak with you."

I was feeling light-headed—images cascading, red lights, roaring trains, my beautiful Italian wife, my infant son. A Madman on a platform, filth-coated arms outstretched, wild hair.

"Coceau—"

"Mr. Orr, I am sorry to tell you that you did not speak to everyone who was on the southbound platform that terrible day."

"Everyone but you."

"And the man your wife was with."

"What?" I felt an electric jolt in the pit of my stomach.

"The man she was with."

I was standing perfectly still in front of the Frenchman. "No one said she was with a man."

"They were behind the pillar. From the platform where I stood, I saw them. Very clear."

"What, they were hiding?"

"No, Mr. Orr," he said softly. "They were kissing."

I opened my mouth but I could not speak.

"I'm sorry," Coceau continued. "But it is so."

I managed, "A friend . . ."

"I don't think so, Mr. Orr. This was *très passionné.*"

I was shaking. "I don't believe you," I said finally.

Coceau stood. "Mr. Orr, I am afraid that you do."

He lifted the glass of water and held it toward me.

"Please," he said. "You must take a drink."

I reached, felt the cold glass on my fingertips. Saw the glass fall from my hand, hit the edge of the desk and shatter as it crashed onto the hardwood floor.

I looked blankly at Coceau, who was coming around the desk.

I felt my stomach clutch, my throat burn.

"Mr. Orr . . ."

I turned, shoved aside the blue curtain, ran past the red-faced man behind the desk and careened onto Columbus Avenue, into the relentless heat.

As I grabbed the parking meter at the curb, I retched and, stumbling between two cars, I vomited into the street.

Coceau came up behind me, reached for me. But I shoved him away.

On the other side of Columbus, patrons seated outside a Mexican restaurant were staring at me, pointing.

I lurched a few feet north on the avenue and tumbled against the next parking meter, its dome hot from the sun's bright rays. I leaned against it, my throbbing head buried in the crook of my arm. My eyes were pounding, my throat felt red and raw.

The sound of a revving engine in the distance. The rush of a car as it sped under a yellow light. A boy on a skateboard, plastic wheels rattling on concrete. He stopped, he looked at me with a combination of curiosity and disgust.

I waited until the sick feeling abated, until the acid subsided, then I stumbled toward the side street and propped myself against the brick wall, next to dented garbage cans, newspapers tied in a bundle.

"Lieutenant Addison, please," I said into the cell phone.

A guy told me he'd signed out.

I dropped the phone as I tried to hook it to my belt.

I stared at it as it lay on a crack in the sidewalk.

9

I knew he was lying. As I walked the five miles from the Upper West Side to TriBeCa, I told myself, again, again, again, that he was lying.

I could not doubt that Weisz had thrown Davy in front of the express train. Thirteen people saw it, and many of them said so, not only to me but to Addison. For me, this is indisputable fact: Raymond Montgomery Weisz killed my wife and child. He has been hiding for five years to avoid paying for his vicious act, confirming his guilt.

Nor did I doubt Marina's love for me, of what we had made together. We had come so far—I never could've become the man I had been were it not for her. Our marriage was sound. Of course it was; why wouldn't it have been? We were raising our children, she was painting, I was writing, we were succeeding. Bella was more than any parent could hope for—bright, curious, charming, engaging. And Davy? A little colic and then never a problem. A cooing, happy baby. Davy was ready for adventure. *Il mio costante compagno,* Marina called him—my constant companion. "I go. He goes," she said one morning as she dressed him in OshKosh overalls for a trip uptown.

She was my light, my teacher. An artist who loved her father, sister, her homeland, nature, her children, her husband, her art. I observed her as she worked, dots of paint on the backs of her hands, a swipe above her eyebrows as she absently wiped her forehead. What a remarkable thing it was to watch her interpret what she saw and create it anew as richer, deeper, more vivid, more vital.

It was as if her brilliance cast its glow upon me and fortified me, helping me to grow as a writer, a man.

I mean, who was I the moment before we met? A boy from Narrow's Gate, New Jersey, with his head up his ass and a basketball tucked under his arm. A jock, with a vague interest in history and old movies. My wardrobe: T-shirts, old jeans, wrinkled Oxfords, sweat socks, sneakers. Under those clothes, I was 6'4" and, at 225, solid, no longer gawky. Aware of my body, but a stranger to ideas.

Then this beautiful woman, a painter who lived in SoHo. I approached her as I approached girls. She was amused.

"No, I don't think so," she said, her dark eyes twinkling. Such skin—olive, flawless. Long fingers.

I had asked her if she had a boyfriend. They always said yes, even if they didn't. Who wants a girl who can't get a guy?

They'd say yes and I'd say, "You want a better one?"

What an asshole.

But it worked, especially if the girl knew me as the star of the high-school team, as a guy on a scholarship to play at St. John's. With those girls, I had all kinds of confidence.

With this woman, who didn't know the ball from the basket, who didn't care about jocks and their snake-oil status, I had no chance.

They were showing *The Manchurian Candidate* at MoMA. Diddio was chasing down some self-inflated rock star, so I was on my own.

She was standing in the lobby, glass of red wine in her hand. The sounds of cordial chatter came from a nearby gallery, one she'd temporarily deserted. A reception in honor of the Italian Futurists.

I had 20 minutes until Sinatra, Harvey, Leigh and Lansbury would transport me from my dull little world.

"Nobody to talk to?" I asked. As if a woman this beautiful, this composed, would be alone by chance rather than choice.

She shrugged, smiled. "They are talking." She gestured toward the gallery with a graceful nod.

That accent.

"About?"

"Oh, Boccioni, Balla, Severini, Carrà."

"Yeah, those guys . . ."

She laughed.

"At least there's wine," I said.

"It's not very good either."

I took the ticket out of my shirt pocket. "Want to go to the movies?"

She said no. "I have to stay," she added. "It's important to meet people."

"You met me." As I said, I was a boy.

"The right people, I'm afraid."

A tall man in an immaculate double-breasted suit and flawless tan appeared at the entrance to the gallery. His manner suggested a self-confidence that even I could recognize as genuine, as the result of achievement, of real status. He was a man, not a boy, a jock.

"I have to go," she said softly.

"Sure."

She went to the man with the tan, the Italian features, the salt-and-pepper hair that draped casually over his ears and on the back of his collar.

Was he scolding her?

No. She nodded. He smiled. He put his hand on her back. They went into the gallery.

I went to the Frankenheimer retrospective.
She was waiting on 53rd when the movie let out.
"Looking for me?"
"A coincidence." But she was smiling.
"Listen . . ."
And that's when I asked her about a boyfriend.
What a buffoon.
But she gave me her number.
And it was perfect from that moment.
Perfect.

I was drenched in sweat, my face red from the relentless heat. The scars on my knee were on fire, my throat was raw from retching, vomiting. I sat on one of the benches in my yard, my back against the wooden picnic table, staring at the cloudless sky. Bella's tomato vines were bare now. Mrs. Maoli's marinara sauce filled a shelf in the basement.

Across the courtyard, behind a screen door, Sheila Yannick played Bach, the prelude to the Cello Suite No. 1.

Coceau is wrong. In his mind, he's created a scenario in which the Madman did no wrong, where the Madman is the victim.

But for his bizarre scenario to work, someone else has to be at fault. If Weisz isn't the villain, who is? The mother. She was ignoring her baby, giving herself to a man who is not her husband. To Coceau, such infidelity required punishment.

The Frenchman can accept infidelity to a spouse. These things happen. But to a family? To put the family at risk? *Ceci n'est pas fait.*

He created this ugly fantasy as he flew from Nice to New York, New York to Paris, Paris to the Côte d'Azur. While he motored across France, Switzerland, the U.K., the U.S., to find posters in mint condition. While he participated in *un petit crime* at home.

He probably did it, the little prick. Brought some counterfeit Cherets into the system. Since they let him walk, he couldn't have been more than the beard for someone with real authority, with public stature. Coceau demonstrated his loyalty by taking the heat and keeping his mouth shut, and that display of *fidélité* created a solution for everyone involved, including Coceau's firm and the museum. His compensation—a transfer to New York, free housing, an expense account.

Such a small man, Coceau. There he is, standing on the other subway platform, observing the horror as if it were a play he doesn't enjoy, that doesn't satisfy his expectations. A Madman appears and throws a baby's stroller onto the tracks. As the Madman vanishes, the mother risks her own life to save her baby. They are both killed, mother and child. The Madman escapes.

No, he prefers this: The poor Madman is misunderstood. He tried to save the baby, who suffers from his mother's callousness. The mother tries to help her baby, but is too late. Or Mother, accepting the consequences of her infidelity, joins her son on the tracks as the murdering train roars through.

He vilifies a victim, a mother, a hero. My wife. The woman I adored.

Why would Coceau do that?

The sky had gone from twilight silver to indigo blue, and I could smell the river, dormant now as if made weary by the long summer and its persistent heat.

I left the bench, limping with my tender knee, confused, uncertain, and went back inside my empty home.

Marina wanted us in this neighborhood and she was pleased when I found this 220-year-old refurbished two-story. We paid a fortune for it. I could hear the mice under the floorboards in my office as I wrote, Marina couldn't find the natural light she wanted until we had the roof above her studio fitted with skylights, and little Bella fell down the stairs twice, landing in the kitchen with a thud and a wail. But we loved the house and what it meant. We were a family and we were fine.

If we weren't, she would've told me.

See, this is one of the reasons I know Coceau is lying. If Marina was unhappy, she would tell me, with a startling exactitude: Here's what's wrong. How are we going to set it right? She couldn't understand people who wouldn't speak up, people who'd simmer and stew. She used to say, "Talk to me, Terry. What is it on your mind?"

She still asks me that. She comes to me and I feel her breath on my neck, her hand on my knee. I hear her laugh, hear the melody of the Italian lullabies she sang to our daughter and son.

If I'm receptive, she appears.

Like this: I'm on the couch, unable to sleep. The house is dark, and it creaks in the gentlest wind and sloshing water runs through its old pipes. Then there is silence and she speaks.

"Terry, what is it you are trying to do?"

I'm sitting in darkness, bare feet on the living-room rug, and I face a blank TV, remote in my hand. "I want to get him, Marina. The man who took you and Davy."

"Is this wise?"

"Somebody's got to pay, *mei carissima.*"

She says, clearly, "Yes. I see."

Harteveld told me she believed Marina might've said something else, something quite different. Like: "Somebody is paying, Terry. Bella. And you."

Now I put my hands on the ridges left by her brush strokes and I stepped back and stared at the white limestone, veins of moss, bush and broom, sea water vanishing into blue sky stroked by Aleppo pines. But Marina didn't appear.

Then I went to the kitchen table and peered across to where she sat, Davy at her breast, warm smile on her face.

"He's hungry?" I asked.

No reply now. Back then: "*È un uomo,*" she said with a shrug.

I went upstairs to Bella's bedroom and retrieved a videotape of a PBS program—*The Future of the Landscape,* an overview of landscape painting in the postmodern era. Marina disliked the show, which compared her to the Dutch landscape artists of the seventeenth century rather than the Italian ideal landscape artists and the nineteenth-century Romantics, whose complementary approaches she felt she fused for her personal style. "A realistic approach to the Impressionists' archetype," declared the narrator, actor Ben Cross. "She finds a natural sense of order and glorifies it to a stunning end."

"Who is this woman?" she asked angrily. "I don't know who she is."

Bella was sitting on the floor, elbows on her knees, chin on her pudgy fists. When the program cut from the purple lines of *Valley of Bovino* to a shot of Marina walking along the promenade in Brooklyn Heights—a totally staged event—Bella exclaimed, "Mama!" Then: "But where's me?"

On screen, Marina said, "What it is we see isn't necessarily what it is. It is what we believe it is. What you bring to your vision is your emotions. This changes everything."

In the living room, dismayed by the sound of her accent, she said, "This woman is a greenhorn."

She stood and left the room. "Call me when there is a movie."

That was a Monday evening. By Wednesday at noon, Judy Henley Harper had sold 11 paintings by Marina for unexpectedly phenomenal sums, laughably high sums. *Valley of Bovino* went to a collector in Bologna for $800,000.

Which was more than enough for the down payment on our new home on Harrison.

I have tried several hundred times to remember what I said to her when she left that morning to head uptown, smiling Davy in tow.

For five years, I heard myself say something like, "I love you, *tesoro.*" To which she replied, "I will be with you tonight, Terry."

But for the past hour or so, I knew it was this: "Bye." "Yeah, bye." Were we so ordinary?

There was one more place to look for her.

I went down to the basement, tugged the thin string to turn on the bare bulb and, from behind an old striped bedspread hung to hide my messy bookcase, took out a stepladder. In the crawl space above the washer and dryer was something I'd hidden five years ago. Several boxes were packed tight against fiberglass, but one of them was different. The others held documents I'd used for *Slippery Dick*. In the last one, a secret.

I took two boxes of files, photocopied letters, notebooks, white pages of false starts and early drafts, and put them on top of the washer. Then I wriggled the third box toward me and took it. When I stepped down gingerly, I left the ladder where it was, tucked the big box against my hip and headed from the smell of detergent and raw wood toward the stairs and up to the kitchen.

It was 10:02, according to the clock in the stove.

I nudged aside Bella's manuscript and undid the box's top, yanking the yellowing tape until it ripped from cardboard.

I opened the box.

Marina wore the uniform when she had to: plenty of black, soft leather, thick-soled boots, white Hanes T-shirts. She had a few tailored suits, including a stunning Versace in deep olive, cut perfectly. Silk blouses Judy ordered from Pink's.

I sent it all to Rafaela. Actually, Diddio did, and Leo. I couldn't. I couldn't bear it.

But about seven or eight months later, I found these dresses in the back of the closet, folded neatly on a shelf that held the extra pillows we kept.

These three simple summer dresses with their floral patterns, roses and honeysuckle, poppies and lilacs, that she wore with pink panties, sandals and, when a breeze threatened, a light sweater tossed over her shoulders. They flowed when she walked, when she turned. They seemed to dance with each step she took.

She was wearing one of these cotton dresses the first time she told me she loved me, on that golden, glorious afternoon on Fifth.

When we were in Italy, a picnic on San Domino among the Tremiti Islands. Dried figs, fennel, juicy pears, a fat loaf of fresh bread stuffed with olives, and a rosé from San Severo. Rafaela put wildflowers in the basket.

With Bella, walking in Central Park, sun on her shoulders. A yellow balloon, string dangling as it lofted toward the heavens. Three-year-old Bella, so pragmatic, not crying. "Oh well. It wasn't going to last much longer anyway."

Marina, two months pregnant with our son, at the lectern at the Viani Dugnani Palace off Lake Maggiore, where she was scheduled to be honored the next day for her work. As Bella and I watched, she stopped the rehearsal of her presentation, bowed her head, choked as she started to speak again and suddenly burst into tears.

Now I tucked my hands under the dress on top, lifted it, ran my fingers along the soft material, my thumb on budding flowers, tender leaves. And then I leaned over and brought the dress to my face and I felt it against my cheek, and, with a deep breath, took in what remained of her scent, faded now, almost gone. But it was there, faint, almost imperceptible, but there it was—the scent of my wife. And I felt her presence, not as a fantasy in which I called her to my side, feeding her lines to echo, controlling her gestures, expressions. She appeared to me as she was when she last wore this simple dress, some five years ago.

And I knew.

I *knew.*

Oh no. Oh Christ, no.

I've always known.

I dropped the dress, and I stumbled back against the chair, my arm flailing as my legs suddenly grew weak. And as I started to fall, I grabbed at the table. My hand knocked hard against the box, sending it, and the dresses, toward the floor. It all landed on top of me.

As I struggled to my knees, I slammed the box against the front door, then grabbed one of the dresses and, screaming, I began to tear it. The cheap cotton ripped easily, and I shredded a second one, and a third, yanking them until they came apart in my red hands, and buttons flew across the room. And all the while I screamed.

And when I was finished, I sat on the linoleum, among the tatters and scraps, the rags and, finally, I spoke to myself.

"You fool," I said, between labored breaths. My voice rang in the barren house. "You insignif— You nobody. You fool."

10

The night had yet to surrender the sky, and Greenwich was so quiet as to be still. I stood on my narrow steps in the early morning chill, my hands in the pockets of my leather jacket, listening to the river as I waited for a livery cab to come and take me up to the Bronx. I probably could've gotten a taxi by the clubs near the old Gansevoort Market or over in the East Village, but I figured I was short on time, despite the early hour. I wanted to be back in the Bronx before sunup, when much of the borough was in a deep sleep, when nocturnal creatures were active and yet at ease.

My illusions were gone now. I was seeing clearly, very clearly.

Did I drive you away, Marina?

"Terry, non sei tu. Non sei tu—"

Excuse me, Marina. A rhetorical question, you know what I'm saying?

Right now, I don't give a fuck.

I'm going to find out what happened to Davy, *il tuo costante compagno.* The giggling baby who lay in his stroller or on a blanket on the floor, playing with a blue rubber rattle, a set of oversized plastic keys, while you were whispering tenderly to your new man in a bedroom somewhere near Lincoln Center.

You, I'll deal with later.

Here's the old black Buick now.

I got out near gate B, off the Bronx River Parkway, and crossed in front of his high beams and watched as he made an awkward U-turn, watched as his red brake lights vanished, leaving me in utter darkness, alone. At 4:17, it was as quiet as it was supposed to be, and I heard him gun his V-8 to hump back onto the highway. As I dug out my flashlight, I wondered if anyone else had heard it—an unarmed security guard, maybe, jarred from his sleep in his cozy shed or made alert while on his leisurely rounds.

The Bronx Zoo is about a mile long and a mile wide and, with few lights to guide night-time prowlers, it was an easy place to get lost in. But, within weeks of Davy's death, I'd learned the wolves were penned off the Bronx Parkway gate and getting to them wasn't much of a challenge. The outer fences weren't much taller than I was. Some, like the first one I took on, had a rail at its center that served as a ledge to boost me over its top. I swung carefully and landed with a light thud. I felt the ripple from the shock in my right knee—a brief spark—but otherwise, no problem. Within five minutes, I'd scaled three other diamond fences and then I wasn't far from where Raymond Montgomery Weisz was found early one morning 20 years ago. No alpha male, 14-year-old Raymond lay outside the pack in their open-air enclosure, nude, caked in mud, curled in a fetal position around a tree stump, apparently undisturbed by the animals that slept not far from him.

I used the thin ray from the penlight flash to negotiate the black path that led toward the wolves' den. I could hear the gurgle of a small waterfall somewhere to my left, but I could see very little. It was deliberately dark in the zoo to sustain the idea of a natural habitat. Perhaps it worked for the bisons or the Père David deer in the park, all of which were raised in captivity.

As I stared into the dull haze under the new moon, surrounded by unseen beech and tulip trees, lazing bison and sleeping deer, I felt the weight of a sudden, unexpected thought. Back with his wolves now, Weisz had an advantage. They'd warn him as soon as I arrived, their yellow eyes narrowing in on me as I approached, the sound of my sneakers on the rutty road, or the scent of my sweat, giving me away. I had to be alert for his charge. He had no way of knowing I only wanted to talk to him, not grind him into pulp, not send a nine-millimeter slug through his brain. I only wanted to know what he'd seen.

I ran the ray from my penlight along the side of the path. The beech tree's trunk resembled an elephant's thick leg.

With the light on the path, on the moist earth surrounding the blacktop, I could see nothing in front of me. If I raised the ray, sending out a narrow, 20-foot quavering beam, I couldn't see the trail beneath my sneakers. And either way, seeing the slender stream of light, Weisz would know I'd come, even before his allies bared their sharp teeth.

I pushed the small button and killed the glow, and I waited for my eyes to adjust, as well as they could, to the blackness around me. Waiting, I leaned against a broad tree.

Of course, he'd return to his wolves. Someone had told Addison that, a police shrink, maybe. About a year ago, the Lieutenant and I had quarreled—I'd been told Weisz was spotted in—

Quiet. *Quiet.*

In the distance, the sound of wings, nothing more. Crows soaring over the zoo, landing in treetops, surveying the land, the skulking animals below.

Squirrels underfoot, more rattling under shrubs.

Addison denied that Weisz had been spotted in Indianapolis, though Tommy the Cop assured me he had, trying for a job tending to animals at a major drug firm. And, during one of our less contentious quarrels, Addison had also told me where else the Madman hadn't been spotted: Peoria, Illinois; Orlando, Florida; Grand Forks, North Dakota; and Green Bay, Wisconsin. Later, I began to wonder why he'd mentioned those four towns and started to look for what they had in common. After a couple of days of following leads to nowhere, I found it: Each had a zoo that housed wolves. Addison was telling me, as he was warning me off, that he'd alerted police throughout the U.S. that Weisz might turn up at their local zoo.

I inched away from the tree and went back to the center of the mottled path. Following it up an incline, moving slowly ahead, I—

"Psst."

I heard it clearly.

"Orr." A whisper.

Then a man's hand clasped tight on my shoulder.

I threw a sharp elbow in his stomach, and I heard the air leave him.

I spun. Before he could draw up, I was on him and I flung him into the bushes on the carved trail away from the blacktop.

Caught in the prickly shrubbery, he struggled to regain his footing, to square himself to charge at me.

But as he pushed away from the bush, I felt the rush of another man coming hard at my side. A bright light shone in my face, and I heard a familiar voice.

"Terry," Addison barked.

He hurried down the path. In the darkness, I couldn't see his black suit jacket flapping behind him, his black diamond tie waving in front of his white shirt.

Twist, who had freed himself from the shrubs, leaped and shoved me hard in the chest. I held up my hands, letting the penlight fall to the ground.

"Rey," Addison said, as he stepped between us.

"You knew Weisz'd be here," I said angrily. "Christ, Luther, you're running him off again."

Twist spit on the path. He adjusted his jacket.

"All right, Rey," Addison said. He told the young cop to meet him at the car. After a few seconds, Twist broke off his stare and headed up the roadway.

"Luther—"

"Stop," he said, as he put his hand on my elbow to lead me toward the area where I knew Weisz had been hiding.

The path to the field was bounded on both sides by wooden posts, wooden rails, and Addison let me pass in front of him. I put my hand on the wood, felt its coarseness, knots, jutting splinters, and I followed it carefully until it led to a viewing station. The diamond fence in front of us was about six feet high—they had raised the fence, I noticed—and seemed to be topped with barbed wire. I knew low shrubs and a flowing stream, serving as a moat, rimmed the downward slope to the ramble and its expanse of earth and trees.

Eighteen years ago, zookeepers found Weisz sleeping about 30 feet from where we now stood.

Addison shone a broad beam of light onto the ramble.

And below me, glaring up at me, standing, his front paws on the tree, was a magnificent tiger, his sharp canines glowing in his wide, impressive head.

"What's going on?" I said, as I pulled back.

Suddenly, the beast let loose a low, rumbling growl, an angry, deep-throated bark, unlike any sound I'd ever heard. He stared squarely at me, relentlessly.

"There are no more wolves here," Addison said calmly, as he steered me away from the beast and toward the path to his car. "They gave them all away."

"When?" I groaned.

"Since the last time you bothered to check," he said. "You let your obsession slip, Terry."

Twist twirled a pair of night goggles as he waited by the unmarked car he and his lieutenant had taken from Midtown North up to the Bronx.

I sat on the steps of a big bird sanctuary. Pale light from inside the hall, and the first blush rays of sunrise, stretched across the surrounding woods.

"Are you all right?" Addison asked, as he returned. He hovered above me.

My heart was racing, but otherwise I was fine. "Sure."

He pushed his thumb toward Twist, who was staring at me, shaking his head. "You thought he was Weisz?"

I nodded. "I couldn't see, and he only said my last name."

The only words I'd ever heard Weisz speak were on a compact disk*: "Thank you," he said, amid roars and cheers, after a performance in Edinburgh, which has a zoo and gray wolves.

"Terry, Weisz isn't here. And he hasn't turned up on Staten Island or in Central Park either. Or Prospect Park. Or out in Queens. Tonight, Raymond Montgomery Weisz is not in a zoo in the five boroughs."

"But you thought he'd come here?"

"No. But I knew you would," Addison said.

"Yeah, I was trying to get something done."

"I told you, Terry. That's no good."

"Somebody had to do—"

Luther dropped his hand on my shoulder. "Before you start in with that, maybe I ought to tell you how you blew it at the cemetery."

"Me? Your guy was sitting on his ass—"

"Weisz was going to walk into the crypt. We had the door rigged so it would lock down on him. It would've worked, but you had to come around."

I looked up at him. "You knew he'd be at Woodlawn?"

"Your Elizabeth Harteveld isn't the only psychiatrist in Manhattan, Terry," he replied, smiling patiently.

Twist sidled up to Addison, his brown loafers scraping slate and stone. "Don't you think we ought to be getting back, Lieutenant?" he said, as he sneered at me. "I mean, you're not going to get anything from this amateur."

*See page 275.

I didn't bite.

"This clown," he said sharply.

I came off the steps and stood in front of the young cop. "Why don't you go fuck yourself, little man," I told him.

"Listen, I ain't no loopy piano player," Twist snapped, jabbing a finger in my face. "Fuck with me and I'll tear you open."

Addison shouted, "Rey, move away. Terry, sit yourself back down. Both of you, now. *Now.*"

Twist looked at me, at Addison, and then let his shoulders sag, his fists relax. "Sure, Lieutenant."

I inched back toward the steps.

"But tell me when you're going to straighten him out," he said. "I'm sick of cleaning up after him."

"Rey," Addison said calmly. "Go back to the car."

Twist waited, then left, kicking across the path.

Across the road, Père David deer stirred as sunrise beckoned. Crafty black crows perched on gray rocks.

"Terry, I want to keep this friendly," he began. "But I want you to listen and I want you to hear."

Behind green eyes and a light complexion sprinkled with freckles, Luther Addison had a direct and forceful personality. Abetted by a temperate disposition, an innate sense of compassion and a real fervor for his work, it made him a hard man to deny.

"You blew it the other night at Woodlawn Cemetery—"

"Maybe if you told me—"

"Terry, all you do now is *listen.* We understand each other?"

I hesitated, then said, "Go ahead."

"I've been very patient with you, son," he continued. "For almost five years you've been in my way. It's your wife and little boy, I understand. But, for all the room I've given you, I get back nothing in return."

"Room, maybe," I said, "but information? Not unless I asked."

"That's right," he nodded. "All I need to tell you is when we got him."

I leaned back. "And that is going to be when, Luther?"

He waited, then said, "Terry, the only reason we don't have Weisz in custody is you. Do you understand that? We'd be a hell of a lot better off if you'd stayed in New Orleans."

"New Orleans? How do you know—"

"Your friend Leo," he replied, shaking his head. "Too bad."

"Look, Luther—"

"No, Terry," he said, with a kind of forceful patience. "Not anymore. You might be a private cop that helped a few people over the years. That's all right. But you have no idea what you're doing when it comes to Weisz. You never did."

I watched in silence as Addison sat next to me.

"You were hanging around the memorial service the other day," he said. "Maybe Weisz saw you, I don't know."

"He wasn't there," I said.

"You saw everyone, Terry?"

I nodded.

"You didn't see Rey," he said, as he dusted off his black slacks. "But he saw you."

"So now it's him after Weisz, instead of you? What good is he?" I asked. "I mean, who does he know?" I was thinking of Coceau, who Addison had spoken to. Or van Kuijk, Harteveld's husband.

"Rey knows everything, Terry," Addison said. "Everything. He's been working on this for two years come October."

I stood. "Does he know Weisz tried to grab Davy's stroller from falling? Does he know Marina was in the arms of a man on the platform?"

He looked away and tugged on his thin black tie. "Yeah, Terry, he does." He turned to me. "Me too. But I'm sorry to hear you do."

I knew it was true when Coceau said it, and I knew it was true when I found Marina's scent on an old cotton dress she'd worn. But something about Luther Addison telling me made it more than true.

It made it real, as if the testimony of an honest man took it from being acutely possible and made it indisputable fact.

"Well, that's right, Terry. I mean, how could they?"

I'd asked him why none of the witnesses I'd spoken to had told me.

"You came to their homes, obviously upset, distressed—"

"They lied."

"Terry . . . They tried to be kind."

"Who saw them, Marina and this guy? I mean, which ones?"

He hesitated. "Schaber, Mr. and Mrs. Holtz, Muhammad Sarwar. The Benjamin girls. And Coceau."

"And they say Weisz didn't push the stroller?"

"Many of them do, not ail," he nodded.

"And none of them went for Davy."

"Happened too fast, I guess."

"And you believe Weisz tried to catch him?" I asked.

He shrugged. "We've got to talk to him. That's why we were at the service, and the cemetery."

"Yeah, but what do you believe?" I repeated.

"I think we have to speak to the young man."

Now Addison was pacing calmly, deliberately, before me. Though the sun was at the horizon line, an empty moon still hung high in the distance.

"Where is he?"

He shook his head. "Terry, go home."

"Luther, you can't be serious," I told him. "I'm going to walk away now?"

"See, you're still not listening," he said. "We had him the other night, Terry. Rey's right. If not for you, he's ours now."

"And what? Bring him in, chat him up and close the file? Accidental death. A standard-issue 12-9."

"Not necessarily. Some of the people on the platform, Healy, Circati, Sylvia Barron, they say Weisz pushed your son," Addison said, as he stood in front of me. "Can we make a case? With Coceau saying Weisz tried to grab him? You'll have to ask your friend Julie Giada."

I'd thought about this, for countless hours, in innumerable places. There's Weisz, entering the courtroom, cleaned up, sedated. High-priced attorneys. His mother's money providing character witnesses. The testimony of psychologists. Then one of the shrinks fine-tunes Weisz's drugs so he goes just a little bit nuts in front of the jury. The verdict: not guilty by reason of insanity. Weisz is to be confined to an institution determined by the court.

And this was before I knew what Coceau would say under oath, and before I saw that it might've been different than I was sure it had been.

"What's your gut, Luther?"

"You mean, did he kill your son?"

I nodded.

"After five years, you finally ask," he said with a wry, compassionate smile.

I looked into his eyes. "Did he do it, Luther?"

He dropped his hand to my shoulder. "I don't think so, Terry."

I turned away and looked across the path to the field where the deer had started to stir.

"With Weisz there's no history of violence—"

"Thirty-nine trips to Bellevue," I said, interrupting him. "That means he was picked up on the street thirty-nine times."

"Vagrancy, harassment, working a squeegee, pissing in public," he recounted. "Took leftovers off an outdoor table at a Greek restaurant in the Village. And since your wife and son were killed, there's been nothing."

"You mean no violence."

"No, I mean nothing. In five years, Weisz hasn't been written up anywhere in the U.S., Canada or Mexico."

"Maybe he left North—"

"Nowhere."

"So his mother set him up somewhere. Got him treatment. An alias."

"That's possible, I—"

I said, "Did you talk to van Kuijk? He was at the service."

"He's out of town, Vienna via Amsterdam. Left last night."

"Strange itinerary," I said.

"His niece had a baby, then he's going to a conference at the Austrian Academy of Sciences. Rey checked."

I looked over at Twist, who was sitting against the black car, his arms folded across his chest. He had removed his jacket and was in crisp shirtsleeves, his French cuffs bearing gold links.

He saw me but didn't change his flat, listless expression.

"What's with that guy?" I said, gesturing toward the young cop.

"I think you've had enough information for one night, Terry."

"He hates my ass. Why?"

Addison paused. "Because he thinks you've been torturing Weisz, stalking him."

"I've been stalking Weisz?"

"He thinks you've been trying to pin your troubles on a guy he sees as defenseless."

"Oh," I said, "Rey Twist is a humanist. An advocate."

"Is he wrong, Terry?"

I pulled back, looked to the darkness.

"Go home," he said, as he stuck out his hand to help me rise off the step. "We're on it. Things are a little clearer now. We'll talk to van Kuijk."

I nodded. I had no idea what my next move was going to be, and I had nothing to say.

"Come on," Addison said. "Let me give you a lift."

I shook my head. "I need to walk. Think." About tigers and a crazy man and a wife who lies. About the wall of obsession I built between myself and the truth. About five years thrown away.

"You're walking home? Fourteen miles?"

I started to move away, to head toward the quiet, leafy streets of the Bronx, before the streets drew legions from the hard-working class.

Then I stopped.

"Luther."

Addison turned and looked across the path at me.

"The guy she was with . . . Did you find him?"

"Not yet, no."

"But you've got a description . . ."

He nodded.

"Who is he, Luther?"

He turned and headed toward Twist.

"Luther?"

Addison didn't respond, and Twist looked at me as he came off the black car. He shook his head sadly, then sent another stream of spit between his front teeth toward the dirt.

I started down along the black lane toward the empty parking lot.

"Terry."

I kept walking.

Addison said, "Regards to Gabriella, all right?"

11

The parking lot at Newark was packed to overflowing, and the yellow cab I was in couldn't get to the ramp that led to the terminal. I handed the cabbie $30 and set out in the harsh sunlight to walk up the long slope. Perhaps inspired by my decision, an Indian couple, both in their 60s, left their taxi and followed me. The wife, short and pudgy under her bright orange *saree,* was struggling with an enormous piece of luggage, as her equally stout husband encouraged her by barking in Hindi. I tried to lift the bag by its taped handle but couldn't, and instead got behind it and shoved it up the ramp and into the air-conditioned terminal. After I wriggled the monument-sized bag onto a roller cart, the Indian man tried to slip me a 25-cent tip.

The luggage area was as crowded as the parking lot. Impatient men gathered at the mouth of the carousel, then shuffled awkwardly to catch up with their suitcases as they tumbled away. Nearby, college students on their way back to Rutgers, Columbia, Hofstra, wherever, used their cell phones to check in.

As I scanned the overhead signs, two National Guardsmen in camouflage and walking a German shepherd parted the crowd, causing a moment's trepidation and sudden silence. "Doggie!" squealed a three-year-old girl in a pink jumper, causing even the cropped-haired soldiers to laugh.

I looked at the harried travelers. Vacation time was over for most of them. Back to work, back to school after Labor Day.

For me, it didn't matter what day it was, what time of year. I could fuck things up in February just as well as I did in August.

But not anymore.

Somewhere between the Tremont section of the Bronx and Harrison Street in TriBeCa, I tossed away my self-pity, and I kept digging through my heart and mind to find the real source of the misery, the bravado, the arrogance, the retreat from life.

Crossing the Harlem River at 155th up by Yankee Stadium on the way to the other end of the island gives a man a long, long time to think about who he is and what he's done.

I did it this way—I stepped outside myself and watched as I worked it out.

Eighty-two degrees at 9 A.M. and there's a man with a leather jacket over his arm, sweat soaked through the back of his shirt, studying old men and boys in baggy bathing suits as they fish off a pier east of the Harlem River Drive.

Now he's sitting on the steps of an abandoned brownstone off First, as cars rumble and quake on the highway.

And he watches firemen hoist a ladder against the side of a crowded apartment building on 116th, as smoke billows from a fourth-floor window.

And all the while, as an unyielding sun stings the top of his head, he is considering how he spent the last five years of his life and trying to understand how, until around sunrise this morning, he was able to tell himself he wasn't wasting his time.

This is a very smart man.

This is a man who despises himself.

Here is a 37-year-old lost boy.

A man with a child to raise.

Who, for five years, did not understand that nothing else is as important as that.

Oh yeah. A very smart man.

I spotted them coming down the escalator single file, Bella out front, then Daniel and Julie, who saw me first and offered an affectionate smile that was tinged with relief.

"Welcome home," I said to my daughter.

"A woman got sick on the flight," Bella announced.

"Seat 12A," Daniel said, nodding. He was carrying Bella's backpack.

Bella, who would not hug me now.

"What's that?" I asked, gesturing to the greasy bag in her hand.

"Here," she said as she passed it to me. "Beignets from Café du Monde."

I looked in the bag. The fried dough had congealed during the flight. "Thanks."

Her brown hair hanging casually around her tanned face, Bella appeared to have grown a few years older in the past few days, and she seemed a bit taller and no different from the college girls at the carousel who conveyed a mix of bubbly enthusiasm and practiced indifference.

"Where's D?"

"He left yesterday," Bella told me. "He never did get back his groove."

"No?"

Daniel said cheerfully, "I had my own room for a night."

"He said he was going out to the bayou," Bella added. "Some band called The New Acadians. Swamp pop."

With a little wave, Julie said, "Hi, Terry." She wore a neat periwinkle blouse with black slacks, and she seemed a little worse for the trip.

I reached around Daniel and took her hand. "Tough flight?"

"I was in 12B."

I grimaced.

"Oh yes," she said with a long nod, "I do need some TLC."

I took her suitcase and rolled it to my side. "Bella, why are we meeting in the baggage claim when none of you has checked bags?"

"'Cause here's where the limo drivers come," she said as she peered past me and scanned the crowded area. "And there he is. Look."

A man in a white shirt, black-and-gray patterned tie and a black suit held up a sign. "Gabriella Orr," it read.

"We go now," said Bella.

Too wide to double-park, the enormous Lincoln Navigator had to pull over at 28th and Second. As I helped Julie out of the so-called luxury SUV, I asked the driver to cut the engine. If I was gone for more than two minutes, I feared the black beast would run out of gas.

"They should have banned those things before we went into Iraq," I told her as I rolled her bag up the tree-lined street.

"I need, repeat, *need* a long hot bath," she said. "A massage, maybe."

I nodded. Having the woman barf in the seat next to me would send me into seclusion too.

"Give me a couple hours to get organized, sort through the mail, call the folks and we can have dinner," she said, as we approached her brownstone. "Something without spice. No rice, no peppers. No shrimp. No Tabasco."

"Sounds great," I said, "but I was kind of thinking of doing something with Bella tonight, Jule."

I needed to tell my daughter about Weisz. Somehow, I needed to tell her she'd been right—that moving ahead was the only way to go.

Julie hesitated. "You might want to ask her, but I think she said she was going to Glo-Bug's. I'm pretty sure . . ."

"Oh. I don't think she told me."

Julie's bag wobbled as it bumped over a crack in the sidewalk.

"Terry, is everything— I mean, I feel there's something wrong."

"No," I said quickly. "Nothing. Not really."

"But it's not us . . ."

"No, Julie. Definitely not." I stopped. "Unless . . ."

She laughed. "Are you kidding? If I was any more obvious . . ."

I nodded sheepishly. "Maybe I've got something on my mind. I—"

"Give me a couple of hours," she said, as she went up on her toes to kiss me on the cheek. "I'll come by. We'll talk."

We got out of the SUV by Daniel's place on Walker. Bella wanted to drop off her disposable cameras before tonight's get-together with Glo-Bug, Grumpy Eleanor, Holly, Benny the Girl, Marcus and, of course, sweet Daniel.

"I never get tired of Daniel," she told me.

Now we were walking in the shade along Hudson, crossing cobblestones, Bella's backpack full of laundry on my shoulder, receipts from the photo shop in her hand.

Her fingers were no longer stout, formless. Her face had lost all its baby fat, and she walked with confidence, with an innate sense of ease. These streets, which had held the power to haunt me, were her home.

"Bella, did you ever go uptown with Mama?"

"Ever?"

"No, I mean, she used to take Davy on these long trips uptown, you know?"

"When she couldn't work, yeah. Sure. I remember."

"Did you go with them?"

"I was in school, Dad."

"Not in the summer, Bella," I replied.

"I was at summer camp."

At the city-run camp at Walker Park. Which is where she was when Weisz—

When Davy's stroller went on the tracks, when the killing train roared through.

"I wonder where they went," I said.

We stopped at the corner of North Moore. An oil truck, getting a jump on winter, backed toward the hydrant in front of an old industrial plant converted to lofts. High above us, nineteenth-century ironwork played host to a family of stout pigeons.

"Uptown," she replied, as we stepped off the curb.

"Yeah, Bella, I know."

"Looking for something to paint, I guess. In Central Park, maybe."

"You think she met a friend up there, maybe?"

"I don't know, Dad. Why? Does this have to do with not finding him the other day? At the church and stuff?"

I nodded. "By the way, Luther Addison says hi."

I skidded to a stop, sneakers catching on the concrete.

She stared up at me, startled. "What? What?"

"Look." I pointed.

An envelope was stuck into the curved door-handle of the Tilt-A-Whirl.

"Probably just a bill," she said. She walked in double-time to get ahead of me, her flip-flops slap-slapping the ground. When she reached the Tilt, she shouted, "It's for Dennis. Should I open it?"

"No."

"Geez, I'm only kidding, Dad."

She pushed the letter at me.

It was addressed to Dennis Diddio, in care of The Tilt-A-Whirl Bar and Grill. "And Grill"? Obviously written by someone who hadn't been here.

The return address was in Baton Rouge, Louisiana. A law firm—Miles Kendricks Toler.

"Toler," Bella said. "That's Willis's last name."

"Miss Mallard's driver?"

"Yeah. Willis Toler. Willis Toler, Junior."

We continued on Hudson, heading home.

"He's my friend," she added, sounding all of six years old again.

The washing machine rattles, Bella announced as I punched
out a phone number. The house doesn't smell right. (That's true. No
pollo con aglio e piselli in the oven, no *pesce spada alla siciliana* on the
stove.) You didn't forward calls to my cell. Turn on the AC.

"Yes, I understand you guys are the agents for the owners of Interstate Properties Limited."

"I believe that's right," the woman on the other end of the line
replied. "But, I'm running out for the weekend. I'll take your—"

"If you don't mind, it's kind of urgent," I told her, as I paced in the
kitchen, moving from the front door to the brick archway. "There's
been a death, you see . . ."

"OK, OK. Hold on." She put the handset down on a desk.

As I waited, cordless phone in hand, I listened to the clatter of filing
cabinets, the flutter of papers. And the rattling of a washing machine.

"Got a pen?" she said when she returned.

I went to the kitchen table and grabbed one of Bella's Cedar Pointe
pencils. "Go ahead."

"Interstate Properties," she recited, "PO Box 1803, Baton Rouge,
Louisiana, 70802."

"Do you have a phone number?"

"No," she said impatiently. She had a Slavic accent, but she'd been
in New York long enough to know how to blow off a pesky caller.
"Look, if . . ."

"A contact name?"

She went silent for a second. "We're not allowed—"

"I'm sorry, but this is—"

"Call back Tuesday," she said. "Happy Labor Day." Then she
hung up.

I went back to my office, did a quick search on the Web for Interstate Properties Ltd., including a look through the Baton Rouge Yel-

low Pages, but came up with nothing. I called the agent's office again and left my name and number on its answering machine, with a request that someone from Interstate contact me.

I suppose I could call Toler myself. It seemed unlikely that he'd know nothing about a hometown business like Interstate, even if it was a shell. But I didn't want to speak to him until D opened his letter.

When I returned to the kitchen, Bella was waiting with a basket full of clean and folded T-shirts, shorts, socks and underwear. Her bowling shirts needed Mrs. Maoli's deft touch with an iron.

"Your punching bag has cobwebs on it," she told me.

"Yes, thank you for observing that."

"I see the manuscript is gone," she said.

"Yeah, I sent it by UPS this afternoon," I explained. "I didn't have time to—"

"I don't care, really," she said as she turned toward the stairs up to her room. "I was just asking."

"Well, it's gone." We'd probably spent 1,000 hours getting her Mordecai Foxx story into shape. Now she doesn't care.

"What do you think your agent will say?"

"Morrie? He'll like it. It's a good book."

"You think it'll get published?" she asked. A glimmer of interest, a flicker of pride, crossed her face.

"I—"

"We need a pen name, an alias, if it does," she said.

"Why? You wrote it."

She made a "get off it" face. "Not really, Dad. You changed it. A lot. You made him a crazy man."

"I edited it, Bella, and tightened up the Tammany plot line. That's all," I said, thinking, A crazy man? I gave St. Mordecai a few books to read, a tic or two and an unusual malady, which made for a clever metaphor. "It's your story. And where's your dress, the one you brought to New Orleans?"

"Julie has it," she said over her shoulder as she hauled the basket upstairs. "She'll get it cleaned, she said."

I looked at the clock on the face of the stove.

"Bella?" I shouted.

"I'm napping," she replied.

"What's the plan?"

"Take your phone," she instructed. "Leave money."

12

Sylvia Barron lived in a high-rise of white glazed brick that sat halfway between Central Park and Lincoln Center. She was a widow, and her tiny one-bedroom was quaint and feminine, in the style of her youth some 80 years ago; the predominant theme—doilies, knickknacks, tchotchkes, Hummel figurines and more doilies. When we first met, her apartment was a monument to her late husband, who had fought in World War II and went on to open a discount clothing chain. Now, vintage Madame Alexander dolls sat on the armchair, smiling beneficently on their proprietor, their cheeks plump and their pinched lips a bright red. Sylvia—she would not *ever* let me call her Mrs. Barron—had moved on by going back.

"You look better," she said as she led me into her apartment, skidding on soft slippers that matched the flowers on her housecoat.

"Better than what, Sylvia?"

"Better than the last time," she said. "You got color."

Must be from walking 14 miles from the Bronx, from querying a roguish restaurateur on the streets of New Orleans.

She sat in the plump sofa, a piece that had been washed out by the sun, by time. A dainty cup and saucer sat on the end table.

The scent of violets and Ivory soap permeated the room, which was immaculately clean.

"Your place looks great, Sylvia," I said, as I sat, and carefully placed a doll on the floor. "Still doing all this by yourself?"

"Who else?" she shrugged. "How's your Gabriella?"

"Great. You know. Too smart for her own good. And mine."

She wagged a finger at me. "You should listen to her. She *knows*, that kid."

"OK, Sylvia."

"She enjoys college, doesn't she?"

"Well, not yet," I answered, "but Whitman is the right high school for her."

"Of course it is," she agreed. "Now, do you have a problem, Mr. Orr?"

"I'm not sure if I do—"

"You're still looking for the awful man?"

"Yes, I—"

"So they still didn't get him," she commented thoughtfully. "By the way, I got Folger's if you want." She held up her cup as if she were in a TV commercial. "I like it. Very easy."

"No thanks."

"You might as well ask your question, then."

I nodded. "Sylvia, what I'm trying to find out is what happened on the platform? I mean, what really happened?"

She carefully put the cup on the saucer. "You know, Mr. Orr."

"I've got some new information."

"After, what is it now, seven, eight years?"

I uncrossed my legs. "I finally spoke to Jean-Pierre Coceau, the man who was on the uptown platform."

She listened intently.

"And since then the police have corroborated what he said."

"Yes?"

I said, "That maybe Weisz didn't push my son's stroller onto the tracks."

"I saw what I saw."

"I know, Sylvia. But people are saying that Weisz tried to grab the stroller, that it rolled toward the tracks . . ."

She shook her head vehemently. "I heard the scream and, that man, that *thing,* he was standing there, with that insane look on his face, and your wife jumped down and he ran away," she said. "Just ran. That filthy, dirty *thing.*"

I went gently. "Sylvia, did you see him put his hands on the stroller and shove it onto the tracks?"

Five years ago, she was the witness who seemed most certain of what had occurred, despite her age. She and Rondell Robinson, the Xerox copy-machine repairman. On the way to the airport this afternoon, before I called Sylvia, I called Robinson. His stepdaughter said he and her mother had gone to Cape May for the long weekend.

"Yes. Yes, I did," she said firmly. As she nodded, the light through the delicate curtains brushed across her thin white hair.

"But he would've had to knock over Marina to do that, no?"

"I suppose so. Run into her, push her out of the way."

"I don't recall anyone saying he did," I told her.

She put her thin, knotty fingers to her lips. "No. She certainly wasn't knocked down, as far as I could tell."

That expression—"as far as I could tell"—is always the opening to a tale of self-doubt, of subtle reinvention.

"But she was right there?" I asked.

"She went down there right away. Didn't hesitate. From a mother, you could expect nothing less."

Sylvia Barron didn't see the man Marina was with. And she didn't know if Weisz actually shoved Davy onto the tracks.

She saw a wild-looking homeless man, dressed in stained, tattered rags, with arms outstretched. What she didn't see, she imagined.

Sylvia was 78 then. Suddenly, all that attention: *Eyewitness News, The Village Voice, The New York Times,* radio.

"I've told this story, Mr. Orr. Complete," she said, tapping on the sofa's thick arm, on the doily, with the palm of her small hand. "I should think I know what I'm talking about."

"I'm sure you do, Sylvia," I said as I stood. "You know I always took your word."

I saw that she was preparing to hoist herself out of the sofa, so I went over and gave her my hand.

In the cup, there was a small mound of crystals, of deep-brown instant coffee, that hadn't yet been put to hot water.

"I told that Negro detective," she said, "yes."

We stood near her coffee table with its figurine of a sweet boy fishing off a dock, an empty basket at his side as he rested against a *No Fishing* sign.

"He told me I was very helpful."

Addison.

"Last year—or was it two years ago?—his young assistant, handsome boy, came to see me and I told him the same thing," she nodded. "He said I had a wonderful memory."

Twist?

"That woman who came to visit, she said the same thing. That I had a good memory."

"A woman?"

"Your friend?"

"My . . ." I shook my head. "I don't know who you mean, Sylvia."

"Yes, you do," she said, chiding me in sing-song. "Your friend. It was right after . . . Oh, you know who I mean. Strawberry blonde. Sweet."

I said no.

"Well, she certainly knew you," she continued. "She knew your name, she knew your daughter's name, she knew your son's name. Where you lived, your books. Everything."

"Sylvia, she came right after Marina and Davy were killed?"

"Yes. Well, a few months after."

"Do you remember, Sylvia, that we didn't meet until more than a year after my son died?"

"Was it that long?" She smiled. "My."

With the exception of my duties with Bella, I did nothing for a year after Davy's death. When I finally came around, it was that day when I had that dust-up with that dumb-ass Tannon at Midtown North, after I stormed from TriBeCa to the precinct house. "Maybe we made the wrong guy," he said, as casually as if he'd just ordered it on whole wheat instead of rye.

"I guess I don't understand how you knew what she said about me was the truth," I told Sylvia. I wasn't getting anywhere here and I didn't want to upset this kind, confused old lady, who had raised three kids and never hurt a soul.

"I don't know," she smiled. "That Negro policeman said nice things about you. He's very nice."

As I was leaving, the doorbell rang.

"They're here," she said cheerfully, as she walked me to the vestibule door. "Finally. Everything is such a mess."

I held open the door for the three tired women in green overalls who were nonetheless ready for hard work.

"Are you the son?" the third woman asked. Her carrier was filled with liquids in squeeze bottles, sponges, brushes.

"No," I told her.

"This lady shouldn't be left alone," she said. "Not no more."

I told her I'd contact her son. He'd be easy to reach. His wife was Lieutenant Governor. Of Nebraska.

Behind the flawless poster of Grün's brilliant globehead in the window, Coceau's shop was empty, except for the fey, red-haired manager. He came from the back of the shop at the sound of the overhead bell and, seeing it was me, frowned in annoyance as he went to his oak desk. On the wall behind him, women in sweeping gowns still swilled cocktails and lithe dancers still kicked their legs high over the moon.

This time, though, he looked up when I stepped between the director's chairs in front of him. "Feel better?" he asked, with a smug smile.

"Coceau around?" The Frenchman might've taken off for the long weekend.

He looked down at the coffee-table book he'd been scanning. Matisse, this time. Collages. The young man was intent on moving up.

I reached over and shut it. Then I took it, tucked it under my arm.

"He's not here," he huffed, "and he doesn't want *you* here."

"I need to talk to him."

"He doesn't *want* you."

"Stop playing rough," I said, "or I'll hit you with this book."

He reached with his right hand for the gold-plated letter opener.

And I slammed his left with the book's sharp edge.

"Ow! You prick."

"You've got paint on your finger," I replied, pointing to his throbbing hand.

"It's ink, Mr. Genius." He used his thumb to rub away the smudge and dull the pain.

"Tell me how to contact Coceau," I said.

His face reddened. "I told you, damn it. He doesn't want to talk to you. Go away."

I wanted to know what happened on the platform. I wanted Coceau to tell me where he was and precisely what Weisz had done to help my boy.

"Give me his phone number," I said.

Frowning angrily, the young man pointed to a stack of business cards in a small gold tray. I lifted one.

"That's his cell number," he said.

"Where does he live?"

He rolled his eyes. "I'm not giving you his address."

I brought up the Matisse book. The young man cringed.

"I don't know it," he exclaimed quickly.

"By Lincoln Center?"

"No. On Riverside Drive," he said, wincing again. "Uptown."

"How far?"

"Uptown," he repeated. "He takes the subway, so it's— Look, I don't know, all right? He never told me."

I tossed the Matisse book on his desk.

"Thanks," I said as I turned to leave.

When I reached for the doorknob, he said, "Be careful you don't get sick out there again, OK?"

He made a curt, sarcastic sound. Might've been his laugh.

Riverside Drive runs along the Hudson from 72nd Street up to Fort Tryon beyond the GW Bridge, but I figured a man like Coceau more than likely had his apartment secured by an agent he'd met through his art contacts or fellow French expatriates and would live south of Barnard, Columbia and the English gothic tower of Riverside Church.

I hooked the phone back onto my belt, having left no message on Coceau's bilingual answering machine, and I looked north, up the tranquil drive. From where I stood, sun sliding slowly to my left, I saw rows of leafy elm trees, the inviting cobbled steps at 79th that led down to Olmsted's Riverside Park, young men and women in shorts, casual tops and easy smiles, their babies in strollers, their helmeted preschoolers nearby on wobbly legs above rollerblades and oversized skateboards, and dozens of dogs straining on leashes—there's a dog run somewhere in the park, I thought, as I started walking slowly north, my pace an indication of my new uncertainty. The dogs were eager and confident under gleaming coats, their pink tongues wagging happily. And many of them were big dogs, meaning their owners had big apartments in one of the city's most expensive neighborhoods.

Riverside Drive was once called a national symbol of wealth. Lined with gray mansions, limestone manor houses with curved façades, stately brownstones that had been single-family homes, and towering apartment buildings with Art Deco detailing and marble foyers, it suggested a time gone by, when the wealthy sought architects with subtle taste and creativity. There was still money here, some of it earned rather than inherited, and these people treated their peaceful neighborhood with the care it deserved.

I passed a uniformed doorman on 82nd as he polished the *Times* honor box.

Coceau takes the subway, the guy in his shop said. The 1 and 9 stopped on Broadway at 96th, which was a little over a mile from his workplace. And the Lincoln Center station was less than a half-mile from the shop. So if Coceau lived uptown on Riverside Drive, then it was likely he was heading home when he saw Davy and my wife on that summer day five years ago: If he was heading back to the shop, he would've walked. If he lived south of the 96th Street station, he might've walked home and he might walk to the office now. Which meant Coceau probably lived north of 96th.

North of 96th, south of 119th. That made it a bit more manageable.

Manageable? About 15,000 people lived on Riverside between 96th and 119th.

On the steps of the Hellenic monument to New York's Civil War soldiers and sailors on 89th, four Asian-Americans rehearsed an ancient ballet, red bandannas on their damp brows, their glittering ceremonial swords catching the sun. On the east side of the street, a woman with a dozen or so Mylar balloons in a plastic bag bounced along, listening to music through big headphones.

I kept going north, picking up my pace, to where the drive split, where raised green islands and vest-pocket parks separated the drive's northbound and southbound lanes. In the distance were Riverside Church and Grant's Tomb, its white dome all but obscured by abundant trees.

．　．　．

I decided to start at the northernmost point and work my way back down. As I reached the monument to Franz Sigel on Duke Ellington Boulevard, still heading north, my phone rang.

"Where are you?" my daughter asked.

I told her.

"Who is Franz Sigel and why is he moving in on Duke Ellington?"

I looked up at the sun-dappled bronze general on horseback. The buildings high on the east side of the drive were soaked in the late afternoon light.

"Anyway, I just wanted to tell you I'm going out," she said. "I'll be home at eleven."

"Eleven?" I kept walking as we spoke. I could hear music, playing not far from where I stood. Two types—a roly-poly calliope and hip-hop dance sounds. A pre–Labor Day block party.

That would explain the firecrackers. More than once I thought someone had blown a tire down on the Henry Hudson.

"Dad, it's the last Friday before school."

"I'm not saying no, Bella. But give me a minute to think about it."

"I'll be with Daniel," she said hopefully.

And I found that comforting, as she knew I would.

"What are you doing?" I asked.

"Movies. Dinner. Hanging out. The usual stuff."

"Take your phone," I said.

I reached 108th and was deep in the shade, under outstretched branches rich with leaves.

"Oh, and Julie's coming over," she said. "She'll be here in a half-hour."

I looked at my watch. I'd still be checking names above bells and talking to doormen on 119th in 30 minutes.

"She'll be all right," she said. "I gave her the code."

"Bella—"

"She loves you, Dad, and I don't think she's a thief."

Now four people have the numerical code to open my front and back doors: me, Bella, Mrs. Maoli and Julie. Who loves me.

"Dad, I'm gone."

"Take your—"

"Take my phone. I *know.*"

"I'm just—"

"You know, Dad, I can take care of myself. Dad. *Dad?*"

Up ahead, near 112th, on the west side of the drive, was Jean-Pierre Coceau. Walking his dog. Some beagle-looking thing, fat, droopy.

He was smoking a pipe, staring out toward the Hudson, wearing a lightweight peach crewneck sweater over poplin slacks and leather sandals, and he had his back turned on a statue of Samuel J. Tilden and a carousel entertaining gleeful kids at the block party. The sound of laughter and boisterous conversation wafted across the drive and over boom-boom rap rhythms and the hurdy-gurdy that accompanied the racing wooden horses.

On the river, sailboats lazed in the mild breeze, and in the Tot Lot on 112th, squealing children scrambled on a plastic jungle-gym.

"Hello, Jean-Pierre," I said, as I settled next to him.

He turned. He was genuinely startled.

His dog, a sluggish thing, sniffed my sneakers.

"What are you— I don't want to see you," he said.

"So I've been told."

"Please go," he said firmly.

More firecrackers shot off behind us. On the drive, cars heading south slowed down to try to catch a glimpse of the festivities under the red balloon arch. A block away stood the solemn gray façade, the archivolts, rose window, of St. John the Divine.

"I have nothing to say," he insisted as he started to walk toward 113th, toward the GW Bridge in the distance.

"Heading home?" I asked. "I'll follow."

"No. No you will not."

He seemed ready to panic.

"Is there a kind of French community up here?" I asked as he walked away, dragging his listless dog. "I mean, Saint John the Divine is modeled on a cathedral in Chartres, and somebody wanted the homes back there to look like châteaux, right?"

"Please go away," he repeated, without turning to me. "I beg you."

From across the drive, beyond the fresh new lawn of the center aisle, the calliope's tinny tune—*The Sidewalks of New York*.

"Wait," I said to the back of his head, his black curly hair. "What's wrong?"

Firecrackers sparked and children laughed. And the blue sky over the river was impossibly perfect.

I reached and grabbed his shoulder.

He turned, his back to the Hudson now, to the cars on the highway below.

"I need to know some things," I told him. "About Weisz, and what happened. It has nothing to do with you."

"You cannot be in my life," he insisted, fear in his voice.

His dog went back to my sneakers.

"I don't want to be in your life, Coceau," I said. "But I need to know . . ."

The goddamned dog was gnawing at the bottom of my jeans, slobbering on my shoes.

I bent down to pet it, to move it away, and I heard a popping sound coming from the east side of the drive, over by the festivities.

And suddenly Coceau collapsed, falling hard on his back, the pipe he held in his hand clattering to the sidewalk. Blood spurted from his chest.

I went to my knees and put the heels of my hands on the wound.

He made a dark sound and his eyes rolled back in his head.

I unhooked the dog's leash from his wrist.

The little Frenchman struggled to breathe, and his lower body writhed. His feet in his sandals twitched unnaturally.

As I shifted to the other side of his body, my hands already drenched in warm blood, I saw a man bolting toward us, crossing Riverside Drive.

Rey Twist, shouting into his walkie-talkie.

He skidded as he came to a stop and shoved me aside without a word.

Blood had soaked into Coceau's sweater. Twist lifted it, looked at the dime-sized hole in Coceau's chest, then tilted him on his left shoulder until he could see behind him. Blood ran in rivers on the sidewalk from the exit wound.

"What did you see?" Twist shouted at me as he returned Coceau to his back.

I edged next to the cop and put my hands back on Coceau's chest.

"Not a damned thing," I replied.

Two men ran at us from the Tot Lot.

I looked around, saw the bronze statue of Tilden, the balloon arch.

Across 112th, the carousel continued to twirl and the stuttering music continued to play.

Coceau tried to speak, but he couldn't.

When he coughed, blood and a sickly white foam came to his lips.

Twist left me, scrambled across the drive and climbed up on the base of the Tilden statue to scan the east side of the street, tall, stately buildings, the curling Cathedral Parkway, 112th north to the church. His hands left streaks of blood on its base, on Tilden's bronze legs.

"*Je*—" Coceau managed, then he groaned painfully.

From the south, a siren: an EMT ambulance, probably from St. Luke's.

"Take it easy, Coceau," I said, as the two men from the playground, hands on knees, stared down at us.

He spoke softly, haltingly. *"Elle a fait de moi un homme malhonnête."*

"What?"

"Elle . . ." He tried to repeat the phrase, but couldn't. When I looked up at the two men, they both shook their heads, sadly.

"Spanish, but not French," added the hazel-eyed man with the mustache.

Coceau coughed violently, then emitted a shallow wheeze.

A patrol car ground to a halt at the curb and the uniforms, guns drawn, leaped out. As they scrambled to Coceau, I gestured with my head toward Twist, who'd bounded off the statue.

"What happened?" asked one of the cops, a stocky woman with red hair.

But before I could answer, Twist came between the two uniforms. He spoke firmly, forcefully.

"The gunshot came from over there, small caliber. Vic was facing east," he said, pointing. "Maybe somebody at the party saw . . ." He looked around, took a deep breath. "Lot of people, lot— And you've got the Swarthmore over there."

The redhead looked up at the apartment building, with its curved marquee, three-globe lampposts and some 12 or 13 stories up to the roof.

"I called it in, so you'll get backup, but move," Twist said. "Like I said, with that party, it's a big job. Go."

The uniforms nodded and ran off, jumping back into their car to take it over to the east side of the drive to begin the process of interviewing 150 to 200 people; most, if not all, were sucking down cool drinks, eating hot dogs and gyros, watching their kids go 'round and 'round. Meanwhile, NYPD was shutting down the Broadway line at 110th Street.

A drive-by, from a car heading south? Would've been a hell of a shot from beyond the green island, trees, Tilden.

Heading north, toward the GW? A good bet, but I didn't see anyone.

I looked down at Coceau. He was out now, struggling to breathe, unaware of the turmoil around him. Blood from his lips flowed onto his cheeks.

Twist turned his back and, fist thrust angrily on his hip, went back on his walkie-talkie. He was barking into it when the squat ambulance, its lights whirling, smacked hard against the curb and bounced up onto the sidewalk.

The two paramedics jumped to action, cutting away Coceau's sweater, slapping large gauze sheets onto the wound. As one tech ran back to the ambulance for the stretcher, Twist gestured for me to join him in the street.

The sirens had brought people from up the hill to the edge of the drive, and they looked down at the scene.

Another patrol car roared north on the drive, passed us and curled around the high green island to get up to the east side.

As calliope music continued its hypnotic chant.

"What?"

Twist repeated his ludicrous charge. "That's right. You walked him into that shot."

And with that, he moved toward me, his head inches from my chin.

"Back away," I told him. Pulsing waves of adrenaline were still coursing through my veins.

As the ambulance siren wailed behind me, Twist said, "You can't help but fuck up, can you? Can you?"

His taunt set me off and, feeling fire, seeing red, I pushed him hard, hands on the shoulders of his white shirt, driving him back, his heels scraping the concrete.

And he quickly withdrew his nine-millimeter pistol and pointed it at me. "On the ground," he shouted. "Now."

I dropped to my knees, then eased my hands, my chest onto the sidewalk.

One of the men who'd come over from the Tot Lot, the doughy Hispanic guy with the dark mustache, said, "Wait. He didn't do anything. I saw him."

I couldn't see, but I heard Twist tell him to back off. Probably pointed his pistol at him too.

Then I felt a sharp pain in my lower back as Twist's knee hit me.

Cramming his gun against my head, he barked, "Give me your hands."

I did as he said, putting them, palms up, behind me.

He slapped handcuffs on me, grinding tight, pinching and tearing skin.

"Get up," he shouted.

I rolled over, sat, then came up carefully.

"What the fuck is your problem, Twist?"

He ignored me and spoke into his walkie-talkie. He said, "I got a 10-50 on Riverside and one-one-three. Confirm 10-85." When he got his reply, he added, "Roger that. Out."

The man with the mustache looked at me, shrugged and went back to his wife and kids.

I peered up at Twist. "You pull your piece on a disorderly person?" That was 10-50 in NYPD radio code, and 10-85 meant that he'd called for backup and, maybe in this case, transportation.

Finally, beckoned by sirens louder than the hip-hop and carousel, a gawking crowd of revelers, paper cups in hand, had gathered. Spotting the pool of blood on the sidewalk, on my hands in tight cuffs, they probably thought I'd killed him. Mothers pointed at me, tsk-tsked, and their children nodded, as they absorbed the warning about the bad, bad man.

"You're finally going into the system," Twist spit.

"Yeah," I said. "Maybe you'll get a big promotion."

With that, Coceau's dog waddled over and started digging at my sneakers.

13

Twist didn't like it, but Addison insisted he go into his office at Midtown North. He insisted by crooking his finger at Twist as I sat next to the young sergeant's desk in the crowded squad room, my hands still cuffed behind my back.

Surrounded by the buzz of activity and the whirr of an old, ineffective air conditioner on the windowsill, I stayed quiet as I waited to be summoned. No sense in complaining now. Seems silence pays: That guy over there, the tub of muscle who looks like every second-rate strong-arm in low-budget mob movies, he got a free Diet Pepsi. Which didn't seem to make him any more cooperative: Refusing to answer questions, he shut his eyes, pursed his lips and folded his massive arms in front of his equally massive chest, stretching the fabric of his jacket until it groaned.

The cop called the big guy Tootie.

Twist kept a neat desk, I noticed.

"Yo."

I turned around.

Twist summoned me in much the way Addison had beckoned him.

"Unhook him," Addison said as I came into the office.

I'd been in Addison's boxy space maybe a dozen times in the past five years, but never in handcuffs.

As Twist undid the cuffs, I thought about commenting on the new framed photo Addison had of his wife Giselle on his filing cabinet, but it didn't seem like the right time. The lieutenant was incensed.

"Tell it," he said, with steely self-control, as he eased himself into his creaking wooden chair behind his desk. His black jacket hung on the coat tree.

He gestured for me to sit on his old cracked leather sofa.

"This guy grabbed Coceau," Twist said.

"'Grabbed'? In what way?"

"He was going at him," the cop replied. "I told you he would."

"I see."

I kept still.

"Then he hit me, so I ran him," Twist nodded.

Addison folded his hands on his desk and looked at me over a row of file folders stacked in a long bin.

"You hit Sergeant Twist?"

I shrugged.

"And what does that mean, Terry?"

I gestured to Twist's shirt, which had my palm prints in blood above his collarbones. "I can see why the sergeant thought I tried to hit him," I replied evenly. "But I wanted to hold him back."

"Bullshit," Twist charged

Addison held up his hand. "Why?"

"A misunderstanding," I said.

Addison frowned.

"I realize now he wanted to get back to Coceau," I continued. "At the time, I thought he was coming at me."

Unable to accept the consideration, Twist waved his hand at me in disgust.

Addison sat back, held up a pink WHILE YOU WERE OUT message slip. "I've got a call here from a Jose Ramirez, who lives on West End Avenue and 120th. Mr. Ramirez here says he saw the entire episode." He looked at Twist. "Which one of us calls him, Rey? You or me?"

Twist took the slip. "I'll handle it."

"Fine," Addison said. Then he looked at me. "Go wash up, Terry, and get right back in here."

I stood and left the office.

I waited outside as Luther Addison dressed down his young sergeant, the pale-green tempered-glass walls rattling as he shouted. I turned away and looked at the squad room, at the cops in shirtsleeves and ties working phones, writing up reports, downing lukewarm Snapple and bad coffee, going at it hard, trying to get things done. In the far corner, a woman in a finely cut business suit cried, pleaded, but the balding cop was unmoved and he kept his fingers flying on the keyboard. Shoplifter, I thought. A career out the window.

The place smelled of dust and sun.

I had blood on the knees of my jeans.

The door to Addison's office opened with a thud and Twist stormed past me without a word. I waited, then went inside.

"Shut the door," Addison instructed and pointed to an old chair on casters in front of his desk. As I sat, he said, "I thought we agreed—"

I held up my hand. "Luther—"

"Not this time, Terry. We've a got a major problem. Rey says you tipped off the shooter."

"What?"

"Rey says you bent down to clear the shot."

I looked at him. He was deadly serious.

"Maybe you think it's Coceau who had to pay," he said.

"Luther, do I need a lawyer?"

He glared at me, his green eyes cold. "You might."

I looked at my watch.

"Going somewhere?" Addison asked.

"Trying to figure out where my lawyer is." Julie was at my house now. She'd know a dozen attorneys to recommend.

"Did Twist Mirandize you?"

"Yes." I nodded.

"What did you tell him?"

I shrugged. "Not a thing."

He sat back. "So . . . ?"

"Luther, if Twist's been following me, he knows what I've been up to."

"You tell me. We'll see if it matches."

I shifted in the padded seat. "I got out at 59th, visited Sylvia Barron and then I walked to Coceau's shop," I said. "When I found out he wasn't there, I set out to look for his place."

"Big city."

"The guy at the shop told me he lived on Riverside," I replied. "I figured he lived north of 96th."

"Your friend Ms. Giada didn't give you his address?"

I shook my head.

"Why not?"

"I didn't ask her for it."

"Really?" he said, eyebrow arched.

He had a stack of CDs on top of the player on his credenza. Miles Davis, along with his favorite, the Modern Jazz Quartet. "I haven't told her much."

I thought I noticed Addison cool down, if only slightly. If anything about me really set him off, it was when I let the D.A.'s office know something I'd learned before I told him.

"And Coceau just happened to be walking his dog?"

I nodded.

"What did you say to him?"

"I told him I wanted to know more about what he saw."

"Weisz," Addison said curtly.

"And the guy Marina was with."

He sat back. "And he said . . ."

"He told me he didn't want me in his life."

"Why?"

"I don't know," I told him. "But he was edgy."

"'Edgy'?"

"Like he was afraid to be seen with me."

"By whom?"

"I don't know." I hadn't had time to ask myself the question.

Addison paused for a moment and dropped his clasped hands on his stomach. "He's not much use to you with a hole in the chest."

"No. That's right."

"But now he can't repeat what he told you about Weisz and your boy's stroller."

I said, "But since he told you, and the Holtzes, Schaber and Sarwar confirm it . . ."

"And Mrs. Barron?"

"She's not really . . . reliable anymore," I replied. I wondered if she'd imagined the visitor who claimed to be my friend.

He nodded. "Then there's the matter of you hitting Sergeant Twist."

I shrugged. "What can I say?"

"You can tell me what happened."

"Luther, I know you. You're not going to let me knock your guy."

He leaned forward and the back of the chair followed. "Go ahead."

"He's up all night at the zoo, then he's tailing me, and I go to Coceau's shop," I said. "So far, nothing. Then I meet up with Coceau, I grab him—"

"You did grab him?"

"No— Yeah, but he was walking away," I explained. "I wasn't angry."

"All right."

"Then Coceau gets hit and your man's blood boils."

"So that's it?"

"Luther, who knows where the shot came from? A moving car, a building a hundred yards away . . . If I don't bend down to push away the damned dog . . ."

"So if it's a setup, you're at risk?"

"Right, yeah."

"Maybe somebody wanted to shoot you," he said plainly.

"Is that why you're following me? To protect me?"

"Terry, today I don't explain myself to you. Understand?"

"Or are you protecting Weisz?"

He smiled scornfully. "I have no reason to believe you will lead us to Weisz."

I got the dig, and I felt a flash of indignation. But instead of snapping at Addison, I took a long breath and, as I leaned forward, said, "You should've told me. You should've told me about her."

He raised his hand. "How was I going to do that, Terry? You were wound so damned tight and you had her perfect."

I stood. "I might've killed Weisz."

He shook his head. "You were never going to find him, Terry," he said, his eyes fixed on me. "You hardly even tried."

I didn't reply, and I stared at the dusty blinds, at the loose threads in the binding. I figured I was at least as tired as Twist, twice as confused, and a bullet had passed within inches of my head.

I wanted out of Midtown North. A man had been shot, a man who'd been afraid to be seen with me in his own neighborhood, who, a little more than 24 hours earlier, had showed no fear. I wanted to find out what had happened to change his attitude.

And then there was Weisz, wherever he might be.

"What about Twist?" I asked. "That guy isn't going to back down."

"Well, you hit him, Terry. Twice," he said. "Rey might be a little green, but in his mind he's got a legitimate beef with you." He tapped his palm on the arm of his chair. "I'll talk to him."

I nodded.

"If I need you, I want to be able to find you," he said. "You understand me?"

He dismissed me by picking up the phone and punching in numbers.

Twist left my cell phone and wallet on the edge of his desk. As I retrieved them, he ignored me, concentrating instead on the pad from which he was transcribing his notes. I knew he'd be thinking of me when the dry cleaner asked him about the bloody handprints on his shirt. As I went down the stairs, I wondered if Luther would still let him tail me.

Not that I was going anywhere but home now.

As I trotted down the stairs, I thought, Maybe I should've volunteered for one of those monitoring devices, the electronic ankle bracelet that they slap on criminals under house arrest.

"Orr."

I turned. The desk sergeant was off his platform, out from behind his big desk.

"This your dog?"

He was holding the red leash that led to Coceau's floppy hound, who was flat on a shady spot on the lobby's scuffed linoleum.

"That's not—"

"I heard it was your dog." The cop was a little guy, shaved head, who was as proud of his hard ass as he was of the American flag behind his station. His uniform fit like Spandex ironed with lasers.

I came toward him.

"Get it out of here," he barked as he shoved the leash at me.

"It's a basset hound," Julie said as I came up the steps, the lazy, 50-pound dog in my arms. "They hunt rabbits."

"Not this one," I replied, as I entered the air-conditioned house. "Too much city life."

I put the dog on the floor and watched as she walked slowly, cautiously, past the kitchen, past the brick alcove, and went into the living room, where she jumped up on the sofa and settled in as if she wouldn't move, ever.

Julie planted a kiss on my cheek as I returned to the kitchen to get a bottle of cold Badoit.

On the table were the makings of a meal—asparagus, Romaine lettuce, red onions, Jersey tomatoes. Potatoes roasted in the oven, and a bottle of Castello di Bossi Chianti Classico was breathing on the counter near the sink.

"You'll tell me, I'm sure, how you came to get blood on you?" Julie asked. She looked good, refreshed, in a pale blue T-shirt, with a low neckline, and pressed jeans.

"Yeah, I've got to change," I replied as I went toward the stairs.

Thirty minutes later, we lingered over the Italian red at the table. We'd had omelettes with fresh asparagus and with a sprinkling of Parmigiano-Reggiano, tiny basil leaves and fresh cracked pepper. Baked potato wedges, tossed in salt and olive oil. A simple salad of lettuce, tomatoes, slivers of red onion and capers. Julie says she doesn't know how to cook, that her mother is the cook in the family.

As I sipped the Chianti, I thought, Yeah, maybe I will accept an invitation to Sunday dinner at the Giadas'.

The dog was under the table, drawn by the promise of the heel of an Italian loaf and a few asparagus stalks. I didn't know how long I'd keep her. Somebody was bound to want to retrieve her, maybe the other person who made up the "we" on Coceau's machine, and then I'd ask that person if he or she could tell me why Coceau wanted me to stay away, why he seemed so frightened.

The little Frenchman wouldn't be telling me anything now.

According to Julie, while I was in the shower Addison called to say that Coceau had died at St. Luke's. It was homicide now, he said, and since Julie didn't need to be told, it was another not-so-subtle reminder that I was to remain far away from 113th and Riverside, and from the shop on Columbus.

I left an awkward message on Coceau's answering machine, after hearing the voice of a dead man. "My name is Terry Orr and I've, er, got your dog. I was with Jean-Pierre when, um, you know . . . Anyway, I've got the dog here." I left my home phone number and hung up.

"Tell me again what Addison said?" I asked now.

She was in my seat and I was in Marina's. "He didn't tell me about the blood on your jeans," she replied as she reached for my hand.

"It's Coceau's," I told her. "I was there when he got it." I touched the center of my chest. "You know, if I hadn't bent down to get the dog off my sneaker . . ."

"You mean you were standing with this man when he was killed?"

"Technically, no," I said, "but yeah. Yes."

"The bullet could've hit you."

I shrugged. But my nonchalance was an act. In the shower, I shook as I thought of a shot traveling just past the top of my head.

Fauré's Violin Sonata No. 1 in A Major danced from the radio above the stove and filled the room.

"But was it meant for you?"

"The bullet? I don't think so," I said. "I was still standing there after he was hit . . . which maybe wasn't the smartest thing."

"My goodness, Terry. What if something happened to you?"

I shook my head. "It won't."

"What if Luther Addison made a different kind of call . . ." She hesitated. "What would I do?"

I held her hand, squeezed it. "It's all right, Jule. Let's let it go."

She moved back, then sipped from the wine goblet.

We listened to the cascading piano, the soaring yet melancholy violin, to a dog slobbering over bread.

Julie said, "For a moment just now, I understood you, Terry. Your feelings about your wife . . . I would be terribly upset if something happened to you, if someone took you from me."

I nodded. I had something to tell her, but now wasn't the time.

She returned the wine goblet to the table and eased out of the chair. "You had such a day." She'd decided to make it light again.

"You don't know how right you are."

She came over and kissed my forehead. I tilted my head back to kiss her lips. The taste of wine, of olive oil.

As she lifted my plate, the silverware, I said, "I think I may have heard his last words, Coceau. Too bad I don't speak French."

"I thought you did."

"Not really. I mean, I can recognize a few words . . ."

"What did he say?"

As she put the dishes in the sink, I tried to re-create Coceau's final sentence. I was sure I mangled it. I had no aptitude for languages, not really. I learned what little Italian I knew from listening to Marina, to Mrs. Maoli, to Berlitz tapes. Bella's Italian was better than mine, and she only used it to gossip with the housekeeper, her surrogate *nonna*.

"Your accent's not terribly bad," she said as she went back to her wine. "But you're sure it was '*Elle a fait de moi un homme malhonnête*'?"

"Sounds a hell of lot better when you say it." I refilled her glass. "Now if I only knew what it meant."

She said, "She made me a dishonest man."

"Really?"

"Roughly, yes," she said. "Dishonest. Dishonorable."

"I didn't know you spoke French," I told her.

"Well," she said slyly, "there might be a lot about me you don't know."

I felt like walking in the fresh air, under a sliver of moon, and she held my hand as we crossed over to West Broadway, went south and came back around to tiny Duane Park, near the old produce warehouses.

Tall brick buildings, proud and defiant remnants of the Romanesque Revival of the late nineteenth century, surrounded us as silent sentries, their high arches barely visible in the street lamps' muted light.

Julie wore her thin, pale blue sweater over her shoulders and, as we sat on a bench facing west, she said, "This is a great old street, isn't it?"

I nodded. "It's my favorite. If we sat here in 1890, what we'd see above the street would be more or less the same." I pointed to the top of 168 Duane. "Look at the curved gable, the trim around the circular windows. Beautiful, not ostentatious. Just great, and it hasn't changed in a hundred fifteen years."

"You love all of this, don't you?" she asked. "The history of it . . ."

I hesitated. Then, as we sat on the bench in the summer-night air, in the small park in the best part of the historic neighborhood, I said, "Julie, I don't think I can look at this place the way I used to. I can't."

"Why not?"

And I told her what I'd learned about my wife, standing and pacing before her as she sat attentively. I told her everything.

And when I was through, she whispered, "I know."

I didn't understand. "You mean you know I can't look at the world like I used to?" In the distance, Weinman's gold statue glittered above the Municipal Building.

"No. I mean I know she was cheating on you."

I didn't know what to say. The best I could manage was a question. "How did you find out?"

"Sharon."

"Christ, who else knows?" I said as I leaned against the wrought-iron fence.

"I think she was looking out for me, Terry," she explained. "She knew we were becoming, you know, involved."

"Luther Addison told her?"

"Probably."

The former head of the Black PBA had reason to talk to Sharon Knight, the highest-ranking African-American in the district attorney's office. They knew each other before I pushed them together.

"Terry, they both care for you."

I nodded. "Oh yeah."

"They do," she insisted, "and don't be cynical."

"Julie, after the past few days, the past *day,* believe me, cynicism is the right response."

"It's never the right response, Terry."

"Even when there's no one to trust?"

After a long silence, she said, "You can trust *me*, Terry."

"Why didn't you tell me I might be chasing the wrong man all these years," I said, as I stood with my back to brick buildings, sandstone façades, robust trees.

"The wrong man?"

"You don't know?"

She shrugged, confused.

"They didn't tell you? Sharon?"

"Tell me what?"

No one had told her about the conflicting testimony of the witnesses. Sharon tipped her off about Marina's cheating, but didn't say anything to her about the case.

I explained. Then I said, "At one time, they all told me that Weisz pushed Davy onto the tracks, and none of them mentioned that Marina was with some guy."

"And Luther Addison believes Weisz tried to help your son?"

"He doesn't know," I said, exasperated. "Nobody knows nothing."

"Terry . . ."

"He believes Weisz is only a suspect."

Julie left the bench, stood in front of me and took both of my hands.

"Terry, you can't keep on the way you have been, you know," she said. "Not now."

For some reason, I couldn't bring myself to look into her eyes.

"You have to think this through and find out what you really feel," she added. "You need to step back."

"I want to talk to Weisz," I said. "To understand."

"This man can't explain, Terry. What can he tell you?"

I was still looking past her, toward the cars barreling north on Hudson, their headlights sweeping across the empty street.

"You say deep down you knew she was . . . unfaithful. Yet your obsession was so strong, Terry." She paused. "You have to think about these things. To understand yourself."

Which was about the last thing in the world I wanted.

"Look at me," she said. "Terry."

I did.

"We'll figure this out," she said with a sympathetic smile.

Later, as we were walking along Greenwich toward my home, toward the convivial sounds of the diners emerging from Pico, The Harrison, The Red Curry, I heard her say quietly to herself, "Poor man."

I had draped my arm across her shoulder and she had me around the waist, her thumb hooked in my belt buckle.

"No more sympathy," I said. "Please."

She looked up at me. "I was thinking about Weisz."

14

I slept as if comatose and woke up groggy at 9:15 A.M., having been shaken by the blaring horn of a trailer that might've been lost on its way to Canal but sounded like it was making a U-turn at the foot of my bed. For a second or two, I thought of nothing except how to get back to sleep. And then it started, with astonishing speed and yet in a sensible sequence: Bella, the dog, Coceau, Weisz, Marina and Davy, and a dreadful feeling that I had to find something to do and somewhere to go.

And then my thoughts raced to Leo. Not Leo the son, or Leo, sibling to the grand, flouncy Ruthie. But Leo, who had been a dear friend, who trudged each night to an empty apartment filled with faulty memories and fantasies of what might've been. Leo, at the ratty four-burner at his Laight Street kitchen, working the flour into the oil, finding solace in what he loved best, what remained, now that Loretta was gone.

I headed toward the bathroom at the end of the hall. To my surprise, Bella's door was open and her bedroom empty. Her covers and Phish throw were on the floor, tossed aside as if she'd leaped from bed.

I knew she was out with the dog.

"Dad!"

Last night, as I was napping, my head on Julie's lap, the TV showing Hopkins as Bligh, Gibson as Mr. Christian, and many fetching bare-breasted Tahitians. But, at the sound of Bella's voice, I sprang up as if I'd been caught at something wrong, untoward.

"I love him!"

When I focused my eyes, I saw she had the dog at her side, down next to her bowling shoes. As always, the damned dog looked exasperated, unmotivated.

"This, this is so great. I'm going to name him."

"It's a her," Julie said, as if that would matter to a girl who wore men's bowling shirts and a man's fedora.

"Beagle. Goes either way," she announced. "Hey, Julie."

"Hey, Gabriella."

"Bella, it's a bassett hound."

She turned and skipped toward the stairs to her room. "Come on, Beagle," she said.

And Beagle, suddenly peppy, followed her. I heard the dog skedaddle up the stairs, nails and pads on raw wood.

Now I came downstairs. Bella's bottle of cranberry juice was on the table, a Pop-Tart wrapper next to it; the *Times,* out of its blue bag but nowhere in sight. Music came from the living room, something jazzy over modulating electronic beats. Diddio could tell me what it was.

Diddio, MIA, I thought as I headed, in shorts, torn T-shirt and bare feet, toward the back of the house. Maybe he found love in Louisiana, some earthy girl out on the swampland, cut-off shorts high up on her tanned thighs, tight shirt tied above the beltline, bare feet in the cool wet grass.

Love on the bayou. Where Leo found it.

Let us pray that D does much better.

I located Bella in the backyard, wearing her PJs—a tie-dyed tank top over a pair of her Whitman workout shorts. Her rainbow of rubber bands was back on her wrist.

Caught in the warming rays of the morning sun, Beagle sat impassively at her bare feet.

"We've got to return her, don't we?"

I nodded. "Yeah, Bella, we do. At least we've got to try."

She looked forlorn, as resigned as the floppy dog.

The *Times* was on the picnic table, next to the empty juice glass.

"I'm sorry," I told her.

Behind her, Sheila ran flawless scales on her cello.

"No, I understand." She came toward me, tugging the dog's leash. "She's loveable, though. Really."

I couldn't see it.

Beagle trailed my daughter as they passed me.

I retrieved the paper and glass, went inside and locked the back door.

As I entered my office, I heard Bella shout from the kitchen, "I'm not going to say goodbye."

For a moment, I thought she was talking to me.

Upstairs, water rushed through pipes as Bella went into the shower.

As I sat and reached down to turn on my computer, Beagle entered the room and, without looking at me, nestled herself under my desk, nudging my feet as she curled into a ball.

I decided there was no rush to find her owner, no reason to run up to Riverside Park and work the dog walks. If her owner needed her for comfort, I'd deliver her uptown soon after I got a return call.

I waited until the shower went silent, then shouted the news up through the floorboards.

I thought I heard Bella squeal in delight.

Beagle hustled off and hopped up the stairs to greet her newest friend.

. . .

I had a feeling he'd be in the shop. Despite his detached air, the redheaded gatekeeper had ambition. He probably moved his stuff into Coceau's desk at sunup, thinking the guys back in Nice would appreciate him keeping the business afloat. Now if he could move one of those Cherets, one of those Bonnards . . .

The door was locked and the sign read "Closed," but the young man was in there, wearing crisp-cut navy-blue slacks, a pale blue shirt with sharp cuffs and a club tie, navy and pink stripes, that matched his braces. His back to me, he seemed harried as he carted a framed poster toward a storage area. The sound of my knuckles on glass annoyed him and he waved me off without turning around.

I waited until he returned from the storeroom to kick the door.

When he saw me, he stopped, tightened his brow to highlight an exasperated grimace, then shooed me off as if I were a buzzing bee.

Without looking at me, he hustled over to his desk and withdrew what looked like a leather-bound log for orders and receipts. He hurriedly flipped through its pages, barely stopping to scan the information on the pink and yellow sheets.

I banged on the door with the side of my fist, looking over my shoulder once again to make sure Twist wasn't nearby.

He found the page he sought, sat on the edge of the oak desk and picked up the cell phone on his brown blotter.

I started kicking the door with the sole of my sneaker. It rattled hard with each blow, and it was only a matter of time until the glass would shatter.

The redhead finally looked at me and, as he readied to dial, realized I wasn't going to go away.

He came over and undid the deadbolt.

"Leave," he said.

"You're sweating."

I pushed back the door and came into the air-conditioned shop.

"We're closed," he said as he stood in front of me. He made an awfully inefficient guard.

"What is your name?" I asked.

"What?" I annoyed him again.

"Your name?"

"Comfort," he said. "Now I need to—"

"Comfort? First or last?"

Frustrated, irate, he spit, "What does it matter? Just get the hell out of here. You know, you really don't know what you're up against."

"I want to talk to you about something," I said.

He put his hands on my chest and tried to push me.

"Wait," I asked. "Calm down a second. I just—"

He screeched, "Get the hell out of here!"

"I want to talk to you," I repeated calmly.

He glared at me.

"Fine," he huffed, and he turned to go to his desk.

But then he pivoted and punched me square on the jaw. It felt like a dry kiss from a maiden aunt.

He stared up at me, horror, fear in his wide eyes.

I grabbed him by the front of the shirt and lifted him.

"First your boss wants me gone and now you," I said. His nose was inches from mine. "What's going on?"

"Please," he said. "Just leave."

I shoved him into his seat, and I looked down at the yellow receipt in the logbook.

Someone had bought the Grün in the window, the poster of the tuxedo-clad man with the globe for a head, *Je Sais Tout*. The only original in the U.S., according to Coceau's hand-painted sign. That's why it cost $12,000.

Comfort frantically scribbled on a Post-it pad. "Here's my number," he said. "Call later and I'll explain. I'll explain everything. Now just—"

As he went to pass the note to me, it slid from his fingers, fluttered to the ground and landed by his high-priced black loafers.

One of his shoes had a dab of orange ink on the tip.

I bent to pick up the paper and ran my finger on the dab.

It was still wet.

As I stood, I said, "What are you doing?"

Comfort had a gold-plated letter opener in his hand, with some vague notion of ramming it into my chest.

"Not again," I groaned as I hit him in the breastbone, hard, with my elbow. He crashed to the shop floor and curled in a ball as he graspled for air.

There was more orange ink on the bottom of his shoe, and it matched the color that was on his finger yesterday, before his boss was killed.

"This," I said, "is bad."

He didn't want to get hit again, so much so that he finally told me his parents named him Roy. But he didn't want to face the wrath of whoever was behind the scam. In the end, it didn't take much to get Roy to move. I told him if I brought the stapler down on the bridge of his nose he'd bleed all over his silk tie, his Armani slacks.

The door to the basement was open. I followed him down.

Under bright ceiling lights was an old-fashioned lithograph press, its wooden frame about three feet wide and twice as long.

Orange, green and black blotches dotted the cement floor.

"You're a lithographer?" I said as he reached the bottom step.

He turned to look up at me. "Not me."

"Coceau?"

He nodded.

"But someone wants you to finish this job." I came and stood next to him, next to the press.

He was trying to duplicate Grün's *Je Sais Tout.* To the untrained eye, it looked like he was doing a decent enough job.

"We're late," he said. "We're supposed to ship today."

This one wasn't going to dry for days. Roy was going to have to ship the piece in the window, replace it with the fake and hope some-one strolling Columbus could be fooled.

"This is only the fourth one we'd done," he said. "Three Cherets and now this."

"Your first?"

He said yes.

"At twelve-K a pop?"

"Just about," he replied, as he walked to the other side of the press, his back to a cutting board, a light table, a row of shipping tubes and other supplies.

"If you pull something, Roy, like trying to stab me with one of those X-Acto knives, I'll shoot you," I said. "I promise."

He stopped.

My gun was lying at the bottom of a lake in Woodlawn Cemetery, but he didn't know it. I might've had one down on my ankle.

"And people believe these are originals?" I asked.

"The first two did." He put his hand behind him.

"Roy, get over here," I insisted.

He slumped, then came around the press. I couldn't tell what he intended to lift from the counter to use on me—scissors, oversized rolls of tape; nothing seemed particularly threatening.

"Who's making you do this now, Roy?"

"I'm finishing the job for Jean-Pierre," he said.

"You're sentimental? I don't think so."

He shrugged, then shifted his eyes to what appeared to be a small bathroom in the corner.

"You know, you're too devious for me, Roy," I said.

I punched him, a short, snapping right hook, on the side of his head. He wobbled, stumbled into the rack of paper towels and sol-vents, tins of Charbonnel etching ink, but he didn't fall.

"Let's stop fucking around," I said as I moved toward him. "Coceau was afraid of being seen with me, and now you are too. Tell it or I'll start smacking you for real."

He rubbed his temple, he bit his bottom lip. He had a choice to make. It was between me and something that might be more painful than a few more blows to the stomach and head.

"Roy . . ."

"She insisted," he said finally.

"She?"

He nodded.

I raised my right hand again.

Quickly, he said, "His woman, the one he lived with. Jean-Pierre."

"Go on."

"She said there were people who contacted the shop via the Web site who knew nothing, not a thing, about La Belle Époque. She could tell. Somebody had told them collecting French poster art was a smart idea so they went online and contacted us."

"Not enough profit in selling the real thing?"

"I thought so, but . . ."

I gestured to the press, to the neatly stacked supplies. "All this is her idea?"

He nodded. "Jean-Pierre wanted nothing to do with it."

"But he gave in."

"He loved her, I guess," he said.

"Had to be more than that."

"She had him under her thumb."

I said, "She made him a dishonorable man."

"Yeah, but this was going to be his last poster," Roy said.

I looked around the cool basement at the surfeit of supplies, the expensive lithograph press. "I don't think so."

He leaned against the wall rack. "Look, I told you what you wanted to know. Can I—"

"Her name. You didn't tell me her name."

"Jasmine," he replied.

"Jasmine what?"

He said, "Jasmine Jones, like a B actress. And, believe me, sometimes she was right out of Tennessee Williams."

"Why's that?"

"Oh, carrying on, her with her big boobs and her New Orleans accent—"

I cut him off. "Describe her."

"Blue eyes. Cheekbones, freckles on her nose. Big boobs, like I—"

"Strawberry blond?"

He shook his head. "Kind of auburn. Could be a dye job."

"She ever use the name Loretta?"

"Jasmine," he repeated. "Jasmine Jones."

"All right," I said, "Jasmine. If Jasmine found out you told me all this, what will she do?"

He sighed. "Put a hole in *my* chest, maybe?"

"You think she did that? Shot Coceau?"

He nodded. "I wouldn't put it past her. She's a nasty piece of work."

I pointed to the press. "Fuck up this job, e-mail me the address of the two other people you ripped off and I won't tell her it was you."

"I can't—"

"I'm going through the desk upstairs," I said, "and I'll find out where you live. Get me the information I want within the hour and you won't see me again."

"She'll know."

"Ship the one in the window, put something else out there and tell her this one's drying," I said.

"She wouldn't go for it."

I gave him my e-mail address. "Just get it done."

I went upstairs to rifle the desk.

I headed to the Columbus Circle entrance to the 1-9 going south by walking down Central Park West, across from the Dakota, the Majestic and several synagogues with young families lingering in animated conversation following Shabbat services. On the other side of the blackened stone walls to my left, the 844 acres of Central Park seemed to overflow with colorfully clad joggers, ten-speed bikers, softball players with old mitts and aluminum bats. Tender lovers walked hand in hand, a few with babies in strollers in front of them, and sun worshippers carried lawn chairs toward the Sheep Meadow. I looked up: A few people were flying darting kites high over the Great Lawn.

Twenty minutes later, I was away from Midtown's bustle and back at Finn Square, heading west along Franklin. TriBeCa was pre–September 11 crowded: Ambling under the bright sun, people seemed in good spirits, enjoying the last weekend of the summer, enjoying each other, dangling an array of colorful shopping bags as they walked along. Time and money spent at Sunrise Ruby, Zoogy, Seam, YHK seemed to put everyone in the right mood.

I dialed Coceau's number.

There could be more than one top-heavy woman in town from New Orleans with high cheekbones and a passion for hounds. And one of those other Louisiana gals, freckles sprinkled across her nose, could've found Coceau, a witness to the death of my son and his mother.

Maybe there are a lot of women in Louisiana with a temperament like that—controlling, ambitious, ruthless.

Pib Owen called her Loretta Jasmine Jones. "I watched that flower blossom," he said. Something like that—flower, blossom, jasmine.

How deep was she in this thing?

What else did Owen say? He called her a tomboy who hunted coon and rabbit. But he said she put away her guns.

Maybe not.

"Loretta, this is Terry Orr," I said. "What are we going to do about the damned dog?"

I gave her my cell phone number before I cut the connection.

Now she knew I'd learned she was Coceau's mate.

At least that much. By now, she might've found out that I knew she'd pushed Coceau back into counterfeiting, and that she killed him because he'd led me straight to her scam.

Loretta Jones, who knew where I lived.

. . .

As I opened the door, I heard the sound of laughter coming from the living room, and then Beagle scurried to greet me, her paws slapping the hardwood. Bella and Daniel Wu bounced behind her, laughing still.

I guess I'm supposed to pet the dog, something.

The garbage can had been turned over onto the kitchen floor, its contents scattered, all remnants of food—the slivers of sugar in the Pop-Tart wrapper, eggshells, asparagus stalks, the tops of the plum tomatoes—had been thoroughly explored and, in most cases, plundered.

"It's evidence." Daniel Wu, who was out of breath after a 30-foot run, thrust a stout finger in the air. "But circumstantial." He laughed.

"She likes it here," Bella added.

"Apparently."

I put my cell phone on the table, grabbed a bottle of Badoit and headed to my office.

After 10 minutes of meandering along the Web, searching for something interesting, something useful, I came across something that was neither, but I read it anyway. There was a fully restored eight-ton Marinoni Voirin editioning press for sale in Menton, France, the kind used more than a century ago by Cheret to create his masterworks. The easternmost town on the Côte d'Azur, Menton was close to Monte Carlo, so it wasn't far to Breil, where Coceau once lived. I wondered if he learned his corrupt trade in Monaco, near the Italian border.

His sordid skills may have lain dormant, the scandal at the Musée des Beaux-Arts scaring him straight, until he met Loretta.

Maybe trading in classic poster art from La Belle Époque didn't bring in enough for her tastes.

Though a place on Riverside Drive had to be better than the old walk-up she and Leo had on Laight Street.

I was thinking of Loretta behind the bar at Big Chief's, flirting with the off-duty blue from the First, when I heard my cell phone ring out in the kitchen where I'd left it.

"Beagle, fetch," I said as I got out of my squeaking chair.

"Dad," Bella yelled. "It's for you."

"Hello."

"Mr. Orr?" I recognized the deep, gravelly voice after only two words.

"Mr. Robinson," I said. "I didn't expect you to call me back."

"My Sherry said you need information."

I headed back to my work space.

"Give me your number and let me call you back," I told him. I didn't know how much Xerox paid, but this good man didn't need to foot the bill for a long-distance call from down the shore.

When I called back I found out he was staying at the Coral Reef Motor Lodge.

"I'm sorry to cut into your vacation," I told him. I was using the phone on my desk rather than the cell. "But I've come into new information."

"Yes?"

"People are telling me that Weisz tried to grab the stroller," I said. "To catch it before it fell."

"Can't say as I saw that."

"I guess the question is, Did you actually see him push the stroller onto the tracks?"

"I have nothing new to say, Mr. Orr. I heard a scream and I looked up to see your son go over the edge and onto the tracks. This fellow Weisz stood there, then, as your wife jumped down, he ran away."

"I see." I put my legs up on the corner of the desk. "Did you notice my wife before that?"

"No, I did not."

"So you couldn't say if Weisz knocked her out of the way to get to the stroller."

"No, I could not," he said. "There is nothing I can add, I'm afraid."

"I appreciate your time," I told him. "Your memory is transcript."

"Not at all."

My remark sparked a flash of something Sylvia Barron mentioned.

"Here's an odd question," I said. "I heard that a young woman was trying to get information from one of the witnesses a short while after the . . . incident."

"Yes. That's true."

"She visited you too? What can you tell me about her?"

"Claimed to be a friend of yours. Or an acquaintance, at least. Said she was helping you. If I recall, I talked to her well before I spoke to you."

"I don't know who she is," I told him. "I wasn't looking for Weisz back then. I wasn't doing anything."

"When I get home I can give you the precise date she visited."

"You remember what she looked like?" I asked.

"Certainly. She was on the small side, petite. Attractive, mid-thirties. Strawberry blond," he recounted.

Sylvia Barron said her visitor was a strawberry blond.

"Did she give you her name?"

"Jones."

"Common enough."

"Had a little bit of an accent," Robinson added. "Louisiana, I'd say."

"Louisiana? You sure?"

"I was stationed at Fort Polk."

Fort Polk must be in Louisiana.

"Her name wasn't *Loretta* Jones, by any chance," I said.

"No . . ."

"Jasmine?"

"Yes. That's right. Jasmine Jones."

I told him about Leo, about his ex-wife.

"That certainly is odd," he replied.

"I wonder what she was doing," I said, pondering aloud.

"Can't say as I know."

I thanked Robinson for his time, his courtesy.

He said what he did the last time we spoke. "I wish you all the best, Mr. Orr. You are in our prayers."

. . .

I took a long pull on the cold, pungent water.

Loretta talked to the witnesses. At least three of them: Coceau, Barron, Robinson, the latter two within a year or so of Davy's death. All three lived in Manhattan, as did the Holtzes, Donna Benjamin, Schaber and Bock. Had she spoken with them too?

No answer at the Holtz apartment. Benjamin's machine had a cute message, as did Bock's. Schaber used Tchaikovsky to set up his.

Weisz won a silver medal at the Van Cliburn competition with his performance of Tchaikovsky's Piano Concerto No. 1, Op. 23.

I wrote it down. I scratched it out.

Paranoia mightn't be a useful ally now.

Did Loretta get what she wanted from Coceau, Barron or Robinson?

I wrote it down: *What did she want?*

Dutilleux, streaming from a radio station in Prague, came out of my computer speakers. Anne Queffélec, a sensitive yet assertive pianist. This post-Impressionist—

Where the fuck is Diddio?

No call, no e-mail. No nothing, as he'd say.

And no e-mail from Roy Comfort.

What did Loretta want from the witnesses?

She gave them information that she could've gotten elsewhere. If what Sylvia had said was close to correct, all that Loretta volunteered had appeared in the *Voice* article on Marina, as had the names of some of the witnesses.

She wanted to know something that hadn't been made public.

What, and to what end? (I wrote that down too.)

Beagle came in, sighed, plopped herself in the desk well.

To use it how?

A nasty piece of work, Comfort said.

Blackmail?

Blackmail.

Who?

She knew how much Leo had.

Did she know how much Ruthie had down in Louisiana?

Of course she did. Nothing I knew about Loretta suggested she'd ignore due diligence when sizing up a spouse.

She didn't marry Leo because she thought he'd become the Prudhomme of the Northeast, Justin Wilson in the shadow of Wall Street.

She wanted the Mallards' money.

Instead, she got what she could siphon out of Big Chief's.

She wasn't using the death of Davy and Marina to get back into Leo's life, into his wallet.

She wanted to get at me.

She knew I had—

"*Dad.*"

I turned.

"I've been calling you."

I blinked.

"You zoned out again."

"No I didn't," I told her. "I was working."

I held up the yellow legal pad.

"Blackmail," she said coolly. "Did you have to write it twenty-five times? Block letters?"

I looked at the sheet.

"Didn't mean to," I said. "So, what's up?"

She sang, off-key, "The best things in life are free, but you can give 'em to the birds and bees . . ."

"How much?" I asked as I dug into my pocket. "And for what?"

"School clothes." She smiled and put her hand on top of her fedora. "And how about you just give me the AmEx card?"

"I don't think so."

"You can trust me."

"Take some of the signed checks." I handed her $125.

"Cool." She put the bills in the top pocket of her blue overalls.

I eased out of the chair. "You need to be careful today."

"I'm shopping. It's not very dangerous."

"No," I said, as I put my hand on her shoulder. "This Coceau thing. Go out the back, go south before you go west, OK?"

She nodded impatiently. Then she brightened. "Can I sleep at Daniel's?"

"Bella, I don't know if that's—"

"He's got, like, four sisters, a mother, a grandmother. A father."

"You're invited?" I asked.

"Always," she said. "They love me."

"Well . . ." Then I added, "Leave me his phone number. And take your cell."

"Thanks."

"And what about Beagle?"

She paused. "I could come back and walk her."

"No," I said. "Don't come back. Call me later. I'll pick you up in the morning."

"Not too early."

"Of course not."

Without another word, she turned, her bowling shoes squeaking on the wood, and left my office.

"Hey."

She stopped, came back.

"No kiss?" I asked.

She went on her toes and pecked my cheek.

"Bella, what happened to all your cash?" The trunk of her Barbie car had at least $700 in it—money she won for an essay she wrote when she was eight; birthday and Christmas gifts over the years; what remained from her summer jobs; the $400 she took from me when she wrote, on a bet, her draft of the Foxx book.

"We bought the CD, remember?"

I nodded, "That's right." In June, we bought a $10,000 certificate of deposit at the Bank of New York, for which I provided $9,750, if memory serves.

"You're not liquid," I said.

She tapped the pocket of her overalls and gave me a wide smile. "I am now."

As I sat, chair creaking, I heard sounds of celebration from the living room, the slap of high-fives.

Curious, Beagle stood, left to investigate.

Seconds later, she and Bella returned.

My daughter stuck out her hand as if to make a deal. "Julie spends the night tonight, right?"

"Bella—"

"She's free. You're free. I'm out," she said. "Come on, shake my hand."

"How do you—"

"*Dad . . .*"

I shook her hand.

As I sat in the kitchen waiting for Loretta's call, the *Times*'s Arts and Leisure section spread on the table, I ate the salad I'd thrown together—tomatoes, shallots, anchovies, lemon juice on mesclun. I felt Marina's presence, peering over my shoulder, drawn by the scent of the dish I'd concocted. *"Cosa stai mangiando, Terry?"* Quickly, violently, pushing her out of my mind, I returned to an earlier thought, something Addison had said, about how I never went at Weisz.

I knew he was right.

I mean, I put together a dossier, after countless hours in the library, countless hours online.

But out in the streets, I shuffled here, scuttled there, crablike.

That's not exactly true. I went to his mother's house and stood on Park like a fool, as if Weisz would stroll out of a luxury palace, walk up to me and, hands high, say, "You win, Terry Orr. You're too clever for me."

I went to Bellevue, talked to a dozen shrinks, maybe more. Got nothing.

And I did go to the memorial service, the cemetery.

I nearly got my ass chewed by a tiger.

As I sopped up the lemon juice and the oil from the anchovies with a piece of Italian bread, I nudged the phone and it spun on the varnished wood, the antenna tapping the *Times.*

Loretta knew I had money. Everybody did.

It's like knowing that Cy Twombly's family's got money, Frank Stella's.

Marina's paintings netted something like $11 million after taxes and fees.

And then there was the money from the option of *Slippery Dick,* the paid-out advance, royalties.

Loretta might've wanted some of that.

Blackmail.

With what information? What did she know?

I put down the bowl, the fork.

Coceau told her he saw Marina with another man.

He told her everything. Loretta turned on her charm and Coceau went for it. And then she found out about his brush with infamy at the Musée des Beaux-Arts.

"You have a predisposition for contravention, my dear," she might've whispered, as they lay in bed, as she toyed with his curly hair, letting him peek at a plump, freckled breast, a pink nipple. "Why not draw upon it to expand your resources?"

Something like that.

Music from Corigliano now, from NPR: Étude Fantasy.

How was she going to approach me with the information about my wife?

"Terry," she might say, cozying up to me as I walked along Battery Park, along Canal, on Seventh Avenue South, by the glittering bronze Prometheus at Rockefeller Center, anywhere. "There are things that you don't know about your wife, my dear."

Loretta liked to say that. My dear. One of her upscale affectations, Pib.

I'd say, looking down into her pale blue eyes as we kept walking, "Loretta, you did what you did to Leo and now you want to *chat*?"

No I wouldn't have.

I would've said, "Really?"

And I would've thought what she was going to tell me would be something that served to glorify Marina, to add to the immaculate legacy I had built in my mind. Something a critic had written, something Loretta had overheard while she was wherever she went after she took off on Leo, killing his business, burying his dreams.

And after I paid her, she'd begin, "Terry, she loved you so much. You remember one Sunday afternoon, after that noisy brunch crowd left, you and Leo were sitting in the sun on Harrison by the kitchen, sucking down Dixies? I was holding Gabriella—such a cute, cute kid, Terry—and Marina told me how much she . . ."

Not Loretta. None of that sappy shit for Loretta.

She wouldn't know its value.

"Marina was playing around, my dear. Big time."

I wouldn't have believed her.

But then I would've asked Addison.

He'd have said, "I'm sorry to hear you know about that."

Then I would've gone home and dug out some boxes, pulled out a cotton dress, brought it up to my face and I would've been certain that it was true.

"I can tell you who it is, my dear."

I would've paid for that. To know the name of the guy Marina was with, the guy who lived near Lincoln Center.

But she didn't know it, or she would've contacted me years ago.

Unless she was happy with what Coceau provided.

Unless she was waiting for the payout after Leo died.

Now Coceau was gone, and there wasn't going to be a check from the Mallards.

Or maybe she did have his name, his address. Maybe she worked it harder than Addison or Twist, knowing someday I'd want to stomp his ass.

Loretta knew my kind, knew me from the moment we met.

She knew I wasn't born into it. That it fell in my lap when Marina and I got together.

She knew how I'd react—from deep inside, without rational thought.

Here's more money, Loretta. Give me his name.

Then that part of it would be over. Loretta would blow away, slink back to anonymity.

No she wouldn't.

Blackmailers always come back.

You get that early in the curriculum in Blackmail 101. Keep tapping the flow.

I'd have the man's name, his address, but Loretta would still have the whip.

"Maybe, Terry, the police would be interested in knowing it was you who beat that man senseless near Lincoln Center. That man your wife was entertaining."

"Entertaining? This is *The Glass Menagerie* and you're Amanda Wingfield?"

"I think the police will know to what I am referring, my dear."

Somewhere between here and the kitchen, Beagle growled.

The assumption is that Loretta interviewed the witnesses so she could find something, some loose piece of information, that she could use to blackmail me.

And she got it from Coceau.

So?

She doesn't have the guy's name. Maybe a description, provided by her little Frenchman.

If she had the name she would've come to me before now.

She would've come when I was foundering, adrift in my self-perpetuated hell, on my planet Misery. (Leo came up with that last one—"How's life on the planet Misery?" Christ, what a mood he was in that day.)

Yeah, I was weak back then.

Loretta could've done me a favor by telling me about Marina. Would've snapped me out of it. Wouldn't have wasted so much time.

Loretta can't work her blackmail scheme now.

I know what my wife was doing on those afternoons, uptown with my son, *il suo costante compagno.*

Who cares if other people know?

I mean, the people I respect—Addison, Sharon Knight and now Julie—they *already* know.

So who can she tell?

Or who will I pay for her not to—

Damn it. *Damn it.*

Of course.

Bella.

Yeah, I was seething and I started pacing until the damned dog began barking, and by the time I got to the kitchen, Beagle was standing over by the front door, staring at it, barking, staring, barking.

"Either speak or shut up," I told her.

She did neither.

I looked through the door's peephole and I saw no one.

Beagle insisted.

Somebody's going to have to shut down Loretta, I thought as I went over to look out on Greenwich. Somebody's going to have to trump her play.

And there, walking east toward Hudson, her immaculate Keds glittering in the noon-hour sunlight, was about the last person I thought I'd see.

I went out and called to her, and she came back. We shook hands as we stood on hot tar in the middle of Greenwich Street.

"Elizabeth," I said, "not only are you the only shrink who works in August, you're the only one who makes house calls."

She offered me a dreary smile.

"Come on," I told her. "It's cool inside."

15

She preferred hot tea and thought Beagle was a good idea.

"It's as I imagined it," she said as she stared up from the mug and looked around the kitchen.

"No, I believe you thought I hung black crêpe over the windows. Candles, an altar. Me, wearing a hair shirt . . ."

She didn't smile. Harteveld was so accustomed to my sharp tongue, my petulance, my attempts to withhold, to misinform, that she couldn't be prepared for a self-deprecating joke. Especially in the frame of mind she was in.

The Inquisitor seemed awfully sad.

And, replying to the crack about turning my kitchen into a dark memorial, she could've said, "You tried to, Terry, and, to some extent, you succeeded. You worked tremendously hard to extend the grieving period and to create illusion, which, of course, seemed quite real to you in time. By failing to work through your—"

"What's up, Elizabeth?"

"I wanted to clarify a few points we discussed the other day," she said.

"About your husband and Raymond Montgomery Weisz."

She was in Bella's seat. I had my back to the sink.

"Yes," she nodded. She wore a long cranberry blouse, open to reveal a matching T-shirt, above baggy khaki shorts. On Greenwich, I'd noticed her legs were tanned and well defined—probably from all that tennis.

"So . . . ?"

She looked at me. "My husband wasn't treating him. He was treating his mother."

"OK."

"He said he never met Raymond Weisz."

"But he knew we were interested in him," I said.

"He did, yes."

"And he said nothing to you?"

"No," she replied.

Beagle shifted on the cool linoleum.

"Well, what can you do?" I said. "If you didn't know . . ."

"But I feel I've somehow— I think it imperative that we maintain a consistency in our relationship, Terry."

"But you're here now, Elizabeth, in my home. Not very consistent. Unless it's the start of a trend."

"I was walking . . . I didn't know if I should come, call. I didn't know. I know it was troubling you and, frankly, it's a matter I prefer to settle."

"You were walking and you found yourself in TriBeCa," I said.

"I find walking very therapeutic," she said quietly.

Me too, I thought.

She lifted the mug, took a sip.

As I stood, tucking the chair under the table, I said, "Thanks for coming."

"Terry, I would like to give you some advice, if I may."

"Go ahead." I leaned against the sink, folding my arms across my chest.

"It's about Mr. Weisz," she said, as she returned the mug to the table.

"The father?"

"No, no. Raymond Montgomery Weisz, who you have consistently referred to as the Madman."

"Who you or your husband don't know . . ."

She nodded, let her eyes drift.

She'd come to clarify my impression of her husband, his faulty ethics. Having done so—at least to her satisfaction—she wanted to do more. I told myself to back off and remember that this was the woman who helped my daughter, who, in her way, tried to help me. A woman who'd learned that her husband wasn't as transparent as he should've been.

What a terrible thing it is to be deceived.

"I'm sorry, Elizabeth. Old habit. Please." I gestured for her to continue.

"I'm concerned about Mr. Weisz, to be frank. As it pertains to you."

"In what way?"

"He's untethered now," she said. "His last link to his family has been severed. His associations—"

"He's been to her grave," I said. "I saw him."

She sat up. "Is that so?"

I nodded. "He got away. Fortunately."

"Why 'fortunately'?"

"And he's not at any zoo in the five boroughs."

"His touchstones," she said. "Now he has nowhere to go."

"Elizabeth, he's been nowhere for five years. Wherever he goes is where he is."

"Yes, but it is not necessarily as it was," she said. "Despite his strong, negative feelings toward his mother, he will be impacted by her death. How he will react isn't known, I'm afraid."

"So you think there's the risk of danger?" I asked.

"Yes I do."

"To who?"

"You, perhaps, but more likely to himself."

I came away from the sink to move around the table. Harteveld followed me with her eyes and, as I sat on the steps that ran upstairs, she turned to face me, putting her arm on the back of the chair.

"Elizabeth, Weisz isn't going to harm me," I said.

"I'm not sure we can say that, Terry. Not with complete certitude."

"She never hurt anyone," I told her. "He didn't push Davy onto the tracks. He tried to save him."

She tilted her head, frowned in confusion. "Terry. Are— How long have you known this?"

"Well, Elizabeth, I suppose it depends on how we define 'know.' Let's say I was told a couple of days ago."

She didn't know how to react. Without her lab coat, files and Cross pen, it was as if she were naked, exposed to the reality of what she was hearing, understanding.

"I don't know what to say, Terry."

"I appreciate that. I really do."

"Perhaps we should explore this."

I shrugged. "Maybe, but you know what I need, Elizabeth? The unvarnished, unadulterated truth. From now on."

"And you feel you haven't had that?"

"I was going to say 'I think that's all we have time for today, Dr. Harteveld.'"

She smiled. "Touché."

"But it's all different now. Isn't it?"

"Yes, Terry. It is."

I offered her my hand as she left the chair. "Thank you, Elizabeth."

She stood and, with Beagle rising to follow her, she went toward the door. "I believe Gabriella will be in this week," she said. "Will you come with her?"

"I might do that," I nodded.

I might not.

"That's a nice dog," she said as she stepped into the hot summer air. "A companion for Gabriella. Where did you get her? A breeder, or did you go to the ASPCA?"

Well, I thought, there was this guy who got shot . . .

The August phenomenon in New York: The later it gets, the hotter it gets, as if someone put a kettle lid over the city come late afternoon. It's nearly 5 P.M. now and the temperature was pushing 90 degrees. Or 120, according to the sun-baked Inca Gold temperature gauge outside the eighth bodega I visited on Amsterdam. As I left, folded sheet going back into my shirt pocket, as I passed under yet another yellow-and-red awning, I could smell the tar, the lingering fumes of the last bus that went by, and the sweat on my brow.

As I trudged south along the upper tip of the Upper West Side, I occupied my mind with thoughts of Julie, who showed up unannounced, with an overnight bag, a smaller companion to the one she wheeled in New Orleans. Some sort of kismet, I suppose, as she rang the bell while I was fixing up the bedroom.

Peering through the peephole, I saw that her face, eager with anticipation, displayed a vague sense of nervousness, as if I might tell her to turn around and go home.

"Hello, Julie."

She held up the little bag. "I've got to get ready for church in the morning. You have an iron, I assume."

"Bella called you?"

She squeezed by me, not before kissing my bottom lip. "I'm not supposed to say. Hey, Beagle."

We decided to divvy up duties. She was down in SoHo, looking for sheets, pillowcases, a thin blanket, a down comforter, new pillows.

I was about to enter Landestoy's Meateria.

According to a hand-painted letter on the door, *Landestoy es la Mejor!* And modest too.

"I remember this," said Roger Landestoy.

A big sign in the crowded window of Landestoy's Meateria announced that, in addition to fresh chicken and pork, produce, Lotto and magazines, he had a fax machine and an ATM waiting inside.

"This woman, she was acting crazy," he replied, his accent strong, unvarnished. "She wanted to send something like twenty-five of those in two minutes or something."

He was pointing at the Weisz obit. On the upper edge of the fax sheet was a numerical code, which included a phone number with a 212 area code and a 799 prefix, which fit the Upper West Side at the edge of Morningside Heights. Neither Staples store in the neighborhood, any of the hotels, or a slew of the bodegas, delis or take-out joints that had a 799 prefix in their phone numbers sent faxes for Loretta Jasmine Jones. I know. I visited 26 places before I arrived here.

"All going to New Orleans, all of them," Landestoy added. "Long distance. I charge her two dollars a minute. She said she didn't care about the money. The waiting . . . She didn't want to wait."

"So she asked you to do it?" I said.

He made a face. Her request offended his sense of order. "I'm not going to do that for nobody."

The aisles in the store were narrow, and from behind his cash register, Landestoy was able to watch his place via convex mirrors in each corner, high above the stocked shelves. The distortion made both of us look like Gumby.

"Could you describe this woman?"

"American, brown kind of hair. *Pecas,* all over the nose." He smiled wickedly. *"Tetas grandes."*

I didn't need to speak Spanish to understand that.

I showed him the photo of Loretta that Leo had willed me.

"That's her, man," Landestoy said. *"Muy caliente, sí?"*

"Oh yes," I replied as I took back the photo. "Charming."

Two hours later, we lay on new sheets, our heads on new pillows, pillowcases.

"I am disoriented," she said. Her dark hair was matted to her damp forehead. Despite the air conditioner's flow, we were soaked in sweat.

"Disoriented?" I asked. "That's a pretty big compliment, isn't it?"

"No, not because of . . ." She brushed off the top sheet and rolled over to face me. Her naked body glistened. "You moved everything around. The furniture, everything."

"I needed a change," I said. "A new perspective."

"It's because you didn't want to think of your wife, isn't it?"

Yes. "No," I said. "I wanted it to be new with you."

She returned to her back with a bounce. "I think you like me."

I closed my eyes, allowing myself to surrender to the allure of sleep—in the past few days, too little of it, and not enough exercise.

"Where's the painting?"

She was sitting up, looking at me.

"Lake Occhito? I put it in Bella's room."

"I was afraid you threw it away."

I laughed. "Jule, that painting would fetch about three hundred thousand dollars now. In Milan, maybe more."

"You would sell it?"

I said no. "It's not mine. It's Bella's. All of them are."

"Does she know that?"

"I never talked to her about it," I said. My eyelids bobbed. "But she knows."

I'd started to slide nicely, slowly, into a soft sleep when I heard her voice.

"Terry, I have a confession," she said.

"Oh?" I had my eyes closed.

"After Gabriella left me here yesterday, I went around and looked at your wife's paintings."

"All of them?"

"If there are four . . ."

"So you came up here." I inched up on my elbows and faced her.

"I'm afraid so," she said sheepishly. "Angry?"

"No," I replied. "But I was wondering how you knew I rearranged the furniture."

"The paintings, they're beautiful, Terry," she said. "I mean, some of them are incredible. In that one—*Lake Occhito?*—you can feel the breeze off the blue water, and the sun on those little yellow flowers . . . It's like you're standing there, surrounded by all this natural beauty. But it's, it's more . . . I don't know, I mean, it's intense yet tranquil."

"That's an artificial lake," I said, edging back to the pillow. "For trout fishing. They stock it by helicopter."

It wasn't yet dark when the phone rang. Twilight flowed through the curtains, sending a wash of silver rays across the bed.

I shot up, startled, once again snapped from a deep sleep. And I didn't know where I was, and then I did, as I heard the shower run, Julie singing low.

When the phone rang again, I thought of Weisz, for some reason, as if he'd suddenly decide to call.

"Hello."

"Give me back my fuckin' dog."

I cleared my throat as I tugged on the sheet.

"Terry, I want Silver Bell. Now."

"Her name's Beagle, Loretta. And she's too good for you."

"That's my dog," she spat. She sounded like she'd run through a few Cajun martinis or a six of Dixies.

I looked at the telephone cradle. Caller ID couldn't make her, which probably meant she was using a cell.

"Where are you?"

"Never mind. My dog—"

"Give me Leo's money and I'll think about it."

"Leo's money." She laughed. "You think I have Leo's money?"

"I know what you did, Loretta. Or do you prefer Jasmine?"

"You're so fuckin' smart, Terry. But there's so, so much you don't know."

"I know that you're not getting a fuckin' cent out of me, Loretta. I know that."

The hiss of the shower water ceased, and I heard the plastic curtain flutter, the rattle of the rings on the rod.

"I'm getting all that's mine."

"Hey, Loretta," I said. *"Je sais tout."*

"What?" Then she went silent. "Did you—"

"Jules-Alexandre Grün," I said. "The poster you had Coceau counterfeit. How many others were there?"

She let out a grotesque sound, a loud yawl that married frustration, confusion and anger.

"You drew me out of New Orleans, Loretta, to keep me away from Leo's family and friends," I told her. "To keep me away from their Loretta stories."

"You—"

"But you were too late," I said, cutting her short. "And then you didn't make sure your boyfriend stayed away from the memorial service. That put me right back next to you, Loretta, when I knew more than I did before. You fucked up. Face it. You lost control."

I had turned and was sitting now on the side of the bed, my bare feet on the carpet.

Julie stood by the bedroom door, a thirsty towel wrapped around her body.

"I will get what's mine," Loretta spat. "The money, Terry, and my dog, and whatever I find at the Tilt. There's nothing you can do about it."

"I don't think so, Loretta. Try this: The cops are going to know you pushed Coceau into that clumsy counterfeiting racket and they'll grill your ass until they find out you shot him to keep him away from me. And you won't get a penny of his money either."

Now, a different sound, a sarcastic laugh, mean, ugly. "I shot my boyfriend?" she asked, as she turned her voice soft and sweet, like an innocent young girl's. "Little ol' me, who's so terribly heartbroken?" She sniffed, then made a crying sound. And then she laughed.

"You know, my dear," she said, as she brought her voice back to its original gritty timbre, "the world does not revolve around you and your ideas."

"Forget it, Loretta," I told her. "You wasted your time—interviewing the witnesses, hooking up with Coceau. You thought you caught a lucky break, finding out about Marina. But from me, you get nothing."

She screamed, "I want what's mine!"

I pulled the phone away from my ear. Julie frowned. She'd heard Loretta's tortured cry.

"Christ, Loretta, if you're in Riverside Park, they heard you over in New Jersey."

"The Mallards owe me and I'm getting it," she said through gritted teeth. "And what Jean-Pierre had is now mine, and you—"

"You get shit," I said. "Nothing from Leo, nothing from Coceau, not a penny from me."

"Terry," she shouted. "Don't you—"

"And I'm keeping the fuckin' dog," I said.

Then I cut the line.

"So that's Loretta," Julie said, as she moved toward the bed.

I could feel the anger boiling within me. "Loretta," I muttered.

She put her hands on my cheeks. "You're hot."

"Fuckin' Loretta," I repeated.

I left the bed. I needed to cool down. I needed a shower. To wipe away the stink of Loretta Jasmine Jones.

16

I woke up to an empty bed. As I sat up, blink-blinking until the cobwebs vanished, I realized I'd slept 12 hours and, with the exception of a dull ache in my ugly right knee, I felt fine. I was rested— Loretta, frothing, hadn't come during the night; or the bloody ghost of Coceau. Or Weisz, his empty eyes no longer the fierce yellow of a rabid beast.

The morning sun that filled the room now came from behind me, rather than from my left, and the wall I faced was bare, though I could see the outline of where *Lake Occhito* had been—gray, ghostly lines on off-white.

And then I realized Bella wasn't home, and Julie had left, and I was alone in the house, and if I allowed myself, if I fell to old habits, I'd be attended to by spirits. A spirit, one who was no longer loving, sympathetic, compassionate. The spirit who had betrayed me with her long fingers, dark-brown eyes, cooing voice, Italian accent, and who had then, for the past five years, continued her deception. And I, a fool, a *fool,* cooperated fully, helping her succeed in keeping me from the truth.

I could've killed Weisz. Or, running in fear, he might've killed himself.

When all he had tried to do was save my son, as my wife was nestled in the embrace of another man.

So intently focused was she on his gaze, on the touch of his hands, the warmth of his lips, that she was unaware my son was about to fall to the hard, soiled tracks and to his death.

I stood and tugged on the string of my pajama bottoms.

Davy should be entering the second grade this week, all suntanned and laughing, toying with a PC down the hall, playing basketball with me in the backyard, building multicolored skyscrapers with his Legos. Watching his sister with admiring eyes.

It's one thing to betray a husband, a grown man capable of taking care of himself, I thought as I wobbled toward the bathroom, my toothbrush, this damned baking soda toothpaste Bella insists I need, the news from the shower radio.

It's another to allow a child to die. Your own child.

That is a sin is well beyond betrayal, infidelity.

Marina, *mei carissima,* you and that man you were with, *il tuo costante compagno,* you are responsible for the death of my son, of Bella's brother, as surely as if you had pushed his stroller onto the tracks yourself.

You, spirit, are gone from my life.

Good luck in hell.

What was that Cock Michaels's lyric D used to quote? Oh yeah: "I'm going back down to where I've been and hell is on the way."

Dante couldn't have said it better. (Yes he could've.)

I grabbed the toothbrush, turned on the hot water in the shower.

Julie had drawn, with lipstick, a heart on the bathroom mirror.

I smiled.

. . .

I decided to get in three before I set out, so instead of showering, I threw on an old Duke T-shirt, shorts and my running shoes. As I came downstairs I was greeted by Beagle, whose expression told me I had a duty that came before exercise. I took her cherry-red leash from the back of the laundry-room door, hooked her up and out we went.

I was surprised to find that a cool breeze off the Hudson had brushed aside the stagnant air that had engulfed TriBeCa for the past several days. The light wind felt good on my face, and I stood and let it wash over me.

To my right, the gleaming sun, which seemed twice its customary size yet somehow less threatening, hovered above a wooden water tank over on Hudson. One of my neighbors had given a long drink to the fragile tree in front of my place, and the trickle of water ran over cobblestone peering through the blacktop.

Not a bad day, I told myself, as I followed Beagle toward West Street.

"Go get 'em, Silver Beagle," I said.

She had a royal spring in her step, an odd sort of dignity.

As we reached West Street, I saw, coming toward us on his way south, Daniel Wu, happily lugging his tubby frame along the highway, a basketball tucked under his arm.

"It is a beautiful day to walk a dog," Daniel said with a bright smile. He wore a Knicks jersey over a black T-shirt and black shorts. Today he had on black high-top sneakers.

Over on the river side of the street, rollerbladers sped by, attacking a makeshift course, hands clasped behind their backs as they made the marble façade of the World Financial Center a blur. A Korean couple sold ficus trees on the concrete island that divided the north- and southbound lanes. Yellow construction cranes rose from the old World Trade Center site.

"Where's Bella, Daniel?"

"All the girls are sleeping," he said, adding with a smile, "except my grandmother."

"You wouldn't lie to me, would you?"

"I suppose it would depend on the circumstances," he replied. "So I'd better say yes."

Beagle sniffed Daniel's sneaker, drooled on the Velcro.

"But you're not lying now."

"When I left, they were sleeping." He looked at me. "Mr. Orr, I didn't realize you were such a father."

"You think it's too late?" I asked.

"For what?"

"Never mind."

I asked him where he was headed, as I reached and slapped the ball out of his hand.

"I'm trying to improve," he said as he watched me dribble the ball fast and tight to the sidewalk. Beagle was unimpressed. "I want to try out for the basketball team."

He was barely five feet, but Daniel was determined. Maybe it could happen.

"Where do you work out?"

"Stuyvesant," he said, gesturing toward Chambers with his head, his floppy mop of hair. "The kids are a little gentler there than—"

"On the city courts. Right."

I spun the ball on my finger and punched it back to him. It hit his unprepared hands and rolled toward the street, the easy flow of Sunday morning traffic heading north.

I handed him Beagle's leash and retrieved the ball.

"Daniel, did you know what Bella was going to do today?"

"I think she was going to try to meet Marcus and Eleanor by the Seaport," he said. "But she would call you, I'm sure." Then he asked, "Do you think she's in danger?"

"Why?"

"She says you want her to stay away from your house."

"Caution," I said. "That's all."

"So it's better that she be away from you than with you," he summarized. "Don't worry. She is safe with my family. When she calls you, tell her to stay at my home. My father will be there, and my sister Wendy. I'll be there before long."

"That's a good idea, Daniel." I patted him on his head. "You're a smart young man. A good friend."

As I got ready to leave, tugging Beagle gently until she rose, Daniel said, "Mr. Orr, I would like to ask you to promise not to tell Gabriella that you saw me today."

"Why not? I mean, sure, but why not?"

"I don't want her to know I'm practicing."

"OK. I promise."

"Gabriella is a good player, you know," he said. "I really can't compete."

"Be as good as you can, Daniel. You'll do all right."

He thanked me and said goodbye to Beagle.

As I started north, I heard him call my name.

"And, no, it's not too late, Mr. Orr. Gabriella needs you—then, now, always."

He nodded thoughtfully, adjusted the ball under his arm, and went off toward Chambers.

With Beagle back in the house, I thought about heading over to Diddio's place on Great Jones and surprising him with an offer to take him for fat walnut pancakes, his favorite, which he ordered with bacon and sausage. But as I stood on Harrison, my hair still damp from the long, sweet shower, his letter from a Baton Rouge law firm in my back pocket, I decided to think it through, to stop wondering what he was up to and try to figure it out. It occurred to me that D hadn't merely been grieving for Leo, though that loss would be a hard one for him to bear. Nor had he been prowling the French Quarter, looking for love in a new town. Diddio had been trying to determine what he was going to do next; specifically, what to do about the Tilt, *his* Tilt, according to the note Leo had left behind. He'd been assessing the opportunity Leo had given him. He understood that Leo had had his well-being in mind. It was as if our friend had told him, "Time for you to settle down, D. Time to make a place of your own."

And if D wondered if he could manage it—as I had—all he had to do, all either of us had to do, was remember that Leo thought so. Leo would never let D fail.

D was running the gauntlet, trying to get to the other side, where his decision lay. I had to give him credit. He was working against his own nature and going hard at his challenge.

He was looking right at it, staring it down.

So I decided D wasn't home, surrounded by his 5,000 CDs, his ragged notebooks, faded posters of rock stars now in their 60s. He was at the Tilt, and there was Leo up on his throne behind the bar, and D was saying, "Leo, man, this place . . . Woof. You know, I mean. It's kind of, like, run-down and—"

"It's yours, D. Do what you will."

"Yeah," he'd chuckle. "Like I know how to do *that*."

I went east to Hudson.

I had Leo's key in my wallet.

Five minutes later, I slipped it into his front door.

"Oh good," Loretta said. "Both of you."

She was holding a gun, pointing at my midsection.

Just below where Coceau got it.

Over by the jukebox, Diddio had his hands on his head. He wore the world's sorriest expression as he shrugged an apology toward me.

"Lock the door, my dear," Loretta told me. When I did, she added, "Now, boys, we're really going to have some fun."

She patted me down hard, turning me around and bending me over the bar, then crammed her hand around my ankles, up my inner thighs, around my groin, all the while keeping her gun pressed against the dead center of my spinal column.

"Get over there," she said, and I went behind the pool table, about 15 feet from Diddio.

"Put down your hands, you dope."

D did as instructed.

"Find anything, Loretta?" Only the red three-ball was on the green felt, and an arched, crooked cue. It wasn't going to be easy to get my hands on either, unless Diddio distracted her.

Loretta looked awfully comfortable with that .32 in her hand.

"I didn't know, man," Diddio moaned, looking sideways at me. "I didn't recognize her."

She had auburn hair, as Comfort had reported. But that was the only difference. She still had striking blue eyes, freckles on the bridge of her nose, high cheekbones, a shapeless body except for the oversized top. An expression on her weathered face that was as cold and hard as marble.

"Still looking me over, Terry?"

I could see Diddio in the old, veined mirror behind the musty liquor bottles. I was hoping he'd catch my gaze. But no. In fact, he'd closed his eyes to make it all go away.

"I guess that's the gun you shot Coceau with," I said. "No more hunting rifles for you."

She didn't reply. Instead, she inched herself up on a bar stool, revealing her bare thigh under the short linen skirt.

"Some shot," I added. "Hit a man with a .32 from, what, at least thirty-forty yards away?"

"Not that good," she said, "since I was trying to shoot you."

Diddio choked back a sob.

Loretta turned to him in disgust. "Listen, I don't want to hear a peep out of you." She looked at me. "What did you ever see in this child?"

"He's not so bad," I said. "Once you get to know him."

I had my hands on the pool table now, leaning forward.

"I don't want to know him," she replied, "but I might shoot his bony ass if I don't get what I came for."

"What's that, Loretta?"

"Money," Diddio cried.

"Find any?" I asked.

"It's here somewhere," she said, waving the gun.

I sat on the edge of the table, thigh on the rail. "Can I help?"

"Terry, you're a charmer, always were," she said with a derisive yet alluring smile. "But you're going to stay right there until we figure things out."

"I told you," Diddio squealed. "We took it all out."

"Not all of it," she insisted.

"But we—"

"Not all of it!" she screamed, her face contorting in an ugly madness. "No you did not."

"Loretta, wait," I said. "Let me explain."

Her face, her throat had turned a bright red. She'd already killed one man with that piece of hardware in her hand. If I didn't calm her, she might make it three.

"Leo left me five thousand dollars to find you," I said, "and that's it. Even the till was empty."

"Five thousand to find me?"

"And bring you to justice."

"Justice." She snorted. "Where's the five grand at? Here?"

"I banked it," I told her. Which wasn't true: I stuck it in my filing cabinet in my office. "I had to write about four thousand in checks just to cover the bills in the desk."

"Is that right?"

I nodded. The cue stick was under my right knee now and the three ball was over by the top pocket to my right. My best bet was to ease over to the head of the table.

I stood. "You know how much Leo knew about running a business, Loretta."

She laughed darkly.

"You ripped him off at Big Chief's, put him in debt with the IRS, the city, state—"

"He told you that, did he?"

"Come on, Loretta. You got the gun. We don't have to play."

She came off the stool and walked toward me, keeping the table between us.

"What if I told you I never took a dime out of the business?"

"Not a dime?"

She had the gun pointed at my midsection again. "Maybe a dime here and there. But big money? Not ever."

I shook my head.

"Ruthie gave it to us with a teaspoon. We were making her rich. Or richer. And what came back? Dimes."

"What are you talking about?"

"Terry, stop eyeing that damned cue stick," she barked. She reached and lifted the red ball with her left hand, tossed it with a snap against the liquor bottles. They rattled and crashed onto the wooden floor behind the bar.

His voice trembling, Diddio said, "Terry, don't do nothing, all right?"

"Maybe," Loretta said, keeping her eyes hard on me, "he ain't as dumb as he looks."

"Ruthie . . ." I wanted her back in her story.

"Ruthie," she repeated. "Ruthie is the one you ought to bring to justice. I sent Ruthie what we owed her each and every month. Didn't miss a single time."

"I don't get you."

"It was Ruthie who didn't make the payments, not me."

"She wanted to bankrupt her own brother?" I asked.

"She never did want Leo to leave home. Not her, not her mama. And not with me, that's for damn sure."

"Christ," I said, "you've got a real grievance, Loretta."

"Damn straight."

"Can you prove it?"

She put her left hand on her hip. "Don't be a damn fool, Terry. Ruthie was setting me up all along. She wanted cash, and I sent it."

"And she was supposed to have checks cut for Interstate Properties."

She looked at me, vast disappointment sweeping across her eyes. "You don't know, do you?"

"Tell me."

She let the gun sag and said, angrily, "I knew you didn't know. I *knew* it. And you had to fuck up my sweet thing with Jean-Pierre."

She'd stayed in New York to find a new meal ticket. When one didn't turn up, she decided to try to come up with something to blackmail me. Which is when she met Coceau. That much I knew.

"Loretta, help me out here," I said. "Make me understand."

"You had a long time to figure this out, Terry. Especially after your wife and kid died and you started up this detective thing. But you never tried."

"Loretta—"

She raised the gun. "You didn't do a damned thing for me, Terry."

"So you tried to kill me?"

"Jean-Pierre," she said, shaking her head, tossing her auburn hair. "*Si bien disposé un homme.* A sympathetic sap. Had to go to the mother's service. Show his support. He led you right to the press in his basement, didn't he?"

"Yeah, more or less."

"I figured they'd blame Weisz for your death." She shrugged.

Weisz with a gun? Not even when I thought he'd killed Davy and Marina. "Did he agree with you on that?"

"Jean-Pierre always agreed with me."

She spun suddenly and pointed the .32 at Diddio.

"No, no," he shouted. "I'm just— I'm— I've got to sit."

He was leaning against the jukebox, pointing at the radiator.

"Sit," she growled.

He did, tucking the heels of his black sneakers down by the cobwebs and dust balls.

"Your dog is fine, by the way," I said.

"I thought about that," she replied, as she pointed the gun at me again. "And I decided to hell with Silver Bell and to hell with Jean-Pierre. I can get me another man and another dog."

She shifted priorities when she sobered up. "Sentimental," I cracked.

I sat on a stool, feeling my way with my hands behind my back. I still had my eye on the cue, but I needed Diddio to do more than sit and shiver inside his black T-shirt.

"Sentimental? Not me," she said. "I leave that to you. You made sure every single New Yorker saw how miserable you were. And all the time you were chasing the wrong man."

"Huh?" Diddio emitted.

Loretta kept her gaze on me as she spoke to him. "Your friend's wife was running around on him, Mr. Critic. She let her baby—"

"Drop it, Loretta. OK?"

She said, "He should hear it, Terry. How your Marina let your son die."

"Loretta," I said slowly. "Let it go."

"How your cool, proper bitch—"

"Loretta, shut the fuck up!" I screamed.

She glared at me, her face going red again as she edged closer, closer. Now she was no more than 10 feet away.

Through gritted teeth, she said, "I wasted my time on you, you self-pitying child. All you had to do was find out that I was hassling your witnesses, come and get me and I would've told you all about Ruthie, and you could've helped me *and* Leo, and I would've been on my way. And Leo would've never known."

She took a deep breath. "But not you, you *child*. Crying to the cops, running to the D.A., getting your name in the newspapers, chasing that lunatic. You lost your fuckin' mind, Terry."

"But you weren't going to blackmail me, Loretta?"

"Only if you decided to be difficult . . ."

"And meanwhile you forgot all about your scam when you hooked up with Coceau."

"You know how it is, Terry," she said with bitter sarcasm. "You fall into it and you start to like it. Flying to Nice, a weekend in Monte Carlo. Fly to San Francisco to look at a rare Cheret. The four-star hotels, the wine. Clothes. You know what I'm talking about."

I didn't reply.

"Dog got your tongue, my dear?"

"Loretta, what are we doing here?"

"I'm getting what's mine. From you, Ruthie, Leo. All of you."

"And you're just going to walk away?"

She nodded, then said, "You just can't imagine anyone is smarter than you, can you? You always thought you were better than me, with your book and your brains and your Italian wife, your house on Harrison. But you're no different than me. You're just a lucky loser who got a ride out of the gutter."

She crept even closer. Now the .32 was about six feet from my belt. If I swiped my hand across—

"And Marina knew it. She told me. You and your rock-and-roll friend—boys. You were going to satisfy her? You were muscle on the side, my dear. A hard body. She needed a man, goddamnit. So while you were running your eyes over every woman in TriBeCa, thinking you were jack-shit because of your money and your stupid book, your wife—"

I heard a shot ring out.

Loretta looked at me with a strange, shocked expression.

Then she fell at my feet, and when I looked up I saw Diddio holding Leo's .38 with two hands.

17

"Oh, Terry," Diddio moaned as his skinny arms started to rattle. He dropped the gun, then he started to cry.

He bent, picked up the .38 and gingerly approached her.

She lay on her back and groaned as she tried to lift off the barroom floor.

I kicked her .32 under the pool table.

"Is she dead?"

"No," I said.

I took Leo's .38 from him, the gun he'd dug out of the jukebox while Loretta was ranting, attacking me.

"I shot her in the back," he said.

"This isn't the Old West, D. You do what you have to."

"Get it while you can?" He looked at me with pleading eyes.

"After a fashion."

Loretta continued to moan. She pedaled her legs, trying to get her feet under her. Her sandals couldn't grip the floor.

"Lift up her blouse," Diddio said.

"What?"

"No, I mean, where's the bullet? You think it's in one of her . . . You know."

Blood oozed onto the front of her beige V-neck polo.

"Let's turn her over."

Loretta's right arm lay at an odd angle, so I shifted her to her left.

Diddio had put a hole in her right shoulder blade. Blood oozed out and onto the floor.

"Put your hand over the wound," I said. "Your right hand. Press."

Loretta hissed.

"Get your hand all bloody," I said. "Put it in the little puddle over there."

He did as I told him.

"Now go wash your hands. Not too good, though."

When he returned, water dripping from his fingers, I told him to call Midtown North. "Ask for Renaldo Twist. Tell him I shot Coceau's girlfriend. Tell him we got the—"

"*You* shot her?" he asked.

I nodded. "And tell him we got the gun she shot Coceau with."

He came over and lifted my cell from my belt.

When I knew D was in Leo's office, I pushed Loretta down until she was flat on her back and I straddled her, my knees on the bloody floor.

She closed her eyes.

"You're not dying, Loretta," I said. "Not yet."

I put the gun under her chin.

"Ow. Shit. Terry—"

"What did he look like, Loretta?"

"Who?" she hissed.

She was hurting, but she could do better than that.

"There's no time to fuck around, Loretta," I said sharply, as I pushed the .38 up against the bottom of her chin.

Squirming beneath me, she said, "He was everything you're not. Cosmopolitan, elegant, European. He was . . . He was not you."

"Coceau said this?"

She nodded.

I looked down at her and she stared directly into my eyes. And she smiled.

"Yeah, you're finally on top of me, Terry," she whispered softly. She thrust her hips toward me, rotating them seductively despite her pain. "Come on, Terry. Come on."

I jammed the gun against her cheek, pressing hard.

"I never cheated on my wife, Loretta," I said. "I'm not you."

She laughed, coughed, laughed again. "You, my dear, are a liar. An awful liar."

"Look at me, Loretta." I waited until she looked into my eyes again. "I did it like I was supposed to, straight down the middle. No deception, no duplicity. I gave my word, I kept my word. And that means you don't know me. You got me? You don't know me. You never did."

Diddio ran back into the room. "Terry, they're—" He skidded to a stop.

I withdrew the gun from Loretta's pale cheek, rose from her prone body.

When I turned, I had fury in my eyes, and my face was bright red.

Diddio looked at me in horror as I put the .38 on the pool table.

"They're coming," he said finally.

There were gauze pads in one of the boxes I'd packed last week. I went for them.

When I returned, Diddio was standing over her, staring down at her.

"She's knocked out," he said.

I kicked her and her eyes flew open.

"She's full of shit," I told him.

We turned her over, packed the wound with gauze and paper towels, all of which turned a deep red in seconds.

I reached under the table and grabbed the .32, using a towel to keep my hands off the cold metal. Then I lifted the .38 away from the green felt.

"Come with me, D," I said as I nodded toward the rack of long-neck empties near Leo's office. "Let's get this thing straight."

"Yeah," he said, glancing back at Loretta.

"Who shot her?" I asked.

"I did—"

"Christ, D."

"You did. You did."

I stopped, turned around.

"Can you pull this off?" I asked.

"I'd better."

"No shit."

"I'll practice," he said earnestly and started yanking on his long hair.

"Go open the front door, stand outside," I told him.

"I'll do that."

"Do a good job."

He nodded sheepishly as I went to wipe down the .38 and recoat it with my prints.

My story did not impress Twist.

"Maybe this .38 is what you had with you at Woodlawn," he said. He wore a dark gray suit, a white shirt and a burgundy tie that matched his spotless shoes.

We were out in the stark sunlight on Hudson. After 20 minutes, the top of my head and my face were starting to toast again. Start traveling with sunblock, I told myself. Something like a 45. At least 30.

Back in the bar, Diddio was getting a gentle grilling from Sanders, the uniformed officer Twist rode with. At the curb, a pair of blue-and-whites surrounded the EMT van near the hydrant, and two other uniformed cops held back the crowd, such as it was. Accustomed to police cars in TriBeCa since September 11, only a handful of people from the neighborhood had come by to watch. I didn't recognize any of them.

I ought to call Bella, I thought.

"If I had this at the cemetery, you would've found it," I said.

"Don't flatter me, Orr," he replied with a sneer.

They had Loretta in the EMT van now, and Twist had bagged her .32. Ballistics would clear up that side of the story.

We watched as the van backed away from the curb and, the siren crying, rode off toward St. Vincent's.

Twist clutched the thick plastic bag that held Leo's .38.

"You're saying this doesn't belong to you," he said.

I repeated what I told him earlier: It was Leo's and Leo was dead.

"And it was in the jukebox." He shook his head. The sun danced on the flecks of gray in his close-cropped hair.

"It was in the jukebox," I said. "That's where he kept it."

"You knew that?"

"We were friends," I said, as I pointed to the bar behind me. "I hang here. Addison knows."

"And you're saying he always kept it in the jukebox?"

"As far as I know."

"Even though there's a whole lot of tape under the bar, right where it would've made sense for a bartender to hide it?"

I shrugged. "I guess I'm lucky it wasn't there. I'd be dead. Loretta would've killed me like she killed Coceau."

He bit his bottom lip and, as he went through his thoughts, ran his thumb under the lapel of his jacket.

"She's going to tell you it was an accident," I told him. "Shooting Coceau."

"Because she tried to kill you on Riverside," he said, repeating what I'd reported earlier. "Tell me again why'd she want to do that."

"You'll have to ask her, but it could've been because I was getting close to her boyfriend's counterfeiting racket."

"Four posters don't make a racket."

"No," I said, "but buying that kind of high-priced printing press does."

"All right."

"Or she might have tried to shoot me uptown because she had a feeling Leo Mallard wanted me to track her down."

"So you knew she was coming here," Twist said, pointing at the Tilt.

"She was already here when I arrived," I replied. "She had Diddio scared shitless, basically."

"What did she want from him?"

I shook my head, shrugged. "Maybe she found out that Leo left him the bar."

"That pissed you off, I'll bet."

"Oh yeah," I said. "I really, *really* want to own a bar. Especially one as prosperous as this one."

"Not everybody's a millionaire, Orr."

"There's that," I nodded. "I mean, that's why Loretta might've come here. She might've been looking to finish off the scam she started five years ago."

I told him how Loretta had talked to at least three witnesses to the death of my son and his mother. He acted as if he already knew.

"She was thinking blackmail," I added. "She didn't know I knew about my wife's affair."

"You didn't," he said, with a faint trace of triumph in his voice.

I ignored him. "Maybe that's why she called me back from New Orleans with the fax about Weisz's mother," I said. "With Leo dead, any chance she had of getting something more out of him had dried up. Maybe she was coming after me."

But that wasn't why she'd contacted me, I knew. She was a conniving shit, but when she was spewing her fury not an hour ago, she'd told me something that made sense.

Ruthie, she said, cut off the flow of funds. Ruthie trapped her own brother in IRS hell.

Which is why she didn't want me talking to Loretta. Ruthie knew Loretta might resurface after Leo's death.

Ruthie could easily discredit any charges Loretta made.

But not if they were made by her brother's good friend.

I had nothing to gain, either way, if the truth about the collapse of Big Chief's was known.

Apparently, Ruthie Mallard did.

"You're not going anywhere for the weekend," Twist said.

"If that's a question, I'll tell you it's a little late for plans."

"And it's not a question?"

"I'm going to Tahiti."

I went toward the bar's green door to find out how Diddio was holding up.

"She's got a lot of stamina, Dad. A big heart, big lungs. She can go for hours and hours."

An old El Dorado bounced along Harrison, then stopped to permit the elderly couple inside to examine neither Bella nor me, but to point to Beagle, who sat proudly if inattentively on the hot concrete, my daughter at the other end of the red leash.

"You're an expert on basset hounds now?" I asked.

"Yes."

Bella was on a good roll. Following my call to Daniel's, she came home to find my former agent had left a message. "Er, Terry? Didn't know you were, er, working on a novel, Terry," Morrie said to the answering tape.

A shy man in his mid-30s, Morrie Steiner had a soft voice, and he spoke in an awkward, tentative manner, as if he always feared he might have to retract what he'd just said. Declarative sentences often ended as questions, making him sound like an eager-to-please teenage girl, or Canadian.

"Didn't know, actually, you were, er, working at all. I had some comments—here and there, here and . . . But I would say you have a winner here? What I would call a real winner? So . . ." And so on.

When I entered the house, she said, "Your agent thinks *you* wrote my book. You can tell everybody you did."

"I didn't. I told you from the start that it sounded like a grown-up wrote it."

"I know, but— Hey, you've got blood on you. Whose?"

"Loretta Jones," I said, as I scrubbed my hand in the sink. "Leo's ex."

"Did you kill her?"

"Maybe I tried to save her, Bella."

"Yeah, maybe," she said cynically.

"Ouch. Teenage sarcasm. And completely unexpected."

"I am *not* predictable," she said.

I draped the damp towel on her head as I passed by.

Now, on Harrison, the old couple moved on, their Sunday drive enriched by Beagle's boastful air of indifference. Bella told me she was going to take her dog to see Marcus and "whoever, you know, shows up." Daniel, she reminded us, was having his customary Sunday meal with his family.

I couldn't tell her I already knew about her Seaport plans.

"When am I going to meet this Marcus?" I asked her.

She cast an uneasy glance at Beagle, who provided no cover, no misdirection.

I added, "None of your other friends are seniors, are they?"

"I've got friends who are seniors," she said, a bit defensively. "I'll be the only sophomore on Varsity."

"OK," I said. I'd forgotten about Whitman's basketball team. But that didn't explain why I'd never met Marcus.

"What time do you want me home?" she asked. "Eleven, all right?"

I couldn't think of a reason to say no. Loretta was in St. Vincent's, and she'd be there for a couple of days. Weisz had returned to the ether. It was the Sunday of Labor Day weekend—there was probably some sort of concert at the Seaport. All the electronic dance stuff she enjoys.

We had to talk, I knew. But it could wait.

Until I knew what to tell her.

"Call me, and Bella, don't make Beagle walk to the Seaport and back."

"I won't— I didn't say I was going to the Seaport."

"That's where you always meet Marcus, isn't it?" I said, recovering.

"Not always. No."

"Excuse me for assuming. Where are you meeting him?"

"At the Seaport."

I dug into my khakis for my thin roll of bills.

"I don't need money," she said. "I got some left over from shopping."

"How much is some?"

"All of it?" she said uncomfortably. "I used the checks."

There would be time to review our finances later. If all was going to go as planned, Diddio was waiting to debrief me at Brothers Bar-B-Que on Varick and, while I talked to him, I'd scarf down some chicken-fried chicken before heading over to the Film Forum for the revival of De Sica's *La Ciociara*. I needed to clear out my head— losing myself in a great movie would do it.

"Come on," I said. "Let's find Beagle a cab."

She handed me the leash. "It's not fair to her," she said. "She'll get tired, all day in the sun and stuff."

"That's very good, Bella. Very thoughtful."

She started to head east toward the other side of the island.

"Dad, don't forget to bring home some popcorn."

As a very little kid, Bella pronounced the Film Forum's popcorn the best in the city. She did so with characteristic certitude. So much of it, in fact, that I couldn't bring myself to tell her she probably needed to go to more than two theaters before making such a declaration.

"Bella, when I walk in, they'll ask, 'Where's Gabriella?' and when I leave they'll put the bag in my hand."

"Yeah, a lot of people know me."

"I got spies everywhere."

She scowled at me as I gave her a big, fat, annoying grin.

The overhead fans, propelled by an intricate system of wobbling belts, gave little in the way of relief from the afternoon heat, and the restaurant's open windows only served to let in city noise: the rattle of chassis as cars thudded into potholes; the squeal of brakes when a cabbie decided to take his taxi across five lanes to nab a fare; the punch and puck of whirring blades as helicopters circled lower Manhattan; and the laughter of scampering kids pouring in and out of the Carmine Rec Center. With the scent of summer heat, auto fumes, even the chlorine from the center's pool, I could barely smell the tangy barbecue sauce.

"I'm telling you, man, I was, you know, like, checking out every third word that came out of my mouth."

Diddio, who said he wasn't hungry, had ordered two portions of collard greens, and now he was reaching across for his third slice of my moist chicken.

I pushed the plate toward him.

"Thanks, T," he said as he dunked the chicken into the pool of white gravy on the mashed potatoes.

I waited, trying not to grimace. Diddio had the table manners of a Rahway lifer just sprung from solitary.

"D, are you sure?"

He nodded as he chewed, sprinkled salt on the already salty chicken. "Oh yeah. You shot her. Gun was in the jukebox. She was getting ready to shoot me. Blah-blah-blah and hi-de-ho. You know."

"Why?"

"Huh?"

"Why did she want to shoot you?"

He gulped down the mouthful, sucked on his teeth. "They didn't ask me that."

"Yeah, but if they do . . ." It occurred to me that Loretta might get one of the guys from the First to talk to D, press him.

Deeply concerned, at least for the moment, he hesitated, then asked, "What did you say?"

"I said she was angry that he gave you the bar."

"Yeah," he cheered, slapping the table with his palm. "I like it *and* I like it."

I took a sip of fizzy seltzer.

"D, you got a piece of collard green . . ." I pointed in vain. "No, over, over. *Over.* Right, good."

"Thanks." He wiped his finger on a paper napkin.

I handed him the letter from Miles Kendricks Toler.

"What's this?"

"Probably be easier if you open it, D."

He put the sealed envelope on the yellow Formica and flicked it back toward me. "You."

I tore the top, then scanned the sheet, which was signed by a Langston Toler, representing Interstate Properties, current owner of The Red Curry, where Leo's Big Chief's once stood.

"What?" he asked, inching off his seat.

"Blah-blah-blah and hi-de-ho."

"You funny, Terry."

I translated the terse, two-paragraph letter from intimidating legalese into English. In essence, it said, Not so fast. We want to talk to you about who really owns the Tilt.

I told D.

"Is that all? That ain't nothing. Leo says yes. Period." He took a big guzzle of his Diet Coke.

"D, do you have a lawyer?" I asked.

"Nope." He had an ice cube in his mouth.

"You'd better get one," I told him as I shook the letter at him.

"Julie."

"Huh?"

"She's my lawyer. Julie."

"Have you told her yet?"

He said no. "I just thought of it. Julie."

I was going to tell him he needed someone who was expert in property, in probate. Toler's letter was a challenge to Leo's right to pass on the Tilt to him.

But Julie would find D the kind of lawyer he needed.

"She don't tell you everything, does she?"

"You mean about her cases? No," I replied.

"Good. 'Cause I—"

"D, what is this need for secrecy? I mean, all of a sudden, you don't want me to know what's what with you? Like, where were you this past week? You disappeared."

"No, T, man," he said quickly, seriously. "Disappeared? No. I was . . . I've been thinking, that's all. A lot. Every since Leo, you know . . ."

"Died."

"Leo died," he nodded. "Here, in New Orleans, here . . . Just thinking."

"And?"

"Basically, I got to grow up. I mean, I'll be forty in about five years."

"Three," I said.

"Right. Wow." Then he said, "Anyway, I got to start doing things for myself."

"D, being self-sufficient—"

"Yeah, I know I am, but only I'm living, you know, like, *small*. Hand-to-mouth. Hustling for chump change."

D once told me he had never earned more than $32,000 in a year, adding that he was grateful he didn't have to pay for music, which was his love and, along with pot, his vice.

"And I can't help you?" I asked.

"No, that's not— I mean, of course and everything," he replied. "I ain't freezing you out, T. Maybe I want to see if I can do it myself."

"Do what?"

"The Tilt," he said as he leaned forward, his long hair rushing onto his shoulders.

I still had the letter in my hand. "You're going to have to fight to keep it."

He hesitated, then he said, "OK. I'll fight. I want it. I'm going to fix it up, make it a place for musicians to hang out."

"Really." So that's the plan he cooked up while he was gone.

"You know what I'm going to do, man? Serve tea."

"Tea."

"All sorts of different kinds of tea. Hot, cold, with lemon, milk. You know."

"Sounds interesting," I said.

"Brainstorm," he replied. "It'll be very cool."

"What'll you call it? In the 1700s, there was a private water supply known as the Tea Water Pump over on Chatham and—"

"I'm calling it Leo's, man."

Tears, and as the lights went up in the pocket-sized theater after Cesira and her daughter Rosetta reconcile, I realized my adrenaline had returned from a boil to its customary steady flow. But tired, feeling vaguely victorious, clearly defeated and now confronted by the bittersweet triumph of humanity in the face of base brutality courtesy of De Sica, Zavattini and Loren, I knew I needed to walk, to think, to reconcile my thoughts.

I didn't know what to tell Bella because I hadn't confronted it myself. And it wasn't until I reached Brooklyn Heights, bag of popcorn in my hand, that I found the courage to look it in the eye.

"Cosmopolitan, elegant, European," Loretta said. "He was not you."

Nor will I ever be any of those things.

Is that want Marina wanted?

Would a woman who grew up in the countryside in the south of Italy, the daughter of a fisherman and a tired, frail woman who worked in an olive grove, seek a man who was cosmopolitan? Elegant?

From Bari, Rome, Florence, Venice, Milan?

Doesn't explain the guy from Narrow's Gate, New Jersey, does it?

Marina wanted to return to Italy. She'd hinted many times. I answered as any American would:

"It's better for the children here," I'd say. "Better opportunities."

Once she replied, "Yes, if I return to Foggia, *sí. Naturalmente.* But if they were to live in Milano, where there is opportunity . . ."

She said if *they* were to live in Milan. Not if *we* were to live there.

Where did she go when we were in Milan?

Bella and I were nudged aside; did we mind? No. As her agent said, this show had to, just *had to,* succeed if Marina Fiorentino were to attract the international clientele her work deserved.

"Shoo, shoo, Terry," said Judy Henley Harper, as she scampered around the gallery, the sleeves of her oversized electric-pink silk blouse rolled above her elbows. "Take your little angel, your *bellisima*— is that right? I could never . . . Oh well. Your wife and I can manage. We *are* managing. Bye. Bye-bye."

Her mother otherwise occupied, Little Bella sat on my shoulders when we visited the Church of Santa Maria delle Grazie and saw da Vinci's *The Last Supper.* As I pushed her along in her stroller, we went to the Biblioteca Ambrosiana, Teatro alla Scala (closed; damn it), the Palazzo di Brera. Bella was giddy with laughter, happy to be in the syrupy rays of the sun, happy to be with her dad, eating merrily in the outdoor *trattoria* (how the waiters doted on her; *"Ecco, bella bambina, un biscotto per te"*), running on chubby legs across the sparse and spotty lawns of the Triennale.

Where was her mother?

Still with Judy at the gallery, preparing for the show?

Her triumphant return to Italy.

"I cannot be certain everyone will understand," she said late one night at the Soperga, as she paced nervously, clenching her hands together, while Bella slept, not on the pull-out in our room, but in the center of our queen-size bed.

"Quality will out, Marina," I said, as I drank Apollinaris from the bottle. "Please, be confident. Your work is superb."

Suddenly, unexpectedly, she stopped and glowered at me. "And what do you know? Really. What?"

Me? Sitting there in my jeans, old T-shirt, comfortable sneakers, sipping sparkling water? I know nothing.

I am the traveling companion, the struggling writer, the jock, the baby-sitter, the American.

I waited, but no apology came, no acknowledgment.

I mean, I could understand that she was tense before a major show . . .

I threw on my sweater and went for a walk.

Looking up from his *Corriere della Sera,* the concierge seemed surprised, concerned as I crossed the lobby. "*Signore,* it is quite late."

"*Grazie,*" I said, and pointed to my wristwatch, to the side of my head.

Surrounded by all that seemed familiar—concrete, blacktop, Fords and Volvos parked under spindly city trees, shuttered bars, neighborhood restaurants with cane chairs upturned on tables, advertisements for Coke, Nestlé chocolates, Marlboro, the *International Herald Tribune*—I knew I was thoroughly out of place, by birthright, by nature, by temperament and, thus, under a blanket of stars in the northern Italian sky, I was alone.

Except for the baby who slept peacefully on the blue floral spread that lay on the big, soft bed.

I kept walking, thinking, brooding.

Anger soon turned to regret, regret to a need for contemplation, investigation.

I walked all the way to the Piazza del Duomo, where I sat on a wooden bench until the *polizia* encouraged me to leave.

I thought about her question, and all that it implied.

About her, I really did know nothing. Or, at most, very little.

What I knew were not facts. They were the illusions of love.

So I sat and thought about her world, where she had come from, where she wanted to go.

And I asked myself an inevitable question: How did she end up with me?

I saw her at MoMA, beautiful as she stood alone beyond the convivial chatter of the reception, and I approached her and, within weeks, to my surprise and infinite joy, we declared that we were in love, and she would paint and I would write and everything would be all it could.

It can happen like that. Everything just so.

Inexplicably, it builds, it builds, it builds . . .

Even if it's wrong from the start.

So then, as I stared at the Duomo, at the pecking pigeons in the square, at the sanitation workers and their worn and tattered brooms, with my fingers interlocked behind my head, my mop of black hair, I asked myself a question that only hours ago would've seemed outrageous as it formed in my mind:

Would Marina have married me had she not been pregnant with Bella?

See, when you ask a question like that you are acknowledging alternate realities, other possibilities. You are creating new worlds, past and future.

One is a new world where there is merely the illusion of true love.

But was it an illusion? I mean, we loved each other, never quarreled, respected each other, shared interests, had similar perspectives.

A woman from Foggia, an accomplished artist, and a boy from Narrow's Gate, an ex-jock, an accomplished nothing, had the same point of view?

Oh yeah. Sure.

I shook my head. As I returned to the walkway of the Brooklyn Bridge, embarrassed by my own stupidity, my own naïveté, I squirmed, shivered as, far below, brown water slapped the brick towers.

Under the late afternoon sun, I went along Chambers, struggling to pull myself away from a hotel in Milan, the Piazza del Duomo; away from outrageous questions and alternate worlds.

True love? What a chump.

I returned home.

Beagle came to the door and, seeing it was me, went back to the sofa in the empty living room.

I needed someplace to hide, and I had nowhere to go. The place I had run to for the past five years, the ideal world where I lived with the perfect wife, had been shattered.

Where do I belong?

I mean, do I even have some kind of *utility?*

Does Bella need me now?

After five years without me, she's learned to live on her own. What was it Harteveld once said? "There's no such thing, Terry, as an occasional dad."

"I'll be there when she needs me, Elizabeth."

Harteveld replied, "How will you know?"

I needed to find some sort of closure, some way to move ahead.

Doing so was the only way to start making up for lost time.

By the time I remembered that Addison had phoned, it was already hours after midnight and I was in bed. Down the hall, Bella slept soundly, after ousting Beagle long ago.

"She *snores,*" she complained, rubbing her eyes as she slouched into the living room.

I was watching TV, a not-half-bad bio of Artur Rubinstein. Cool grainy black-and-white footage, plenty of music.

"Dad, make her stay with you," Bella whined. She wore an old

Marquette T-shirt of mine over men's boxers she'd ordered online. On the baggy shorts, big, bright goldfish swam happily, bubbles floating from their grinning mouths. The dog, who'd followed her downstairs, looked at Bella, at me, Bella, off into the distance, me.

"Beagle, stay," I said, as Rubinstein offered a charmingly delicate Chopin Nocturne, Op. 15, No. 2.

Bella turned and dashed toward the stairs, leaving behind the strawberry scent of her shampoo.

Beagle jumped onto the chair next to the sofa and nestled in.

Now, as I stared at the ceiling, I wondered if the dog was in the same spot, snoring, dreaming of overturned garbage cans, chasing rabbits across a green glen, walking with Coceau along Riverside Park.

I was wondering about a lot of things as I turned, tossed, wriggled in the dark. My mind raced, senselessly.

I hadn't come within a hundred miles of finding closure, and I started hating the word, if not the concept.

Tracking down the guy she was with and kick his cosmopolitan ass? Satisfying, but not very productive in the long run.

Purge my memories? Not possible, and I had already discarded too much of what was mine.

Start working with Harteveld and get my head on straight? Now, that might work . . .

The sounds of the house toyed with me: water, creaking boards, windows as they deflected a light breeze off the Hudson, the central air as it sighed, shut down.

Thoughts of Bella: "Thanks," she said when I handed her the bag of popcorn. Chomp. "Still the best," she added, walking away.

Julie.

Such a sweetheart.

When she called tonight, speaking soft, tenderly, speaking of us, I was thinking, Please, Julie, please don't say "I love you."

Love is anguish, betrayal, abandonment.

Julie, let's not destroy this good thing.

Now, 3:36. I went into the bathroom, I stared at my face in the mirror, tiny scars, crooked nose, forehead red from too much August sun.

Where can I go?

I need someplace where my thoughts won't find me. A place that would give me peace, if only for a while.

Art. Yes, good. In art, there are so many places to hide.

For instance, the Rubinstein bio.

I climbed back into the bed, jostled the pillow, tugged on the top sheet until it covered me.

Even before he came to America, Rubinstein was famous: the Chopin scherzos, the nocturnes.

He played with fire, imagining each note, never repeating himself, approaching the music as if he'd never seen it before and, thus, had to consider every passage, every phrase.

He was the anti-anti-Romantic, bringing not only an element of daring to his performances, but charm, personality.

What I ought to do, I thought, is listen to a Chopin nocturne, a peaceful piece of piano music that is quietly expressive—

I shot up in bed as if I'd been jolted by a surge of raw electricity.

Weisz. *Weisz.*

Christ. It's Labor Day.

I hustled out of bed, went to my closet, unfolded a pair of jeans.

I knew where he was.

Harteveld is right. Weisz, untethered, cannot go to his familiar touchstones—his mother's house, the family mausoleum, wolf dens at New York City zoos.

But he can go to his music.

Art. Where there are so many places to hide.

Christ, I not only knew where he was, I knew what he'd be playing.

The poor man. Poor, haunted man.

18

I came out of the 66th Street station and crossed Broadway. At 4:30 A.M., I had the rarest of New York experiences: In the silver darkness before dawn, I looked south, north, and I saw no one on the wide street, not a living soul. Not a lonely cabbie cruising for a fare, a cop on the beat or a delivery driver looking to unload his morning newspapers. On the street, beneath soaring buildings, no one but me, in jeans, sneakers, *Slaughter at Kinmel Hall* in the pouch of my black hooded sweatshirt.

On 66th, there were two publicly accessible entrances to Alice Tully Hall, the smallest theater in the Lincoln Center complex—the loading bay and, farther west, the artists' entrance. Weisz, I told myself, probably knew of a few other ways into the underground concert hall, through sewer lines, drainpipes and tunnels known only to the homeless seeking shelter or solitude. If Weisz was doing what I thought, I had no choice but to smuggle myself in through one of the entrances.

Before I went west, I walked over to the front entrance of the hall, tucked beneath the steps to the Juilliard School, and yanked on the front door's copper handles. Locked.

Crazy to think Raymond Montgomery Weisz, son of Harold Arnett Weisz and Eleanor Montgomery Weisz, would have a key, no?

As I headed toward Amsterdam, walking along the building's tainted white marble, I found the loading bay on 66th no more promising. Its steel gate was clamped tight to the sidewalk, and the lights inside the artists' entrance were turned off and the glass doors were locked.

I continued west and found a receiving dock for the Juilliard School, directly across from Balducci's. A deep bay, it had a security booth on the platform to my left, and there was someone inside it— the flicker of lights suggested the guard was watching TV. I couldn't tell for sure: The view to the booth was obscured by Dumpsters filled with packing crates, cardboard and other bulky trash.

Which meant he couldn't see me.

I ducked down, moved inside toward the dock, slithered onto the platform, passing under a rumpled American flag, and crawled to the open door.

I was inside Juilliard, standing near a freight elevator, a hand truck. Now I needed to make my way to Alice Tully Hall.

Dusting my hands on my jeans, I headed down a dimly lit corridor, its walls an odd mustard yellow. I followed the corridor with my fingers on the cinderblock walls for 30 feet or so until I came to a fork: In front of me, a framed poster of Leonard Bernstein, conducting with typically outsized energy; to my right, a glass door that, with a gentle tug on the handle, I found was locked; and to my left, a double door, steel, painted a dark, military green. It had no handle, so I leaned my palms against it. The door moved; as I gently rocked it, the deadbolt slipped from its worn port.

Moving cautiously, I stepped into what I assumed was a floor above

Alice Tully Hall and continued along a dark, musty corridor until I came to another portal, a glass door that was unlocked. It led to a concrete stairwell. I went to my left, passing vertical water pipes and a fire extinguisher, and headed downstairs.

Aided by a single red lightbulb on each of the two landings, I made my way down, hand on the painted steel banister, to a door that I opened carefully, carefully, until I lost the fusty scent of confinement and felt the warmer air of the hall, until I had the sensation of entering a larger space. I stepped into the darkness, one small step, another step, and I heard what I had expected to—the shimmering, romantic melody of Rachmaninoff.

I was in the wings of the hall's wide stage.

Lit by a single flashlight, which he'd placed on the low end of the keyboard, Weisz was at the concert grand he'd rolled to center stage, and he was well into the second movement of the Russian's Piano Concerto No. 2 in C Minor, Op. 18.

Of course. In September 1982, two years after her son's debut at Carnegie Hall's 268-seat Weill Recital Hall, Eleanor Montgomery Weisz rented Alice Tully Hall and presented her Raymond, who performed two solo works—the *andante dolce* from Prokofiev's Eighth Piano Sonata and Liszt's Mephisto Waltz No.1—and then, with the New York Philharmonic Orchestra, the Rachmaninoff. A ludicrous vanity: Thirteen-year-old Raymond was not ready, technically or emotionally. The repertoire was too ambitious for even most seasoned pianists, and the orchestra was much too overpowering in the hall, which holds about 1,100 people. Confronted with the somber muscularity of Prokofiev, the complexity of Liszt, the majesty of Rachmaninoff, and challenged by the brawn and command of the orchestra, Raymond was lost, though he struggled valiantly and, according to the *Times,* reconfirmed his promise in the face of overwhelming obstacles. He sobbed during the polite ovation he received from the invited guests.

Immediately thereafter, Mrs. Weisz was scalded, both in the media and in the fur-and-fudge salons of the Upper West Side.

Poor Raymond. Such a gentle soul.

His father would *never* have permitted this.

Two nights later, he vanished. Or, as the *Post* put it, WHIZ BOY GOES AWOL.

He turned up at the Bronx Zoo.

Imagine what the headline writers at the tabloid did with that.

I slowly inched back and, careful not to ruffle the heavy curtains, felt my way to the stairs that led down to the auditorium.

Weisz sat in his familiar position—hunched over the keyboard, his hands seemingly extending not from arms, but from his torso.

He'd cut his red hair, crudely and close to his scalp, and he was wearing a filthy, once-white T-shirt, tattered khakis and, if I could see in the dim light below the keyboard, torn sneakers.

And as my eyes adjusted to the shadows beyond the spot he'd created, I saw on the right thigh of his pants an uneven splotch of blood. He had crammed something—old newspapers, a rag—under the frayed material to stem the flow.

I had nicked him in Woodlawn Cemetery, grazing him with a bullet from the nine.

Four inches to the left and the shot would've taken him down.

Six inches to the left, sixteen inches higher, and I would've shattered his spine.

He'd have been on the cold ground in the empty cemetery, and I would've had him, to do to him what I'd wanted to for five long years, before I knew what had really happened on the platform, as my son tumbled onto the tracks.

I shook my head at the thought, as I eased into a seat in the fourth row, stage left, directly below the boxes.

I would've killed an innocent man, a tortured soul I now wanted to help, as he had tried to help my Davy.

Weisz was playing magnificently, moving with confidence through the movement's main theme.

As I stayed in the shadows, I asked myself if he could hear the woodwinds, as they repeated the triplet figure he'd played earlier. Did he hear the tender, arching sweep of the strings?

Weisz seemed hypnotized, as he raised his head, his eyes closed as he played another moody passage.

Suddenly, he hunched over again and, after creating a cascading flurry of delicate notes, he stopped, as Rachmaninoff had prescribed. And then Weisz issued a furious eruption in the mid-range, followed by a confident and dazzling exploration with his right hand that dwindled into regal single notes that recalled the theme.

He began to rock and sway as he continued to play gracefully, sensually. Then he offered rich chords in a steady tempo, again, again, with the slightest variations, raising, lowering, toying, leading.

And then, with clearly articulated single notes, he brought the adagio to its splendidly logical and thoroughly satisfying end.

I resisted the temptation to applaud.

Weisz hesitated as if suspended between moments. Stooped over the keyboard, his breathing labored, his concentration still in command, he could not move.

I shifted quietly along the row of seats, edging closer to the center row of the auditorium.

Then Weisz raised up on the bench, slowly, until he attained a formal posture.

He turned to face the auditorium and stood, his right hand on the piano's black lacquered case.

And he started to stammer and cry.

"I can do better, Mother," he said, staring into the blackness. "Please let me try to do better."

He came forward, leaving the shallow spot his flashlight cast.

"Mother?"

Christ.

"Mother, please."

I stood.

"Raymond," I said, "it was magnificent."

He was perhaps 40 feet from me, this man I'd sought for five years. The Madman, the cruel, savage specter who I'd thought emerged from the mist only to take my wife and son from me—he was standing in front of me, and we were alone. Weisz, the object of a hatred so raw, so intense, that it had overwhelmed me, almost consumed me.

He was right there.

I saw his outline, backlit by the dull light's reflection. He tilted his head.

"Yes," he said deliberately, softly, in response to my comment, "but is it perfection?"

He ran the back of his hand under his eye.

"It was superb, Raymond," I said as I stepped into the aisle.

"I'll do it again," he replied, nodding, "yes."

As he backed toward the piano, I proceeded to the lip of the stage and watched as he reentered the light and sat, finding his ideal place on the bench.

I saw the blood on his pants.

He stared at the piano's keys, as he attempted to summon his formidable focus. His body stiffened.

"Raymond," I said. "You can relax now. You've done it."

He blinked in confusion, frowned and, with a mechanical rigidity, turned toward me.

Then he lifted the flashlight and shined it on me.

His eyes grew wide.

And, in less than an instant, he sprang off the bench and, dropping the flashlight, darted behind the piano and dashed toward the wings.

I leapt onto the stage, grabbed the light and followed.

I heard a door rattle, bang.

Weisz was racing upstairs.

I followed him as he sprinted past the steel doors, down the mustard-colored corridor and out onto the Juilliard loading dock. Despite the wound, he ran furiously.

The startled guard was shouting when I barreled into him, losing the flashlight. The burly guard fell, I tumbled over him and then scrambled off the platform and ran onto 66th Street.

Weisz was running east, his threadbare sneakers flapping on the bulging tar as he blew past Tower Records.

I was going to catch him. Despite the wound to his leg, he was quick, but we were running in a straight path, with no obstacles in our way. By the time he reached Broadway, I was no more than 10 feet behind him.

He bolted toward the entrance to the subway station.

By the time I reached the station, he was on his knees at the bottom of the steps: He'd jumped. And now, with alarming grace, he bounded over the turnstiles.

Ignoring the shouts of the wiry old man in the token booth, I went over the turnstile too. The paperback book fell out of my sweatshirt pouch and skidded across the concrete platform.

Weisz was down on the tracks, darting around pillars, leaping to avoid the hot charge of the third rails.

"Raymond," I shouted.

My voice rang through the empty station.

Backlit now by the lights on the uptown side, Weisz stopped, turned. He glared at me through wild eyes.

I held up my hands.

"I want to talk. Please," I shouted. "I know you didn't—"

He let out a loud, gruesome howl and he started scurrying north along the center track, moving toward utter darkness.

I slid down off the platform. Running awkwardly, sloshing through puddles and grime, trying to keep my feet on the wooden ties, I was well behind him now and saw I couldn't keep up. But I kept on.

"Raymond," I screamed. "I can help you."

To my surprise, he stopped, stared at me and he again let loose another guttural yowl.

When he was done, Weisz darted to his left, crossed the tracks I was on and vaulted back onto the platform, charging in my direction.

I tried to do the same, but instead caught my knee, tumbled back into the mire, then rolled onto the platform just as Weisz was racing by me.

I stuck out my arm, jamming it between his legs.

As he fell, I scrambled to my feet and dove on top of him.

My chest and stomach were hard on his scrawny back. My full weight held him down.

He smelled of piss, iodine, sweat, insanity.

Dirt was caked on the back of his neck, on his scalp.

He was all bone. Sick scent and bone.

"Raymond, listen," I said as I gasped for my breath.

He growled and tried to wrestle free.

I scampered, shifted and put my knee into the small of his back.

"Raymond, I do *not* want to hurt you."

A deep, rumbling purr.

"I will *not* hurt you."

He made not a sound.

"Raymond, listen. I know you didn't do it."

He turned his head to the side.

"Mother is my angel," he said. "Mother is."

And then I heard the train, behind me, in the distance.

"Let me get you to a doctor," I said anxiously.

I wanted to hold him down, keep him still. The man in the booth had called the cops, I was sure of that. I was going to pin down Weisz until they arrived.

And I was going to tell them to help him. He was all alone and he needed help.

"You're safe now, Raymond," I said.

I was lying on the platform, no more than 10 feet from where my son died, my wife died.

He tried to help them.

Despite the fierce grip of his debilitating mania, Weisz tried to do what was right.

"Raymond. There is no one to threaten you now," I whispered, drawing close to his dirt-crusted ear. "Let me help you."

"Mother is my angel," he muttered quickly, each word a staccato burst. "Father's gone and mother is my angel."

"Oh, Raymond. You don't—"

He snapped his leg behind me and caught me hard with his heel.

As I pitched forward, he wriggled free and quickly jumped off the platform.

And he looked down the track at the incoming train, staring hard at its white light.

I turned. The train appeared to be about 100 feet away and it was bearing down on him.

"Raymond, please."

He spun toward me. "I know you. I know you. Your house, your daughter, your house, your baby." He repeated what he'd said, in a rapid-fire, single-word spurt. "Yes. Your baby. Your house. You, you. I know you."

He danced in place, shifting side to side.

"No, Raymond. You don't. Please."

"Mother told me. Mother said, Mother said."

"Raymond, let me help you."

We both glanced toward the train.

He roared at it.

"Please." I held out my hand, desperately. "I promise to help you."

The engineer punched the train's klaxon and the blast of sound hit us. Then I heard the harsh screech of brakes, metal on metal. I saw sparks, smelled the burning.

Despite the rattling sound of the brakes, the train kept coming, squealing, sliding on the shining tracks.

I raised my hands, once again showing Weisz my empty palms.

"I'm sorry, Raymond," I said. "Let me make it up to you."

"Oh no. No, no," he replied as he fidgeted frantically.

I backed away to give him room. "Come up here, Raymond. Come on."

The train rushed toward him, orange embers, metallic squeals.

"Raymond, please," I screamed over the din. "You can be free, Raymond. You *are* free."

Weisz suddenly sagged and stared at me with a look of total resignation, of bottomless misery.

I stepped toward him, stretched out my hand.

"All I have seen," he uttered.

He turned and started to run toward the skidding, sliding train.

I lunged and grabbed the back of his flimsy shirt, and I tried to pull him toward me.

I heard the sound of impact, a dull, sickening thud, despite the ugly metallic bellow of the brakes. Then I felt the rush of the train as it barreled by me.

It stopped finally, its last car about 15 feet beyond the platform.

Weisz's blood had splattered onto my face, shoulder.

19

I answered their questions, but only after they let me go up into the fresh air. As I wiped the blood off my cheek, one of the uniforms handed me a cold bottle of Poland Spring water and I drank it, desperately, as the walkie-talkie clipped to his collar squawked unintelligibly.

"Thanks," I said, as I ran the back of my hand across my moist lips.

He nodded indifferently and tossed the empty bottle into a trash can.

I hadn't processed it all yet, but I was starting to feel a bit better, starting to get my feet under me again. Maybe it was the signs of life around me—in the violet light of morning, Midtown was beginning to wake up. Some sort of early run had been planned for Central Park, and men and women in shorts and T-shirts were milling on the island between Columbus and Broadway, stretching as they waited for friends to join them. The pudgy man in a turban at the newsstand over by Tower was stacking his papers, and an elderly couple walked their fussy little dog. The Disney Store was getting its windows washed for the holiday crush.

Then I saw a blue-and-white, siren on, lights whirling, rumbling toward us down Broadway. It crossed 66th and skidded to a jarring halt, next to the squat EMT truck.

Rey Twist jumped out of the passenger's side and, eyes pinched in fury, raced toward me.

Barreling between the two cops, he grabbed me and slammed me against the thick green rail of the subway entrance.

"You killed him," he screamed as he held me by the sweatshirt's shoulders. "You fuckin' prick. You finally killed the poor bastard."

He tried to catch me with a short right, but I got my hands up in front of my face.

The stunned uniformed cops jumped into action, and then his partner Sanders came up and grabbed Twist from behind, pulled him away.

Twist spit as he shouted. "You fucker. I'm going to nail your ass."

The wiry old guy in the token booth scurried toward the furious Twist. "You got it all wrong," he shouted frantically.

One of the uniforms blocked the token vendor's path.

Eyes wide, face ashen, the old man shuddered. "Second time I seen something like this," he said before he went off to return to the ugly scene below Broadway.

Sanders kept struggling to hold back Twist. "Rey," he said urgently. "Rey."

Twist shoved him too.

"Come again," I said, "and I'll snap your neck, you little shit."

Twist dove at me.

But the uniformed cops got between us.

Sanders kept his hand on my chest and I stayed against the railing.

"You hounded him and finally got him, prick," Twist shouted as he tried to wrestle free from the other cops' grips. "And now you're gonna get me."

Suddenly, Twist stopped spewing, and I felt a strong hand on my shoulder.

I turned.

"Come on, Terry," Luther Addison said calmly, directly. He nodded at Sanders, at the other cops who held me. They let me go.

"Come on."

I squeezed past one of the cops to follow Addison.

Addison walked me away from the crowd, his hand on my elbow.

"Did somebody look you over?" he asked, nodding toward the whirling lights of the EMT truck.

I shook my head. "I'm all right."

He looked past me, back toward the glass-encased elevator on Broadway. I turned to follow his gaze.

They were bringing up Weisz on a gurney, an IV line hooked into his left arm. His right arm was gone, I was sure of that, and his right leg had been torn off at the knee. I'd gotten him away from the train, but not before it slammed into his body, not before severe, irreparable damage had been done.

As I lay on the platform, his blood on my face, his shirt in my hand, I'd thought I had lost him, that he had been crushed by the rushing train.

Then I heard him moan behind me, and I turned over to see the carnage where the right side of his body had been.

He passed out before he could speak, as I wrapped my belt around his right thigh.

Nothing could be done for his arm, now a gruesome stump. I didn't know what to do—blood was spurting from his shoulder. Finally, I stepped on him near his neck, but it didn't help. He was dying as I looked down at him. We were both helpless, and I wanted him to be all right.

Addison said, "Let's take a walk, Terry."

"Is he . . ."

"No, he's alive. But he's in a bad, bad way."

I nodded absently, but waited until they quickly rolled Weisz to the van.

Someone had dropped my copy of *Slaughter at Kinmel Hall* on the white sheet that covered his bloody torso.

I looked down at him as he passed us. He was out, his dirt-caked eyelids shut, his sore-covered head wobbling as the gurney's wheel found cracks in the sidewalk. But he had color in his gaunt face, and in the fog that surrounded my brain, I thought maybe they did get to him in time to save what was left of him.

As they hoisted him into the van, Addison tugged at me, pulling gently on the back of my sweatshirt.

"Terry?"

"That book is out of print," I said, as they sealed the doors shut behind Weisz.

"I'm sorry," the lieutenant said quickly. "I didn't get you."

I shook my head again. I couldn't believe what I'd just said.

"Let's walk," Addison said.

The ambulance siren split the morning silence.

We went to Amsterdam Avenue and back, slowly, without exchanging a word, and then Addison got them to let me wash up in Balducci's. A nice manager went and got me an orange, and I thanked her. I folded my bloody sweatshirt and carried it under my arm.

Then he brought me down into the station. Nothing much had changed. Someone had put up a lot of yellow tape, but the train was still off the end of the platform. Blood still coated the grimy concrete, and red footprints led to the turnstiles.

"What happened?" Addison asked.

"I tried to help him, but he ran. He was frightened."

Addison pointed to the security cameras on the station's ceiling. "That will confirm what the man in the booth said." He nodded.

The old token clerk watched as Addison led me to the edge of the platform.

"What happened before you got here?"

I told him all of it—my hunch, the Rachmaninoff, the flashlight, the agonizing appeals to his mother, the race along 66th. "'Mother is my angel,'" I repeated.

"How'd you know he'd be there?"

I said, "Harteveld told me he had nowhere else to go."

"So he went to his music."

"Where it all came apart," I nodded. "Maybe he wanted to see if he could get it back together again."

"He say anything?"

I repeated what Weisz had intended to be his last words.

"'All I have seen'?" Addison shrugged. "What the hell does that mean?"

"I don't know," I said. "He was howling, screaming and then, just when he knew the train was going to kill him, he said, 'All I have seen.' Clearly, lucidly."

Addison nodded. "His nightmares, maybe."

"Or what goes on in his mind."

Addison peered toward the train, then cautiously peeked at the tracks.

"It was right down there, wasn't it?" I asked. "Where you—"

"Yeah." He turned, stood next to me. "Impossible to forget, even after five years."

"I bet it is," I said.

Earlier, when the uniformed cops arrived, and then the EMT guys, I pulled back and looked at my bloody hands and Weisz's bloody clothes, and as I turned away from the grotesque carnage and stumbled toward the mud, filth and oily black water on the tracks below, I saw my son, I saw Marina. Which is why I sobbed on Amsterdam.

"Your nightmare," he said now.

A little man in a suit led a bunch of MTA cops into the station, and

I could overhear their conversation: This mess had to be cleaned up fast. The man in the ill-fitting suit, a Crown Prince of the Subway, couldn't afford to have the Broadway line backed up all the way to the Bronx. He wanted action and he wanted it now.

"I'll drive you home," Addison said.

As we walked toward the officious gaggle milling around the suit, I said to Addison, "Those security cameras, were they here five years ago?"

"They had some, but they weren't worth a damn back then." Then he asked, "Why?"

"I don't know," I said. "Maybe the guy she was—"

He put up his hand.

"Terry, this story is over," he said. "Let it go."

We went around the group and to the stairs.

"Listen to me, Terry. For once, listen. It's over. Let it go."

He let me lead and followed me up the stairs toward the pale morning light.

I sat on my front steps and took off my sneakers. Covered in blood, grease and rat piss, they had to go, so I left them by the curb. A silent wager: They'll be gone by 9 A.M. and it won't be a homeless guy who jacks them. It'll be somebody squeaking by on $250K. If they don't fit, he'll wash them, give them to Goodwill and take the write-off.

I kicked my jeans and soppy socks down into the laundry room, and tossed my sweat top down with them.

Beagle watched as I went upstairs and scrubbed my hands and face in the sink. And when that wasn't enough, when all that rubbing, digging and grinding wouldn't make it go away, I went into the shower and scrubbed some more, and then, hand on the overhead nozzle as steaming water flowed down my back, I couldn't keep it in any longer and started to sob again and I sobbed and hung my head, shook my head, until I was no longer certain what I was sobbing for.

Now it was over. I'd lost my son, my illusions, my mission. A sad, troubled man was critically injured, terribly damaged, and I had no idea what I was going to do.

I had to figure out who I was, and I didn't want to do that. I was afraid to know.

"You've got some hard days coming," Addison said as we passed the ass-end of the post office at 31st.

I stared at the countless bricks in the apartments on Ninth, at a shirtless man who rolled a flat tire along the west side of the street, at a doughnut shop where Smokey's used to be. My uncle Eddie took me to Smokey's. We had ribs, brisket, fries. He let me have a beer, though I was only 16. It was a good time, before I found out my uncle was scum.

I heard myself say, "Luther, how far back am I going to have to go?"

"I'm sorry," he said. "I didn't get you." We'd reached the north end of Greenwich.

"Never mind." I saw my home, the empty sky where the World Trade Center used to be.

Addison seemed to look for potholes to clobber.

When the rattling stopped, he said, "Giselle is going to call you. You and your Julie, we want you to come over. Just relax."

"Sounds good," I said.

As I reached for the car's door handle, he said, "Go slow, Terry. You can't hurry this."

I let the hot water wash away my tears. By the time I'd finished shaving, almost all the red was gone from my eyes.

She opened the door, peeked out.

"Dad, what?"

She'd been taken from a deep sleep.

Beagle looked up at her. As I knocked on the frame, the dog barked, scratched at the wood.

"We need to talk."

"'*Need to*'?" Her eyes were slits. "Now?"

"I think so," I told her. "We can do it while we walk Beagle."

"Am I in trouble?"

I shook my head.

"You walk Beagle," she said as she brushed long strands of hair off her face. "I'll meet you in a half-hour."

Thirty minutes later, she was at the kitchen table, the *Times*'s Arts section spread before her, three green rubber bands in perfect ovals on the varnished wood. A photo of Charlie Watts, standing calmly in front of his regal estate, drumsticks in hand, stared up at her.

We had no treats for the dog.

"You'd better get her some food," I said, as I removed her leash.

"We don't know what she likes," Bella replied, without peeling her eyes from newsprint. She was still in my old T-shirt, her goldfish boxers.

"Well, she's not too damned discriminating. I had to wait while she sniffed other dog's butts."

"Actually, Dad, there's a small sac around the anus that contains scents unique—"

"Thank you," I said, holding up my hand.

I found an old fortune cookie in the cabinet above the dish drainer. Without the little sliver of paper, it made a good snack for the dog.

As I sat, inching my chair away from the sink toward the table, I read the fortune, which told me that distant water won't put out a fire close at hand.

"Dad, if it's about Weisz and everything . . . It's not my thing, if you know what—"

"Bella, I was . . . I was with him today, Raymond Montgomery Weisz."

"With him?" She reached for one of the rubber bands and stretched it between her thumb and pinky. Frowning, she asked, "How?"

"I found him at Alice Tully Hall, playing," I said. "Then he jumped in front of a subway train."

She stopped toying with her rubber band. "You saw it?"

I nodded.

"What happened?"

"I got him out of there," I said, grabbing at the air. "But he was hurt bad." I ran my left hand down my right arm. I pointed at my right calf.

She let her eyes drop to the music reviews and the big ad for J&R. Then she said, "You helped him, Dad?"

"I tried."

She sat silent for a moment. "That's unexpected," she said finally, flatly.

"I told you that there was a possibility he didn't push Davy," I replied. "He didn't. He tried to save him. It was an accident, Bella. Davy's stroller rolled away and fell."

She bit the pad of her thumb. "How do you know?"

"Addison."

That seemed to satisfy her. Bella admired expertise in a good man.

"And Mama? Where was—"

"It happened really fast, Bella." I snapped my fingers. "There was a crowd on the platform, and the pillar was there, and people . . . She did everything she could."

She nodded. "So Weisz tried to save Davy and you tried to save him. I mean, you actually saved him."

Now I hesitated. "Something like that."

She shut the newspaper and asked me if I had my wallet on me.

I leaned to the side, pulled it out of my back pocket.

She took it, opened it up, dug in behind my driver's license.

"You won't need this anymore."

She held up my PI license.

"No, I guess not," I said.

She collected her rubber bands, snapped them back on her left wrist and pushed out of her chair. She took the flimsy license as she went to the stairs.

"Bella, listen," I began. "We should talk about what happened. About things . . . since Davy died, and your mother."

"Dad, there's nothing to talk about," she said, her bare foot on the first step. "It's all gone. All those days." She shrugged. "Sorry."

"And what will happen. We have to talk about that."

"Who knows, Dad, but it will happen."

"Bella, you can't be flip about this."

"I'm not being flip, Dad," she said evenly. "I've been kind of looking forward for a long time now."

"Just like that?"

"Not really," she replied, as she went up a step or two, her hand on the banister. "But it's OK. I'm not upset or mad or anything. Everybody is different. I know that."

"Bella, I'm not asking for forgiveness. I'm just saying that it had to be the way it was."

"No it didn't. Look, I said I'm not mad, so if you don't mind, I'd just rather let it go."

I leaned back, tilting my chair until it touched the sink, and I locked my hands behind my head.

"Is that what Dr. Harteveld thinks?"

"That I should let it go? No. But I made up my mind. I wish Mama and Davy didn't die. Really. But there's nothing I can do about it."

"Bella, why be the world's only fifteen-year-old stoic?"

She didn't reply.

I watched her, studied her face, and I realized it might be possible that she wasn't angry, that somehow during the past five years she'd learned how to move on without her mother, brother and, in many ways, without me.

And then I felt a different type of sadness, of loss.

"Are we still having the barbecue today?" she asked.

"Sure. It's a good idea, right?"

"Then I'll see you later, OK? I'm going back to sleep."

Beagle watched as Bella headed up the stairs, flapping my license against her bare thigh.

I said, "I'll see you then."

Her bedroom door opened, shut.

And that's how we left it, my daughter and me, even when Addison called at 5:30 A.M. to warn us of page one of the *Post,* which carried a grainy black-and-white photo of me, my head hung, streaks of blood and tears on my face, the lieutenant's comforting arm slung across my shoulder. The headline: VICTIM SAVES WHIZ BOY. The bold, italicized subhead: *RISKS LIFE WHERE WIFE, SON DIED.*

They could've done better. Must've had the B team working the holiday.

I might've told Addison it was going to happen—reporters from the four dailies and local radio and TV outlets tried to ruin our Labor Day fete, and they interrupted the delicate introduction of Diddio and shy Sheila Yannick, who we asked over for burgers, salad and beer.

"D, let me run this by you," I said, when he came to the door, full of his customary bounce, courtesy of Sinsemilla, Maui Wowee, White Widow, whatever's popular these days. He'd apparently put aside the fight we were going to have with Toler and Interstate, and seemed to have forgotten what I'd told him about Weisz.

"I was thinking of inviting Sheila Yannick to join us," I said.

"The cellist? You know her?"

"She lives right behind me," I said. "You've heard of her?"

"Sure, man, she's great," he replied. "She played with Cock Michaels, man."

"Move over, Yo-Yo."

"Don't be so cynical, T. There are four thousand cellists in New York City and she got the gig."

"Point taken," I nodded.

After a producer from CNN called, I took the kitchen phone off the hook and crammed the cell phone into my sock drawer. When Julie's cell rang—an industrious producer from *The Today Show*—we surrendered. I called Tom Coombs at the *Times* and gave him all I had. His piece, an exercise in controlled breathlessness, ran in Wednesday's Metro section. By then, everyone else in the press had forgotten about me.

"Says you're a hero, Dad," a harried Bella chimed as she scarfed down a cold Pop-Tart and a jelly jar of cranberry juice while scanning the *Times* and gathering her books, her laptop, her basketball stuff for the second day of school. "Why don't you let Morrie get you a book deal? You know, *I, Hero.* That kind of thing."

"No thanks," I replied.

Beagle and I watched the 15-year-old whirlwind in a sunburst T-shirt, white carpenter's jeans and flip-flops. Bella hated an early wake-up, but the girls' squad could only get the gym at sunrise. The boys' team, which went 5–19 last season, had it reserved for after school.

As she hoisted her backpack on her shoulder, nearly dislodging her fedora, Bella asked, "What *are* you going to do with yourself now?"

"Well, I've got to finish this thing for Leo," I replied. But not at 6:15.

She pinched her pretty face and shook her head. "No, I mean forever."

I had no idea. None. "I could write. Maybe."

"Like what?"

"I don't know. Something about Andrew Johnson's incoherent inauguration speech in March of 1865," I said. "A biography of George Jones, editor of the *Times* in Tweed's day. There was a boxer I knew in Narrow's Gate . . ."

As she double-checked her rubber-band rainbow, I took a sip from the bottle of Badoit, the sparkling water I first drank in a café in Montmartre with Marina across the table from me, smiling warmly in the late afternoon sun, light dancing in her brown eyes.

"The only person worth writing about now," I said, "is Raymond Montgomery Weisz. That poor son of a bitch . . ."

Weisz remained in critical condition until Friday, when he was upgraded to "serious but stable."

Julie heard that Weisz presented a problem. He wound up at St. Luke's–Roosevelt, where he was recuperating nicely, until somebody realized the dialysis center at Beth Israel was named after his paternal grandmother.

"Your Weisz is a millionaire, Terry. Several times over," Julie said, as we sat on a bench near the old Five Points and shared a platter of Middle Eastern–flavored chicken and rice with too much white sauce. "He's sitting on a pile of cash."

"And the hospitals want to fight over who has dibs if he dies?"

She nodded as she sipped from her sweating can of Diet Coke. High above the courthouse, the bloated sun hid behind a string of thick gray clouds. Two days of rain had left lower Manhattan as soggy and steamy as New Orleans. To our left, pigeons pecked at the puddles on the concrete, luxuriating in the occasional splashes of dark water made by flapping wings.

"I suppose Mrs. Weisz left a will," I said.

Julie managed to shrug and nod at the same time.

"But would she leave him money?"

"For his care and treatment, perhaps," she said.

"He'll need it." The plastic fork was useless with rice.

"He'll need representation when they authenticate," she said.

We sat in silence for a moment or two, watching a delivery van painted with Chinese characters struggle to make its way past double-parked cars on Mulberry.

"You know somebody who can handle that?" I asked. "Someone who's an expert on wills, probate and stuff."

"Terry, don't you think you've done enough for this man?"

"I wasn't thinking about him," I told her. An image of Diddio, scratching his head in confusion, floated across my mind.

She handed me the Styrofoam platter. "Enjoy."

Her name was Eunice Cope and her wobbling, nicotine-stained croak of a voice made her sound like she was 114 years old. But Julie said she knew what she was doing, and I felt her authority when she told me that neither my opinion nor presence was required in the matter of Leo Mallard, Dennis Diddio and the Tilt-A-Whirl v. Interstate Properties or whatever they were going to call it.

"I'm just following up," I said, trying to explain as I paced the kitchen. "To see if there's been any progress."

Beagle looked at me, curious but not at all sympathetic. Upstairs, Mrs. Maoli worked on the bedroom, resigned finally to its new configuration.

"As I said, Mr. Orr, we will consult you if necessary," Cope said.

Have another Camel, you tyrant, I thought as she cut the line.

I walked over to Hudson to drop in on Diddio, who was stubbornly hanging out at the Tilt, taking the cobwebs off the molding, scrubbing the urinal, planning ahead.

"No, Eunice is great, man," he explained. "Tell Julie thanks."

"But she hung up on me, D."

"I guess she's busy, you know, fighting bad guys. Something."

Leo would've been on my side.

Diddio had his hair clipped up on top of his head, and the sweat rolled down his face as he slopped Mr. Clean near the bar rail.

"D, it's gone," I said, pointing. "The blood."

He said no. "I seen this TV show. They spray some shit and blue spots turn up. Spooky, man."

I didn't recognize the music from the jukebox, but its wavy, psychedelic guitar screamed San Francisco circa the Summer of Love. I would've thought it'd be Barber, Britten, Bartók, something that featured the cello. The morning after Labor Day, D told me Sheila Yannick was better than Mallomars.

"Maybe you should tell Ms. Cope that I can help," I suggested.

"She knows what she's doing, T," he replied. "Man, I wouldn't be cleaning no floor if I thought it was going to end up like Big Chief's did."

I pulled a stool off the bar and sat it near the front door, away from the slimy gray strands of the mop, the harsh medicinal smell. As I hopped on the stool, I noticed that Leo's final FedEx package was still on the counter. D had dragged the dust rag around it.

"Still thinking of the tea thing?"

He smiled. "Can't you see it, man? It's going to be great, ain't it?" He let the mop handle fall, and it hit the damp floor with a dense thwack. "I'm going to shine this place all up, and back over there will be . . ."

And on he went, full of energy and boyish enthusiasm, and while he yabbered, drawing blueprints in the air with his bony fingers, I was thinking that Ruthie and Toler were going to steamroll him and Eunice Cope. They had the resources, they were amoral predators who were not likely to compromise and, if Loretta flew anywhere near the truth during her diatribe, this dream Diddio had cooked up, this reflection of his new, life-altering ambition, wasn't going to happen. Somehow, they were going to take the Tilt and do what they did with Big Chief's, which might've been smart from a business point of view, but was a miserable way to do family and friends.

Little Daniel Wu had it right on the flight down to New Orleans. "Someone who is a thief and a liar has no regard for property or promises," he said. Which could also mean that someone who had no regard for property or promises is a liar and a thief.

In Eunice Cope, Julie had chosen someone who'd approach it as she would—by the letter of the law, with a finely tuned code of right and wrong, of morality versus expediency. Buttoned-down, with formality, courtesy. Strong, resolute but with a sense of propriety.

But this thing wasn't going to get done over martinis and bone china, with carefully worded subpoenas and firm but respectable orders to suppress evidence, testimony.

Leo's last wish—to turn over the Tilt to Diddio—was under assault.

I was going to help Leo, whether D wanted me to or not.

I mean, what else did I have going on?

"Mind if I open this, D?"

I gestured toward the FedEx package.

"You want to read a two-week-old newspaper?" he asked rhetorically as he lifted the mop handle. "Go right ahead, man. I got work to do."

But he was looking at me as I zipped open the packet and pulled out the folded newspaper, as another envelope tumbled from the fold of the newspaper and onto the tacky floor.

"What the fuck . . . ?"

When he unsealed the white, letter-sized envelope, Diddio found a short stack of $100 bills, not unlike the neat pile Leo had given me.

I followed him as he went to spread out the cache on the pool table.

"Five thousand bucks," he said.

"More or less."

"What's it for?" he asked.

I took a guess. "Uncle Sammy. Miscellany."

"Mortgage?" He looked up at me, brow bent in bewilderment.

"We didn't find a mortgage book, did we?"

He shook his head.

"Ruthie sends Leo five thousand dollars . . . how often?" I asked.

"Not every day."

"No, D. I don't think she sent him five thousand dollars every day."

"I guess not," he replied. "That would be, like, eighteen billion dollars."

"Something like that."

"Maybe once a week . . ."

Which would make it more than 250K.

"That's still a lot of money," he said.

"You think?"

"Terry, man—what's going on?"

"Give that to Ms. Cope," I said. "Call her now and tell her."

"Er, T . . . I can't, like, keep this? You know, to get some stuff. Cups, mugs? Teapots? They got brochures . . ."

"Leo didn't say you could keep what was in his envelopes," I said, as I rapped a knuckle on the pool table. "Only the Tilt."

"Yeah, but the envelope is in the Tilt, right?"

I backed toward the door, stopping only to put the rickety stool back on the bar.

"Call her," I repeated.

He nodded, not bothering to hide his disappointment. "Where you going, T?"

That packet of hundreds iced it for me. I was going back to New Orleans.

"I'll call," I said.

I hopped the same 9:05 A.M. flight out of Newark, only this time on a Sunday. Bella said she'd go to Mass with Julie, eat with Julie's folks, bring Julie back to spend a night or two at our place on Harrison, and walk and feed Beagle, and that Marcus was an asshole and she didn't care if he fell off the planet. Asshole, and she said it like she meant it.

Bella has a boyfriend. Christ.

I brought along a copy of John Feinstein's book on Patriot League basketball and devoured it, stopping only to ignore the cardboard bagel and watch a bit on a blind windsurfer on the tiny overhead screen. After a few bumps and a forced-smile sweep by the flight attendants for errant coffee cups, we descended toward Kenner and once again, only the ospreys and herons saved the gray, murky swamps surrounding the airport from resembling something Asimov imagined. I was in the terminal before noon local time, lugging one of Bella's backpacks, which contained two documents, a razor, shaving cream, deodorant, three pairs of underwear and five T-shirts. I wasn't planning on staying for more than 36 hours, but I was prepared to sweat as much as I had to.

At a Mardi Gras–themed bar, boisterous men and women in black and gold waited for the Saints' game to kick off, allowing me to wonder, while I sucked down an icy club soda, what kind of fans came to an airport to watch sports. I ponied up and, heading toward the rental-car counters, dodged a cart that moved two elderly women along the crowded terminal toward their gate. Under high blue hair, they beamed, queens on a float in their own parade.

The *Times-Picayune* kept only a month's worth of back issues at its offices on Howard Avenue, but the switchboard operator told me the city library on Loyola had every issue since 1914 on microfiche. Since the library was closed on Sundays, I took a practice run out to Thibodaux, to Ruthie's house, cutting the air conditioner, opening the windows and letting the wind off the bayou surround me. The pebble-and-sedge-bracketed back road off 310 was nearly empty, and I slowed down to take in the earthy scent of the marshes and to watch Spanish moss on cypress trees sway languidly in the afternoon breeze. As I puttered by, silver spots danced on the brown water as the sun filtered through thick fronds, and stout gulls suddenly burst from the rushes as an airboat piloted by two shirtless men split the silence. Like an excited kid, I was hoping they'd wave at me, that they'd be real-life Cajuns on an alligator hunt, and I knew I looked like the goddamnedest tourist in my white Chevy Cavalier, New York City chip on my shoulder melting in the steady heat. But I didn't care. I couldn't have been more interested if I'd driven to Mars. It was all new, I was alive, I was doing something worthwhile and, suddenly, unexpectedly, I could feel all of it burbling within me.

Only having Bella at my side would've made it better. And Davy in back, a curious six-year-old craning his neck as I pointed to birds whose names I didn't know, to trees that looked like creatures waiting to pull up root and run off.

And Leo to guide us. Acerbic Leo, who would've put aside his cynicism, his sardonic wit, to show a friend the home state he loved but had had to escape.

Sweet Julie.

Julie, who spent a couple of lunch hours and one long evening digging through records of real-estate transactions in TriBeCa. Julie, complicit now.

"Just call Toler's office, pretend you're Cope's secretary and ask for a meeting at Ruthie's for Monday afternoon," I said, pointing to the bedroom phone.

Moments earlier, she had been lying naked on the bed, letting the evening sun and the delicate breeze off the Hudson bathe her moist body. Now, sitting with knees up to her chest, she tugged the bright yellow top sheet up by her neck.

"I can't do that, Terry."

"It's unethical?"

"It's not *right*," she asserted.

"Oh, it's right," I said.

I pulled into Thibodaux a little after 2 P.M., wriggled onto North Canal and wound my way until I found the Mallards' home.

Yeah, it's a mansion, I thought as I went west, hung a U-turn and reexamined the question-mark-shaped driveway, the long, unencumbered stretch of lush grass that swept toward the building's Greek Revival façade, its tall white Ionic columns, the evergreen oak that stood alongside the placid body of water out back.

To the left of the main building, next to a garage, was a small cottage. I made that as Willis Toler's residence, where the chauffeur kept and cleaned his .38.

The garage door was open, and the big, metallic-green '51 Fleetwood was gone. I wondered briefly if a man who carried a gun did chores—food shopping, pick up the dry cleaning, drop off a bill at the BellSouth office.

Probably not. Maybe the elder Toler was tooling around La Fourche Parish, getting Ruthie her Sunday constitutional. I could see her, majestic in pink as she lounged on the vast rear seat in a cloud of sweet perfume, singsonging her opinions, totaling up her accounts, getting ready for her 2:30 meeting tomorrow with Eunice Cope, figuring how to work Leo over one last time, telling her driver all about it. Not a pleasant thought, but one I'd nurture and toy with on my ride back toward New Orleans—I'd even fill out the dialogue, using what Loretta told me to get it right. Ruthie's theme: Leo had to pay for his intemperance, his disloyalty, his particular form of arrogance. I had to put him in his place now, didn't I?

I needed it, needed to stoke the fire so I'd be red-hot when I turned up tomorrow, well before the planned meeting among Ruthie, the lawyer Toler, and Cope, who'd be in her office in Brooklyn Heights, unaware of the ruse. As I headed back to North Canal, I started working it up, and it didn't take much.

I was going to enjoy interrupting her lunch.

I put in about two hours the following morning rounding it off and stitching together a pretty good history on the Mallards. And I learned a few things about Langston Toler that told me I'd made the right choice, that going at it head-on, with gloves off, was the only way these two would understand.

The son of Willis and Ethel Toler, originally of Nebo in LaSalle Parish, Langston Toler was a freeholder in East Baton Rouge Parish, an elected position that was sort of akin to a councilman for a county, but one that put him amid key decisions made on public works that impacted the local branches of the multinational petrochemical companies, as well as the soybean and sugar producers in the region, many of whom were represented by Miles Kendricks Toler. In addition, he served on the boards of several local museums and charities, sponsored a Little League team, was active at Tulane, his alma mater, and had managed to get his face in the *Times-Picayune* about once a week since the century turned. At best, he was ambitious, civic-minded. More likely, he was fattening his résumé as well as his wallet, with an eye on statewide and, perhaps, national office.

The Mallards' story made for more interesting reading; like Eleanor Montgomery Weisz's, it had the sweep of fiction, with the sort of touchstones that precede the commercial breaks in made-for-TV movies. Regarding the Mallards, Pib Owen summed it up best: "There's oil out there on the bayou." And near Olla in LaSalle Parish, where Leo's grandfather moved his family in 1917. I smiled and shook my head as I read several profiles of the original Leo Mallard, who was born in 1882, grew up in Caddo Parish, worked on the robust derricks and pipelines that dotted the landscape of his birthplace until the boom went bust in 1914. The workingman found sudden prosperity when oil was struck near his patch of property in Olla, and Leo Mallard, who fished the Catahoula Lake for a living, pocketed his fortune and squeezed it tight until his son Earl proved he could multiply the windfall through savvy investments in oil and gas concerns that blossomed throughout Louisiana.

Earl and Big Ruthie, 18 years his junior, were married in 1957, three weeks after the first Leo succumbed to throat cancer. They had three children: Earl Jr., Ruthie and Leo, the baby. Earl Jr. died at age two in 1961, and Earl moved the family to Thibodaux shortly thereafter, where they found companionship among other second-generation millionaires who tried to emulate the old money on the Bayou Lafourche plantations.

The Earl Mallards, who apparently had an almost religious belief in an endless supply of oil in the wetlands, suffered during the bust of the 1970s and again in 1985, having failed to buy in on the expansion to the Gulf of Mexico. In the first instance, the family more or less recovered, but by the mid-'80s, Earl had suffered his fatal heart attack and Big Ruthie had had to turn to outsiders to manage the family portfolio, with Leo off in New York City, working in the kitchen at Gris-Gris on Ninth Avenue, and Ruthie still growing into the woman who'd supplant her mother as the Mallard matriarch. The money in the pot had dwindled, but the Mallards owned the home in Thibodaux and the *Times-Picayune* alluded to other real-estate ventures.

Yeah, I thought, as I checked my watch and gathered up the microfiche. Like the property The Red Curry and the architectural firm Alexander, Andrews & Cowens now occupied the space where Big Chief's once was.

Out on Loyola, I unlocked the Chevy and headed toward the French Quarter, where I needed to pick up some protection for the afternoon's activities. Last night, between films on Turner's James Mason festival, a 30-second visit to reception had told me I could get what I needed at any of several shops on Bourbon Street.

I parked on Bienville, walked in the stark noonday sun to Bourbon and chose from among the kinds of places that used to line Eighth near 42nd Street. Under crackling zydeco music, a guy with a safety pin through his cheek sold me a leather sap without hesitation, pulling it from a dark spot in the glass counter and pausing only to count the cash as I tried to avoid his collection of dildos and crayfish ashtrays. I told him to keep the brown bag and I stuffed the weight in my back pocket. On the way out, I saw a T-shirt that showed a pair of frogs trying out the Kama Sutra. I thought, What else would you need to know about a guy if you saw him wearing that?

I jumped back in the car, got on Rampart to take 90 out to the Mallards'. My watch and the clock in the dash told me I had about 90 minutes to get to Thibodaux.

Langston Toler must have had his father pick him up in Baton Rouge, because there were no cars but the big Fleetwood in the scoop in front of the Mallard mansion. In a crisp cream shirt, and minus the bow tie and shoulder holster, the wiry chauffeur was casually buffing the Cadillac with a thick chamois glove, and with each easy swipe, the sun shone just that much brighter off its glittering green finish.

I circled back on North Canal, parked across from a Howard Johnson's, a short rack of newspaper honor boxes and a tobacco store that featured mint snuff, and started a 10-minute walk toward the white house and its opulent lawn.

Two black-and-tan hounds lazed near the chauffeur, who had his back to me as he worked the driver's-side door. As soon as I passed under the cypress trees framing the wide lane, one of the dogs lifted its head, glanced at me, and went back to daydreaming. But the other straightened up and let out a yelp, and Willis Toler turned. I waved to him as if he was my oldest friend. As he quietly chided the dog, he removed his chamois glove and withdrew his black bow tie from his breast pocket.

I kept walking toward the house, staying on the pebbled drive, coming up on the back of the car. The thick hounds fixed their eyes on me, and one, the one that had cried out, seemed particularly alert.

When I called on the day of Leo's funeral, Julie said Bella and Daniel were playing with the hounds. I was chancing that she was right, that Toler's companions were playful beasts.

I'd hate like hell to have to sap a dog.

"I wasn't sure you'd remember me," I said as I continued toward the elder Toler and the hounds.

"You are Mr. Mallard's friend from New York City," he said directly, as he clipped on the tie, straightening it until it was perfectly level.

He folded his hands behind his back.

"I guess I'm early," I said. "I was supposed to meet Mrs. Cope at the Howard Johnson's . . . I just thought I'd come over."

He nodded cautiously. Julie had told a secretary at Miles Kendricks Toler that Eunice Cope would make her own arrangements for transportation.

"I know," I said, as I pulled about 10 feet from the back of the Caddy. "T-shirt, jeans. But I was drenched in sweat the last time."

"Yes sir."

"But it's kind of cool here," I added as I edged toward him, "with the breeze, the water . . . Listen, I have to confess I'm a bit scared of that dog you got . . ."

"Mr. Orr," he said evenly, "I think it would be best if you waited here for a moment."

"Sure, but not with that dog."

"T-Bone won't trouble you," he said. "Now, please wait—"

I reached out and grabbed him hard by the throat.

"Look at me," I told him. "Am I fucking around?"

He stared into my eyes.

I lifted him. Veins bulged at his temples, and his face had gone red.

"The gun," I said.

He shook his head.

But I saw his black suit jacket folded carefully across the Caddy's back seat.

"The gun. It's under the jacket?"

He refused to say.

"Old man," I said, staring into his bulging eyes, "don't make me put you down."

I slipped the leather sap from my back pocket and held it high.

But his allegiance, pride, his stubbornness wouldn't let him give up the piece.

"Hands on the trunk," I told him as I eased him down.

He retreated slowly to the rear of the car, placed his long brown fingers on the gleaming green car.

T-Bone and her companion watched with bland curiosity as I tossed aside Toler's jacket and snapped the snub-nose .38 from the holster.

He inched closer to the back seat, intent on trying to stop me. When I stood, I pointed the barrel of the gun at his lean face.

"I will shoot you," I said.

He looked at the gun in my left hand and the leather sap in my right, and he said, "No, sir, I don't believe you will."

He was right, of course. I'd come back to Thibodaux for 20 minutes of productive conversation, not to add to my P.I. résumé the one element it seemed to be missing—a body made dead by my hand.

"What am I going to do with you, old man?"

T-Bone dropped at my feet, her thick body crunching the pearl pebbles.

"In the trunk," I told him, nodding toward the Caddy.

"Sir?"

"Get in the trunk."

"It's—"

I lifted the gun as if to strike him.

He backed toward the trunk, leaned down and popped it open.

With only a few flares, a first-aid kit and the spare tire in the space, Toler had plenty of room to lay out.

"In," I said, with a wave of the gun.

"The heat," he replied, as he lifted one black shoe into the well.

I returned the sap to my pocket and scooped up the red flares. "Take off your tie."

He nestled himself in the trunk, and I shut the lid with a hollow thud.

If it went as I thought it would, I'd be back in less than a half-hour.

Longer than that, and I'd be in trouble. And I'd have to tell them I had Toler and that they needed to let me walk away in order to get him back.

I came in through the kitchen, and a heavyset cook, who dominated the room despite old, restaurant-style appliances and a menagerie of well-seasoned pots and skillets hanging above her, looked at me, looked at the .38 and dutifully sat on a stool at the long table. On the stove, chicken necks, backs and feet boiled with celery, onions and carrots for stock, while a smaller pot of gumbo rested on a flameless burner. A pan of cornbread was covered with clear plastic wrap, and on the table, fresh parsley lay near a wood-handled mezzaluna. A few pieces of china were in the deep sink.

"I'm Leo's friend," I said, "from New York."

She nodded.

"I'm not trying to hurt anyone."

Though her eyes were calm black pools, she nervously kneaded her dark fingers on the tip of her white apron.

"You think she did him right?" I asked.

She looked down at her hands.

I moved toward her. "You'd better come with me."

She stood and led me to a swinging door.

The dining room had lime-green walls with pale yellow trim, gold drapes, a china cabinet that bore silver commemorative plates, and a high ceiling that wore a glittering chandelier above the long table, and Ruthie and the lawyer Toler were sitting next to each other, she in the head chair, and he with his back to the kitchen door.

Ruthie seemed annoyed with her cook until she saw me enter behind her.

"Please," I said to the worried matron, "sit."

The woman looked at Ruthie for approval, as Langston Toler pressed his napkin to his lips and began to rise.

"Gun," I said.

"We see," Ruthie said dryly. With a terse snap of her head, she told her cook to drop down at the ass-end of the table.

I went to the thin, light-skinned black man, crisp in his blue blazer over a baby-blue shirt, canary-yellow slacks and white bucks, and offered him my hand. "Terry Orr," I said, as he shook it. "Let me guess: Langston Toler, up from Baton Rouge."

"Isn't he cute, Langston? With his blue jeans and his T-shirt. Track shoes."

Toler looked at me, at his client. He needed a cue to know how it might unfold.

"Is this how heroes behave, Terry Orr?" Ruthie asked.

I moved behind Toler and chose the seat closest to the corner, to the sliding doors to the grand foyer. I patted the cook on her hand as I sat.

"You saved that man," Ruthie continued. "That man everybody thought killed your wife and child. That took every kind of courage, Terry Orr. But this . . . This is so *unusual,* so heavy-handed, don't you think?"

I looked at Toler, who'd returned to his chair. "Does she do this singsong thing when it's just you two?"

"Mr. Orr," he cautioned, "you have forcibly entered this home, a pistol in your hand . . ."

I put the blunt .38 on the table. "Last resort." What was it Tommy Mango told me a year or so ago? You don't ever want to go to your last resort. Though he did, and killed two men.

"You should have called ahead, Terry Orr," Ruthie crooned. "We would have set down a place for you."

The gumbo appetizer had given way to what looked like shrimp pie, a potato salad with scallions, and cornbread. Ruthie and her lawyer were drinking iced tea.

"If this kind woman cooks as well as Leo did, I'm sure I would've enjoyed it," I said.

"Yes," Ruthie said with a faux smile. "Your friend Leo."

The pink chiffon dress was back in the wardrobe, and today Ruthie wore a navy-blue skirt, a business suit for their meeting with Diddio's lawyer. Her white blouse had a big bow in the front that rested comfortably on her heavy bosom.

"Mr. Orr," Toler said, "I must say that gun is making me terribly nervous."

I nudged it toward him, then yanked it back, my finger on the trigger guard. It slid easily on the polished wood.

"You recognize it?" I asked. "It's your father's. He's fine, by the way. Though I notice you didn't ask."

"Then that is not the gun you used to shoot Miss Loretta Jones," Ruthie said.

"No. That was Leo's."

"How he would have enjoyed that," she replied. "And how is my dear sister-in-law?"

I snapped my head toward Toler. "He hasn't spoken to her yet? Somehow I doubt that."

"You didn't quite get rid of her, did you, Terry Orr?"

"I didn't try," I said. "You're the one who needs her gone, not me."

"Mr. Orr," Toler said, "is it possible that we be civil here?" He calmly adjusted his starched collar, ran his thumb and forefinger along the crease in his yellow slacks. He wasn't really nervous about the gun. Nothing made this guy sweat.

"Depends on what you mean by civility, Mr. Toler. If you mean a display of courtesy, it seems to me that you and your client have no intention of showing Dennis Diddio the courtesy he deserves. Or Leo, for that matter."

"I'm sure I don't understand you, Mr. Orr."

I slid the chair back into the corner and brought the gun to my lap.

"You know Leo wanted to leave the Tilt to him and she can't bear that," I said, nodding toward Ruthie.

"Langston," Ruthie led. "Let him see it."

The lawyer held back the flap of his jacket and silently asked for permission to reach inside. When I nodded, he dipped in his inside pocket, came up with a photocopy of a letter and passed it to me.

I knew it was from Leo before I unfolded it. Something had to have moved them to write to D.

Ruthie:

Dennis Diddio is a very thoughtful young man who has been helping me since I was taken ill. Over the years, he has proven himself time and again to be a trustworthy individual. I would like him to be rewarded for his compassion and loyalty. In the event of my death, I am instructing you to be sure he gets to take over the Tilt to run any which way he wants to. I'm sending a copy of this to Langston Toler, so he can make sure it happens like it's supposed to.

I know you will be very careful to make sure Loretta gets nothing, which is fine by me. But I want you to take care of Diddio. Leave him be and let him do the best he can.

Leo

"Great," I said as I returned the letter to Toler. "Now we all know what he wants."

"That," she said, pointing at Leo's missive, "is the product of a deranged mind. And we cannot say for certain if he wrote it—'trustworthy individual,' 'taken ill,' 'rewarded for his compassion.' Don't sound like Leo to me. Maybe you did it."

"Not my style," I said. "But I know the sentiment is your brother's."

"The key phrase, in my estimation, is 'gets,'" she continued. "What does it mean? 'Gets to take over'?"

"That's funny," I replied. "I thought 'take over' was the key phrase."

Toler started to speak but Ruthie cut him short.

"Well, be that as it may, Terry Orr," she sang. "All of it is out of the question. Absolutely out of the question."

"I know," I said. "That's why I'm here. You threatened Diddio, and you're all set to bury Leo's last request."

"There's been no threat, Mr. Orr," Toler said.

"I don't know the legalese," I told him as I squirmed to reach into my front pocket. "But I took this letter as a threat."

I gave him a copy of the letter he'd dictated and sent to Diddio, admonishing him to stop any and all activities related to the Tilt.

"I'm sorry if you and your friend were offended," Toler said. "But Miss Mallard has a clear and unmistakable right to protect her investment."

"Yeah, but Leo wants him to have the Tilt," I said. "You've got it in writing, and so do I."

The cook, still twisting the end of her apron, watched as I handed him the other letter I'd brought along, the one Leo wrote to me before he died.

As he read it, I said, "And there's Leo's letter to Diddio." Cope had that one now.

"No one is ever going to believe my brother wrote this twaddle," Ruthie spit, waving the back of her hand as if chasing off a housefly.

"I guess the question is, What was Leo's interest in Interstate Properties," I said to Toler.

"I'm not at liberty to discuss Interstate," he replied, "other than to assure you that Miss Mallard has a controlling interest. I'm sorry to tell you that Mr. Mallard's position is irrelevant."

"It may not be," I said. "Especially if your client relies on the income from The Red Curry and any other property it holds. Who knows how long that money will be tied up while this thing plays out?"

"Terry Orr, you can't possibly believe we will allow this boy, this *hippie* to operate that property," Ruthie said, with a heaping dab of scorn.

"I don't see where you have a choice," I told her. "I mean, Toler here knows more about this than I do, but I think you've got Leo's last request in writing in at least three different documents. For all I know, there may be more. Leo might've had his own lawyer. Enough of them came to the Tilt."

To shoot pool and listen to D's music. If they started talking shop, Leo shooed them out, sometimes with broom in hand.

Analyzing the bluff, Langston Toler tugged on his cuffs but kept quiet.

"So you can't do a thing until Leo is heard," I said. "It's a just reward for you, Ruthie. It's what you get for orchestrating his decline."

"His *decline*. Is that a fact?"

"Which is how he wound up in that dump of a bar."

"To operate that dump, Mr. Orr, was his choice," she told me. "He could've just as easily opened another restaurant."

"Really? With what? The five grand you sent him now and then?" I shook my head. "That was to pay off the IRS."

"The IRS," she scoffed. "Your dear friend Loretta is the one who is responsible to—"

"And to keep your investment in the Tilt above water. I mean, you pay the mortgage out of Baton Rouge, just like you do with the Harrison Street property. So Leo needed cash for vendors and other things. Pocket change."

"Miss Mallard has been very generous toward her brother, Mr. Orr."

I kept an eye on Ruthie, who nodded exultantly at her lawyer's flattery.

"How long was Leo running the Tilt before you moved in?"

"Miss Mallard acquired that property to support her brother," Toler said.

I said no. "To control him. That's right, isn't it?"

Ruthie hoisted herself out of the chair. "Terry Orr, what is it you think you know?"

I said, "You wanted me to stay away from Loretta, not out of any sense of propriety, but because you feared she'd tell me about how you threw down Leo."

"You had to find her, didn't you?"

"She found me."

"But you went looking," she said. "Interviewing people in New Orleans."

Pib Owen. Of course he called Ruthie. I'd expect nothing less from a man who'd boast of nailing his friend's girl.

"Loretta." She rolled her eyes. "Such a solid citizen, such a worthy soul."

"Fuck Loretta," I said. "But thanks to her, I know about your role in your brother's fall, and that gives us the leverage we need to get the Tilt transferred to D."

"Oh, really?" she asked as she moved along the table, drawing closer to her lawyer.

"Mr. Orr, precisely what is your point?" Toler asked. "I mean, why are you here?" He nodded toward the gun in my hand.

"You don't want D to have the bar. Leo does," I replied. "It should be easy for you to straighten this out. But it's not. So you'll scare him off. Or tie him up until he can't move."

"It can happen that way, yes," Toler replied. "In this instance—"

"He wants the bar. He's getting the bar. There's nothing more to say."

"Terry Orr, let me tell you something," Ruthie began. "That boy is not getting that bar and all the guns in the United States and all the New York lawyers aren't going to change that one bit. My brother simply did not know what he was thinking when he wrote those crazy letters. He was incapacitated in some manner."

"As I understand it," I said, "it's simply a question of intent, and it's clear enough that Leo intended to transfer the business to Diddio."

"Mr. Orr," Toler said, with a trace of urgency, "it seems to me we can come to an accommodation."

"Diddio wants the bar."

"Yes, but he is *not* getting the bar," Ruthie chimed.

I said, "Yeah, he is."

"Ridiculous," Ruthie scoffed.

I turned back to Toler. "Did you know Loretta made her payments to your client? In cash?"

He didn't reply.

"But Miss Mallard didn't forward the payments, either to the original owners of the property or the IRS and New York City and State," I said. "And now Interstate owns the place where Big Chief's used to be."

"Those are unsubstantiated allegations, Mr. Orr," Toler said. "Interstate purchased the property after we were made aware of the financial hardship the owners faced."

"They had hardships," I said, "because they didn't get their rent from your client here. I'll bet it was the same with the Tilt. Leo couldn't make it work and you moved in."

Ruthie said, "We were simply opportunistic. The property became available and we purchased it. I believe that is called capitalism, even in New York City."

"But you had to fuck over Leo to do it," I said. "Even though you had all this."

I gestured with the gun toward the chandelier, the china in the breakfront, the rest of the vast house.

"Leo could've come home at any time, Terry Orr."

"Which is what it was all about from the jump," I said. "Control. Like your grandfather controlled your father, you wanted to control Leo."

"You don't know a damned thing about my daddy," she shouted, dropping any trace of the singsong she'd used.

"I know he didn't have the nerve to marry your mother until after his father died." As I stood, I added, "Good for Leo that he pried himself away from you."

"Let me tell you a little something, Terry Orr." She jabbed a stiff finger toward me, as I edged toward her lawyer. "I raised that boy and he ran off with that piece of white trash Loretta Jones and I told myself that someday . . . Well, someday came, mister, let me tell you. And when it was time to pay, he paid, goddamnit." She sneered, "Leo paid, like he should. That dumb, soft-hearted bastard."

At the end of the table, the cook recoiled at the bald contempt in her employer's spitfire words.

I dropped my hand on Toler's shoulder. "Sweet, isn't she? What do you think—the IRS sets up shop in here? Or do they move into a few cubicles at your offices in Baton Rouge?"

Under the rhetoric, the wordplay, I was seething. Leo deserved better than all this, this mockery of his kindness, this assault on his compassionate nature. He knew D needed a home, and something to do with his life other than trawl rock clubs and recording studios.

D had to get the Tilt.

"You people in New York," Ruthie continued, contempt dripping from each ugly word, "you all think you're all so high and almighty, like you're all kings of the modern world. And you draw a man like my Leo—"

"It wasn't what Leo was drawn to," I said, "but what he was running from."

"That is not—"

"And that's what does it to the people who don't cut it in New York. It's not the city, and it's not us. It's what comes at them from back home. And in Leo's case, it was a controlling, money-hungry cretin who has a calculator and balance sheet where her heart is supposed to be. You could not bear to have him succeed."

Ruthie went silent, her mouth agape. But anger still raged in her eyes.

"Yeah, it was Loretta, sure," I said, as I moved toward her, pointing with the .38. "But it was you too. You."

Toler stood.

I said, "That poor sweet man. What chance did he have with a shrew like you for family?"

From the end of the table, I heard the cook sigh to hold back a tear.

Ruthie snapped a glare at her.

"Mr. Orr," Toler said, as he stepped between me and his client. "Please. There is no simple resolution."

"Sure there is," I replied as I looked down at him. "The license to do business will be transferred to Diddio per Leo's instructions."

"That will not happen, Mr. Orr, I assure you. The owners must assert their prerogative."

"Yes," Ruthie said as she returned to her seat. "Indeed, yes."

Toler continued, "Please be aware that we are eager to compensate Mr. Diddio for any hardship that Mr. Mallard's misinterpretation of his rights may have caused."

"Yes," Ruthie chimed in, mocking. "Poor little Mr. Diddio. So forlorn, so absolutely alone."

"That's not going to work," I said.

"Perhaps you have forgotten the real value of a dollar, Terry Orr," she said. "For you, with all your wife's money, an envelope with five thousand dollars once a month doesn't mean very much. But maybe to Mr. Diddio, it is a considerable sum."

She was right. An additional $60K a year would change his life.

"Just how much do you think you'd get for that piece of property?" I asked. "Must be sizable, if you're willing to offer a man in his late thirties sixty thousand dollars a year for life."

She smiled wickedly.

"I don't believe Miss Mallard was suggesting Interstate would reimburse Mr. Diddio in perpetuity, Mr. Orr," Toler added quickly, urgently.

As he spoke, I went to the window on the other side of the table and pulled aside the thin curtain. The Fleetwood was still in the scoop and the trunk was sealed shut.

"It doesn't matter," I said, as I let the curtain sway. "He wants the bar. Leo gave it to him and he wants it."

"Mr. Orr, unless you intend to shoot us all—which will not further Mr. Diddio's claim—I don't see how we can achieve anything here," the lawyer said. He tugged on his jacket until it lay as perfectly as it did when his tailor did the final fitting. "I suppose we will see each other in court."

"Toler, how can this benefit your political career?"

"I am pursuing the best interests of my client," he replied.

"I'm going to summarize," I said. "You represent a woman who has intentionally driven her brother out of business in order to acquire a property. She did so by defrauding the Internal Revenue Service, among others."

"Mr. Orr, your inference is—"

Ruthie interrupted him. "No one is interested in his *inferences,* Langston. How boring this all will be to the folks in Baton Rouge, I can assure Terry Orr of that."

"And then we add to it Loretta," I said. "Man, can she tell it or what?"

"My sister-in-law," Ruthie mused. "Murderer. Tax cheat. Brazen hussy." She tapped the table with her chunky finger and the china rattled. "A very reliable witness indeed."

I stood next to Ruthie. "Driven to murder by her greedy, heartless sister-in-law," I said. "It'll play. The *Times-Picayune* will eat it up, the TV news. One of those tabloid TV shows."

And the way Toler looked at Ruthie told me he knew it would.

"Freeholder Toler becomes State Senator Toler on his way to the U.S. Senate, the governor's mansion," I counted. "I don't think so."

"Terry Orr," Ruthie said, "you simply do not know Louisiana politics. No one from your neck of the woods can possibly ever."

"Maybe I'll write it myself," I mused, as I walked over by Toler. "From the inside."

Toler looked at his client. He must've known about my *Slippery Dick,* my ancient reputation as a writer.

"Yeah, it'll play," I said. "As a matter of fact, it's all kinds of juicy:

Loretta, and then you add to it that Miss Mallard here has been paying you off, Mr. Toler, by keeping your father on the family tit. Then
there's poor Leo, a good ol' Louisiana boy, making good up there in
New York City until his sister jumps on him."

Toler was lost in his calculations. He was trying to figure how
much it would cost him to give up Ruthie Mallard.

"Am I right in thinking that you have a piece of Interstate, Mr.
Toler?"

"Terry Orr," Ruthie said. "Maybe you ain't as smart as you think you
are. Maybe there are things people would want to know about you."

"The last person who said that found a .38 slug in her back," I
replied.

At the end of the table, the cook groaned.

"Maybe I will just go to New York and pay my sister-in-law a
visit," Ruthie said with a curt nod. "Find out if there's more I need to
know about you."

"She'll be glad to see you," I told her. "But make sure she doesn't
have a shiv in her cell. If she made bail, check for a .32 in her hand-
bag. Remember, she got her boyfriend in the chest, dead center."

Ruthie huffed, looked up at me with another mean dose of deri-
sion. Then she said, "Langston, tell this man . . ."

"We had better discuss this, Ruth," he replied calmly.

"Langston." Her voice was sharper now, and the raw anger had
returned to her stout face.

"I'm gone," I said, thinking that real fireworks were about to
begin.

"Hold on," Ruthie said. "You walk into my house with a gun and
you think you are just going to walk away?"

I looked at Toler. "Tell her," I said. "You don't want me talking to
the sheriff either, do you?"

"*Our* sheriff?" she laughed. "You think you're going to tell *our*
sheriff—"

"I'm not naïve, Miss Mallard," I said. "I know money buys friends.

But something tells me a woman like you has a whole bunch of people just waiting to see you fall."

"Mr. Orr," he said. "We will contact Mrs. Cope."

"By the way," I said. "She's not coming."

"Yes," he replied. "I gathered as much."

I looked toward the cook. "I'm sorry for the disturbance, ma'am."

She nodded nervously at me, her eyes fixed on her snarling employer.

"If you're looking for me," I said to Toler, "I'm going to the cemetery. I've got to say good-bye to my friend."

With the two thick dogs yipping at my heels, I popped open the trunk and was glad to find the chauffeur soaked in sweat but in good shape. He blinked several times, used his arm to shield his gray eyes against the midday sun. When I offered him my hand, he took it to hoist himself out of the big vehicle.

I apologized to him, and said, "This was for Leo. I'm sure you'll hear enough about it when you're driving her around to know that's true."

He dusted off the front of his black slacks, but didn't reply.

I pointed with the .38 toward the house. "You'd better check with them before you come after me," I told him.

He reached out and shut the open trunk.

I gestured for him to turn over the keys to the Caddy.

"I'll park this thing in front of the Howard Johnson's in town," I said, as I moved toward the driver's-side door. "The gun is going in the bayou."

That was my thing now—throwing perfectly usable guns into bodies of water.

"One more thing before you decide to come after me," I said. "Ask yourself: Where are they now? I mean, they're not out here checking on you, are they? Like Leo's mother would've been. Like Leo."

He stood straight and folded his hands behind his back.

"Yeah, you know all about it, don't you?"

He said nothing as I tapped T-Bone under her chin, jumped into the Caddy and, after an awkward U-turn, moved the big green rig along the drive, heading toward the arching cypress trees, the fragrant Spanish moss.

"How is she?" I asked.

They had called the Newark flight, but I needed to hear a loving voice, the ring of compassion, of sincere affection.

"She's doing her homework," Julie replied. "She's very serious about it, isn't she?"

I heard Bella's voice in the background.

"She's singing?"

"Yes."

I said, "Ouch."

"Terry, you have something to tell me?"

I couldn't say it. Not yet.

Over by the gate, security was confiscating Starbucks coffee cups. At the first checkpoint, a man protested when a guard wanted to seize his Montblanc pen. Something about the sharp nib.

I was glad I'd dumped the sap down a drain at the Halfway Cemetery.

"You're great, Julie," I told her. "I mean it. You—"

"Terry," she laughed. "I meant for you to tell me about the meeting with Miss Mallard and Langston Toler."

"I think they understand the compromise," I said.

Julie was the one who pointed it out. Interstate keeps ownership of the Tilt while Diddio runs it, as Leo said, "any which way he wants to." And Ruthie keeps kicking in the monthly $5K until the place runs a profit above prime or until three years pass, when she can kick D back into full-time rock 'n' roll.

"You can tell Ms. Cope to expect a call," I added.

I wondered how much it was going to cost me to keep D's tea-and-music venture alive.

"And you were reasonable?" she asked.

"I'll see you at midnight or so," I told her.

"You dance, Terry, when you have to."

"Kiss Bella for me," I said as I stood, replaced the receiver, lifted the backpack and headed toward the gate.

22

I'd dozed off on the sofa and woke to the sound of the door-knocker on wood. As I sat up, comically confused, *Slaughter at Kinmel Hall* tumbled to the floor. Swinging my legs around, I imagined Addison chiding me—"I went to the trouble of getting you that book out of Weisz's bloody effects and you fall out while you're reading it?"

Beagle followed in curiosity as I went to answer the call.

"Happy Friday," Julie said. "Hey, Beagle."

I rubbed my eyes.

She wore a camel-colored suit with a brown silk blouse that matched her shoes. In one hand was her briefcase; in the other, a shopping bag that brimmed with food. Haas avocados were peeking over the top, nudged to the side of the sack by yellow corn in thick green husks.

I took the shopping bag. "Hungry?"

"For the weekend," she replied as she entered. "Is Mrs. Maoli still here?"

"I sent her home," I said, stifling a yawn. "Why?"

"I don't want to invade her kitchen," she replied as she kicked off her shoes. "She still hasn't made up her mind about me."

She went on her toes to kiss me.

"I just woke up," I said as I pulled away.

"I'll settle for your cheek."

And she did. Her fresh, clean fragrance left a faint trace of lemon in the air.

I watched her as she put her briefcase on Bella's chair, took off her jacket, undid a few buttons on her blouse and took the paper sack to withdraw tortilla chips, fat-free yogurts and a quart of skim milk—the stuff Mrs. Maoli neglected to buy. Even when doing the simplest chores, Julie exuded life, optimism, anticipation. Sharon once called her "a good girl, and happy." She was much more than that.

And only she could've sold Eunice Cope on the idea that Toler had decided to do right by Diddio and honor Leo's wish.

"Any more news on Weisz?" she asked.

"You mean do I agree to go and see him?"

She nodded.

"Not yet."

"Which means . . . ?"

I shrugged. "Not yet."

I had an idea—to give Weisz a copy of Wittgenstein's etudes for the left hand. But I wanted to run it by Harteveld first. She'd find out if it was an appropriate gesture, especially from me.

"And Loretta?"

"No," I said, "I don't think I'll call her back."

No bail for Loretta, who was recovering at Riker's. A penitent Twist told me that.

"Good," Julie said. "Let her stew. She's where she belongs."

Julie believed in heaven and hell, in redemption and grace. The good eventually found their reward, while the unrepentant suffered for eternity.

Could be. Who knows?

She dug into the bottom of the bag and pulled out a bag of Ruffians, some kind of bacon-and-liver-flavored knots for dogs.

"That's a good idea," I said. "She's probably sick of Chinese."

Julie knelt down to hand one to Beagle, who sniffed it and walked away.

"Oh, you snob," Julie said.

"Don't feel rejected."

"Me? It'll take more than that." She put the soft twist on the floor. "She'll be back."

With an appealing bounce, Julie went toward the stairs to the bedroom. "I'm going to change," she said.

"Not too much, I hope."

She stopped, turned, smiled. "My clothes."

"OK," I replied. "I'll brush my teeth."

We walked west on Harrison and I could see my house in the September twilight, the pale green river as it rocked easily, casually under a trim sailboat gliding north. The end of summer, I thought, the end of this year's golden days. And the beginning of what? Autumn, of course.

Terry, let's not play, I told myself. Put away the jokes, the flip comments, toss aside the cynical mask. Answer one question: What are you going to do with yourself now? Without the daily crawl toward abject misery, toward pointless revenge, what are you going to do?

I had a kind, tender woman, a bright, caring woman on my arm.

And at least one good friend: Back at the Tilt, pulling linoleum, promising to dress up for tomorrow night—his first real date with Sheila, as the four of us would go see the Electric Light Orchestra at

Irving Plaza—Diddio was off in fantasyland, imagining crowds queuing for his "super-duper tea, man. Earl Grey, can you believe it? Oolong. How cool is that? *Oolong.*"

And over by my house was Bella in her carpenter's jeans and fedora, urging Beagle to pick up her pace, and Daniel Wu, struggling with his basketball.

Said Daniel, "It's not too late, Mr. Orr. Gabriella needs you."

I can see Davy now. He's clear in my mind—his bright eyes, bud of a nose, his glittering lips, his pudgy fists, ball of a belly. How he giggled in delight when I entered the room. How he grabbed at the tennis ball I rolled to him. That little boy loved me, and I love him still.

I think about my children as I walk around TriBeCa, Little Italy, Gramercy Park, as I run along West Street to the Javits Center, or around to the Seaport. A beautiful boy who deserves to have a father who will do him proud.

And a bright teenager who needs a father to stand behind her, to take her hand, share a laugh, wipe a tear.

Can I make something out of all this?

I can't imagine it's a bad place to start.

And maybe I could be a real P.I., instead of the half-assed one I was. That might be interesting.

Of course, I'd have to find where Bella hid my license.

A writer?

"Terry," Julie said, "I've got a question for you."

"Go."

"What do you think of us?" she asked.

" 'Us'? Me and you?"

"No. Women," she replied. "What I mean is, after few weeks, has your view of women changed?"

She was keeping it light, so I went with it.

"Depends on what you thought my view was before."

"Yes, I suppose there's that."

Daniel dropped the ball again and it rolled toward Harrison. With the dog's leash on her arm, Bella retrieved it and easily flung it behind her back to Daniel, who, unprepared, reacted as if she had passed him a hand grenade.

Beagle's dour expression didn't change.

"I like women," I said.

"That's it?"

"It summarizes my position."

She stopped, let go of my arm. "Terry, Leo's sister is manipulative and cruel, his ex-wife is a murderer and a thief, Weisz's mother drove him to mental illness and suicide—"

"And I learned that my beloved wife was running around on me and my kids."

She looked up at me. "So?"

"You're serious? OK." I went over and sat against the side of a parked Hyundai. "The world is filled with women I've never met, right?"

"Yes, Terry," she laughed. "Very good."

"I admire Sharon. Harteveld's OK. I like you."

"You like me?" She came to me, punched me on my shoulder, kissed my cheek. "Thanks."

"My sister can be all right."

"You have a sister? I didn't know that."

I pushed off the car.

"Yeah, well, there might be a lot about me you don't know."

She took my arm and we continued across Greenwich, moving toward the water, my daughter, my dog, Daniel, my home, my future.

Such as it was. Whatever it will be.

Three recordings by Raymond Montgomery Weisz were issued during his troubled career. All are currently out of print and, as of the date of his accident, none has been transferred to compact disk from the original analog source.

Introducing Raymond Montgomery Weisz, issued in 1981
(a reprise of the repertoire he performed at his Carnegie Hall/Weill Recital Hall debut):

Prelude and Fugue in C Major (from *The Well-Tempered Clavier*)	*Bach*
Fantasy, Op. 116	*Brahms*
Valse Oubliée No. 1	*Liszt*
Sonata No. 7 in D, Op. 10, No. 3	*Beethoven*

  I. Presto
 II. Largo e mesto
III. Menuetto (Allegro)
 IV. Rondo (Allegro)

Raymond Montgomery Weisz in Edinburgh, issued in 1988
(recorded at The Queen's Hall in Edinburgh):

Impromptu ("Nocturne")	*Liszt*
Mephisto Waltz No. 1	*Liszt*
Piano Sonata No. 8 in B-Flat, Op. 84	*Prokofiev*

  I. Andante Dolce
 II. Andante Sognando
III. Vivace

Russian Nights—The Artistry of Raymond Montgomery Weisz, issued in 1994 (recording of his performances at the Van Cliburn competition, for which he won a silver medal):

Piano Concerto No. 1 in B-Flat Minor, Op. 23   *Tchaikovsky*
   I. Allegro con Spirito
  II. Andantino Semplice
 III. Allegro con Fuoco

Piano Concerto No. 2 in C Minor, Op. 18   *Rachmaninoff*
   I. Moderato; Allegro
  II. Adagio Sostenuto
 III. Allegro Scherzando